The Eden Tree

Peter Worthington

Clink Street

London | New York

Published by Clink Street Publishing 2016

Copyright © 2016

First edition.

ISBN: 978-1-911110-18-7
eBook ISBN: 978-1-911110-19-4

Disclaimer

Acknowledgements

Over 30 years ago, an evangelist with CfAN predicted that Wesley's story would go around the world. I believe it will!

It is also dedicated to my family, from whom I have learned so very much. They have been consistently loyal.

To my wife, Meg, who *is* from south Wales, but she has auburn hair, not black. She fills my life with joy and is the kindest person I know.

To my daughter, Rachel (nearly Rebecca as in the story), and her husband Andy, with their two children, Rose and Ellis. I have learned so much about being a granddad through them. Rachel and Andy have given me wisdom and encouragement.

To my son, Calvin, and his wife Amy, with their baby Max Harry. Calvin is a computer buff and has been since he was a child, although unlike the character in the story, he is not a hacker. Also his hair is dark, not ginger. I have learned so much from him and his wife. We get on well, and both play World of Warcraft®.

I should also mention friends and associates who have greatly helped my writing. The board of my local housing association, Bromsgrove District Housing Trust, of which I remain a board member at the time of writing. The trust has been supportive in many ways, and the executive officers always ready to support an Indie writer.

My thanks to Great Ormond Street Hospital, whom I intend to benefit from my book.

My thanks to friends in church and religious circles who have helped enormously.

Thanks to my World of Warcraft® online friends, especially my guilds. On Stormrage I am Mercedez (Ally) and on Lightbringer I am Durzle (Horde). You know who you are!

Mention goes to friends on FanStory for all the great reviews and advice they have given me over the years.

A mention of search engines and social media, which provide such useful information, without which my knowledge and writing would be much weaker.

And a final mention to my Creator and Saviour: Jeremiah 29:11 (NIV): "For I know the plans I have for you," declares the LORD, "plans to prosper you, and not to harm you, plans to give you hope and a future."

Contents

Prologue

In 1992, in Jaffa, two brothers made a remarkable discovery, one that treasure seekers around the world would envy if they ever found out. The discovery was a box.

Joseph and Simeon Latchman were property developers, specialising in house clearance. Owning several houses in other parts of Israel, the brothers had bought a property in Jaffa overlooking the sea.

"What do you think of it?" Simeon asked as he surveyed the dilapidated white building. "We can't rent it, that's for sure." He inserted his hand in a crumbling wall.

"It looks old and we bid beyond our price, so let's hope we can recoup our investment," Joseph replied. "We've done well so far with our portfolio. Let's take a look inside."

The door creaked as Simeon pulled the door handle. Grey clouds of dust swirled and spiders' webs quivered in the breeze. The sun warmed their backs as they left daylight behind and entered a cold, dark room.

"Look at this." Simeon's torch beam illuminated a wooden sign sparkling on the whitened wall. The sign of the fish appeared to point to a thick blanket curtain.

"It's the early Christian sign, probably made smooth by many hands stroking it," Joseph stated, "they used it to announce a gathering. There might be a cellar."

Simeon nodded, confident in his younger brother's

knowledge. "So…the followers of the carpenter met here. Come on, let's see what's down there." Simeon pushed through a blanket curtain and clattered down the wooden stairs.

"Be careful, brother," Joseph said, as he followed, testing each wooden slat.

Yellowed circles of light from hand-held torches came into view on the walls and dusty floor. Joseph coughed and placed a white handkerchief over his mouth. His fingers touched the icy cold wall and he used his torch to check his bearings.

"There might be more history down here," Simeon rubbed his hands. "We might have got a bargain." Amidst the thick musty darkness, a torch beam fell upon drag marks on the floor.

"It looks like something heavy has been moved from the corner recently." Joseph stroked his beard. "The owner mentioned they had cleared some furniture."

Simeon shrugged his shoulders. "This is weird though. Look at that mound, it looks like someone was either hiding it or unaware of it."

Joseph's eyes followed the beam. "It might just be a pet's grave," he said. "But I'll fetch the trowel." His steps echoed on the stairs.

Kneeling down in the dirt, Simeon carefully excavated under the mound, clawing at the sand laboriously with his bare hands, sweat stinging his eyes. Joseph knelt beside him, placed a cloth to kneel on the pressed sand, and dug with the trowel, then he passed the trowel to Simeon. They lay their torches on the ground and a matrix of light illuminated their excavation. They both clawed and scraped until the hole was about twelve inches deep.

"There's something here," Simeon whispered, his voice trembling as he felt the trowel touch a hard object.

"Shush…careful," Joseph looked over his shoulder.

A circle of sand grew at their knees. Like two children at the beach, they dug eagerly.

"By all that's holy!" Joseph scratched his head, paused, and rested.

Both brothers' foreheads glistened. Dark stains appeared on the neck of Joseph's starched white shirt. In unison, they gasped in bewilderment and finally uncovered an old wooden box: an antique. An intricate pattern of green leaves and golden angels was engraved on the lid. Moisture dripped across their bearded cheeks and fell onto the sand.

"What on earth is this?" asked Simeon. "It appears to be a lid," he said expectantly.

"Be careful, Simeon," Joseph cautioned, "we don't know how old it is or what's in it. We don't know what it's worth." Both brothers looked over their shoulders and listened.

Simeon lifted the box out of its nest, like a nursing mother with a newborn baby, and placed aside the lid. The brothers peered into the box.

"*Oi vey*, be still my heart," Simeon gasped in astonishment as he knelt on the cellar floor inspecting their treasure trove. On top of some very ancient scrolls, manuscripts and parchments there was a white cloth bag with drawstrings. Simeon gently pulled the drawstrings and opened the bag. With a mystified look, he showed Joseph the few ounces of dark brown powder inside.

"It can't be hashish," Joseph pronounced, "not lying here all this time." He sniffed carefully. "It smells like pine or some herbs, but an unusual smell."

He rolled the powder with his fingers. Both brothers looked right and left and were silent. Putting the pouch to one side, Simeon took out the documents one by one; the torch beam gave the manuscripts a translucent appearance. Joseph joined him, eerie haloes reflecting on the cellar walls as the beams shone through the ancient parchments. Simeon deftly rolled them open revealing drawings, detailed maps and ancient script, some with hieroglyphics.

"I recognise some of this," Joseph took the first scroll in his hand, "it's like text in our synagogue's archives."

Joseph rolled open the scroll and attempted to decipher the heading, slowly tracing the text with a nervous finger.

Following the first-century Aramaic with deep breaths, Joseph read, "The last will and testament of Simon Peter…yes, the last will and testament of Simon Peter." His face was contemplative as he breathed deeply.

"What?" Simeon shone his beam on Joseph's manuscript. "This belongs to the rabbi's follower?"

"Yes, brother," Joseph said, tapping his brother's head. "It goes on I think to give some background and history, but it clearly states the scroll belongs to Simon Peter, disciple of Jesus Christ of Nazareth."

The brothers knelt in silence. Joseph said, "So we're guessing his followers met here and this box has remained hidden all this time?" His face was deep in thought. "Two thousand years?" They tenderly examined each parchment and replaced them with the small bag.

"It'll be like winning a lottery, brother." Simeon's eyes glowed with excitement. "We've worked so hard over the years, clearing houses of their junk. Now after all these years we've hit the mother-load!" He rubbed his hands together.

"True, brother," Joseph answered. "But the box and its contents need to be assessed. We need an expert to take a look; someone that we can trust."

"Someone who can keep a secret," Simeon said, and then added, "possibly Uncle Caleb?"

Joseph approved with a bow of his head.

With amazing providence, their uncle Caleb in Cairo lectured in mythology and archaic languages at the University of Egypt. They would seek his help.

*

Simeon and Joseph waited apprehensively in the hallway of the University of Cairo's Department of Ancient Languages and Mythology. Simeon held the ancient box bundled under his left arm, a white sheet draped tightly around their possession.

He tapped a ringed finger on the wooden arm of the bench;

the sun's rays bounced off the gold. Next to him, Joseph surveyed posters on a wall opposite. His gold-rimmed glasses perched on a substantial nose as he periodically placed his fingers in his shirt collar and pulled. His curly black beard glistened in the light streaming through a window behind him. They had called their uncle and taken the first available flight to Cairo the day after their find. It was midday when they arrived.

A brass nameplate on a dark brown door a few feet away shone in the sunlight: Doctor Caleb Weingart Ph.D. Dipl. Arch. The door swung open and a head appeared. A young man dressed in black cords and a light blue denim shirt stepped into the hallway and beckoned the brothers with his hand, saying, "Dr. Weingart is waiting." He strolled down the corridor with books under his arm, the sound of his sandals slapping against the mezzanine floor.

An aroma of pine polish and musty books filled their nostrils as the brothers entered. "Shalom, are you both well?" Caleb rose from his chair to meet them. The brothers' uncle circled his desk and greeted them, hugging and kissing them on both cheeks. "Please sit."

A black leather couch squelched as they sat and took in their surroundings. Wooden shelves filled with books of all sizes spanned the wall behind their uncle. Papers and magazines were piled precariously high on one end of his mahogany desk. Silence in the room except for the squeaking of Caleb's chair.

The professor's chair rocked on wheels as he moved his generous girth, his hands folded on his stomach. A grey cardigan stretched around his sizeable form, the buttons straining. He seemed a man easy to converse with. On his nose perched rounded bi-focal spectacles. The soft leather couch sucked them in as the brothers shifted uneasily.

"Do you think we should break the ice?" Joseph whispered.

"Yes, I hope this journey is not in vain," Simeon said, and leaning to his brother's ear he added, "surely if anyone can help us, Uncle Caleb can?"

Certificates gleamed in frames and set forth Professor Caleb Weingart's expertise in myths, religious document translation and ancient languages. After a few minutes, Caleb coughed and took the lead.

"It's good to see you, Simeon and Joseph." His eyes were questioning. "Is there a special purpose to your visit? You were quite vague and, if I may say, evasive on the phone?" Caleb's eyebrows rose and he extended his palms.

Simeon extracted the parcel from under his arm. The white sheet dropped to the office floor. Like a magician bringing a rabbit out of a box, Simeon placed the treasure down on Caleb's desk. Caleb carefully pushed aside several stacks of papers and examined the box gleaming under the office strip lighting. A stack of magazines toppled and clattered to the floor, the pages opening haphazardly. Caleb didn't appear to notice.

"Mmm, what have we here?" their uncle asked. He twirled his greying beard with his fingers as he held the box in both hands and minutely examined it. He removed his glasses and pulled a magnifying glass from a desk drawer. "The etchings on the lid are exquisite; created by the careful hand of a master craftsman, probably a carpenter." His questioning face looked towards his nephews.

"Please take a look inside, Uncle," Simeon interjected. "Help us if you can".

The professor's expression as he lifted the box lid changed from curiosity to puzzlement and delight. He opened the bag, sniffed the contents and stroked his beard. His fingers sifted the ground leaves and his eyes opened wide.

Magnifying glass in hand, he inspected the manuscripts. Parchment by parchment he unfurled the scrolls, documents and maps, muttering to himself and tracing the script with his finger. He scratched his head and resumed his detailed scrutiny with fascination. His inspection over, after at least 40 minutes, he exhaled and placed all the contents back into the box and then replaced the lid.

He took a breath. "Have you boys understood any of the text or maps and drawings? Do you understand what the pouch claims to be?"

"No, Uncle, most of it's a mystery to us," Joseph said. "The reason we brought it is to discover its truths. We don't understand what the powder in the cloth bag is, or what the maps are for."

Their uncle took a further deep breath and held up one hand, then the other, palms upward, as if weighing something. He leaned forward and replaced his specs. The brothers leaned forward with interest.

The uncle glanced at the box and then focused on the brothers. "OK. Here it is," he said, "I know my summary will be unbelievable and startling. But please listen...try not to interrupt."

The brothers nodded and moved to the very edge of the couch, exchanging excited glances.

Caleb extended his hand, "What I'm about to reveal will sound like *mishegas*...craziness. I ask not to be judged until I've finished."

Joseph and Simeon nodded their assent again and were quiet, indicating to Caleb to continue.

"The parchment scrolls appear to contain the last will and testament of Simon Peter, disciple of Jesus Christ. Two thousand years ago, Peter was eager to leave persecuted believers a further legacy to his letters: now part of the Christian Bible. I know the story sounds very far-fetched but don't dismiss it as a hoax. We have the obvious age of the box and scrolls, and the location of your find in Jaffa. History confirms that Peter was in ancient Joppa – now Jaffa – for a number of years, until his imprisonment in fact. Please let me explain in a nutshell what you have in your possession." The professor took a deep breath.

"Carry on please, Uncle." Joseph leaned forwards, hands on his knees, almost tumbling off the couch.

Caleb continued, "Simon Peter had been one of the confidants of Jesus Christ along with James and John. During their days and nights with Jesus, he apparently gave them this box. A box made by him in his carpenter's shop in Nazareth. He etched an intricate pattern of leaves and angels on the wooden lid. In the box, Jesus placed maps, drawings and text detailing the exact location of the ancient Garden of Eden surrounding the Tree of Life."

"What?" Simeon said, his eyes widening with shock. He brushed his fingers through his hair.

"Please let me continue," said the professor, "it's very important you understand the whole story."

"Of course, Uncle." Joseph placed his finger on his lips.

"Amongst the scrolls," Caleb continued, "the rabbi placed in a bag ground leaves from the Tree of Life. The leaves have special healing powers: the ability to cure diseases. James was beheaded by the Romans and John moved away to Patmos, so Peter was apparently left alone in Joppa with the box. Jesus had given his three closest followers specific instructions not to use the contents of the box for their own use; they were to heal the sick by prayer, but not to use the leaves. The box was to be entrusted to a man with the pattern of the leaves and angels on his hand. He would ask for a cure, and be honest and courageous. Any deviation of these laws would unleash terrible harm to any who disobeyed."

"We need a man with a tattoo then?" Simeon said, with a questioning shrug.

Seemingly annoyed at another interruption, Caleb raised his voice, "In his last years on earth, Peter had waited diligently but fruitlessly for the man who would inherit the box. Knowing that he was about to be arrested by the Romans he carefully buried the box in his cellar: the place where Christians met in Joppa."

"The fish sign, Uncle," Joseph said, his face brightening, "there was the sign in the house."

"There you are then." Caleb looked pleased. He sat back in his chair and exhaled, a heavy load discharged. He mopped his brow and wiped his spectacles with his cardigan sleeve.

"Thank you, Uncle." Joseph eased back into the soft leather. Simeon sat deep in thought, his expression crestfallen.

Caleb's room became a muted shrine. The sun streamed through a window behind him. The ancient find was the most significant event in the brothers' lives, an event with consequences: but not theirs to keep? They spoke in whispers.

"The huge potential for the leaves and maps is obvious," Simeon said. "The world would be our oyster. We must think carefully before we give it to anyone. Even a museum would pay us a fortune!"

"Yes, that's true, but what about the warning?" Joseph replied. "The awesome judgmental power of the God of Abraham, Isaac and Jacob is real. Think of our history!"

Caleb seemed to sense the nature of the brothers' hushed reasoning. "You should leave the box and its contents with me," Caleb said, "let me research it."

The brothers weighed up their options for some time until Joseph and Simeon announced they would return to Jaffa. Caleb reasoned strenuously to leave the scrolls with him, but they insisted upon returning to their homes. They assured Caleb they would adhere rigidly to the instructions of the scrolls.

*

For years, they waited for the person with the lid's image on his hand.

Alas, no person appeared with the identifying mark or characteristics. Years after the discovery of the box, Joseph moved to England. Simeon remained in Jaffa with his daughter, to whom he told nothing. He placed the box securely in a safe-deposit box in his bank. Over almost 20 years, the box had remained unopened: a secret.

Wesley John Morgan

One morning in May 2005, our daughter Becky, biting her lip, asked if she could "have a moment". Glancing at Liz, I raised my eyebrows and we sat together at the breakfast bar holding our coffee mugs. Stew bubbled on the gas ring a few feet away.

Sucking in her breath and fidgeting, Becky seemed to search her mind for the words. She finally blurted out, "I'm pregnant."

Liz's coffee spilled as she set down the ceramic mug. My stomach sank. I felt the blood drain from my brain and the kitchen floor appeared to wobble. I watched Liz walk to the gas hob and accidentally turn the knob higher, sending stew bubbling over and steam and the smell of vegetables and onions into the air before she turned it off.

Wiping the maroon counter repeatedly with a kitchen cloth, Liz turned to Becky. "Are you sure, sweetheart? What about uni?"

Her face blotchy, the floodgates opened and Becky sobbed, "Yes, Mum, I've had the tests." Liz and I weighed up the formidable costs of a teenage pregnancy and, we suspected, those of a single parent. We saw on her face that Becky had thought about this too.

We hugged Becky who was weeping, her shoulders convulsing. Liz's tears joined Becky's. Wanting to ask about the father,

I nevertheless decided to bite my tongue. 'Useless bugger,' I thought, 'where is he now?' I had other questions.

The first few months of her pregnancy, Becky stomped in and out while we tiptoed around. She slammed the phone down when friends and family tried to rally. One person who did not rally or give any support was her boyfriend Jason. I think the "inconvenience" persuaded him to steal away in the late spring.

"Just give me five minutes alone with that toad," Sean snarled, making a scissor movement near his groin. "He won't father any more children." Sean was my best friend, an ex-paratrooper, a retired SAS officer, and the security advisor in our business, Morgan Steel Limited, in which Liz and I were 50/50 shareholders.

"I know what you mean, Sean," I said, my fist clenched, "join the queue." But I knew that violence rarely solved problems.

"Getting a straight answer from that bloke is like catching a fart," Sean said.

His succinct humour summed up what I felt: anger tinged with disappointment.

Jason's rapid departure obviously upset Becky, but I'd never rated him. Jason Gould seemed to me to be as slippery as an eel stealthily slithering away from steady sentiment.

With his departure, Becky appeared to tumble into a black hole of uncertainty. I watched her stroll aimlessly around the house in a white bathrobe, no make-up, eating not enough to keep a gnat alive, and giving vent to uncontrolled outbursts.

"Come on, darling, you must eat something," Liz pleaded one lunchtime. She placed a bowl of piping hot soup on the kitchen counter.

"I just don't want it! OK?" Becky pushed the food away. "Stop fussing!" Thumping the swing door, she stormed out, taking the stairs two at a time. A bedroom door slammed, reverberating around the hallway.

One morning Liz and I were in each other's arms in the kitchen.

"She seems crushed, John," Liz sobbed, her tears wetting my shirt. "Instead of being full of maternal joy she's so gloomy, and it's so unlike her to be so prickly. I think her self-esteem is bruised."

Becky slouched into the kitchen from the lounge, her eyes piercing. My cheeks went hot, sensing we'd been overheard.

"Why don't we go shopping, sweetheart?" Liz said. "You need some new clothes and the baby…"

Becky shrugged. "No thanks."

I caught snippets of phone conversations and sensed her friends' words and ours were ignored. With heartache, I saw Becky withdraw to a life of solitude, shut away in her room and growing bigger week by week. For three long months, her morbidity gave us the fear that depression had established a stronghold in Becky's mind, and with no apparent saviour.

But an unlikely saviour came in the form of a dog, a chocolate-coloured puppy, her 18th birthday present from my mother.

The Labrador, aptly named Bourneville, offered unconditional love and a childlike irresistible happiness. He chewed slippers and played with magazines that littered the hallway. His perpetual wagging tail slapped the furniture, leaving scuff marks and dog hair clinging to every piece of furniture. But we accepted his trail of damage, watching with surprise the change in Becky.

The dog grew from misbehaving puppy to tireless friend, drawing her into his world of fun. The sound of his persistent yapping echoed at the door until she walked him out onto the lawns.

"All right, I'll get your lead," Becky yielded, and walked him to the lakes.

He nudged a despondent knee until she stroked his head and then he licked her hand. Bourne – his name abbreviated – dispelled the angst. With my own eyes, I saw his sunshine scatter her cloud of despondency. After weeks in limbo, Rebecca Morgan stepped back into life's arena to face all contenders.

"I want a long soak in the bath," Becky announced one day, "and where's my lippy?"

Sporting a little bump and looking radiant, Becky shopped and shopped again, returning with Mothercare bags and new clothes from Mark & Spencer and Next. A new wooden cot arrived in a Habitat van.

"Fetch Tony," I said, referring to a family friend, and looking at the cot, mystified. "These instructions are in Chinese."

Sean laughed, but I knew both he and I were useless at DIY.

From the nursery ceiling hung coloured mobiles, which whirred in the breeze, flashing in the sun's rays. On a white shelf a can of talc, baby wipes, creams, a steriliser tank, and feeding bottles were organised. The walls painted lilac gave a soothing feel and one wall was adorned with a mural of a tree with white, red and blue flowers, its tantalising green leaves spreading in the wind. 'The nursery looks amazing,' I thought. 'Everything is ready for the arrival.'

On Jan 4th 2006, I heard, "John, you can come in now." Liz held the door open, her face beaming. We were in the maternity wing of Knutsford and General Community Hospital. I strolled into the room and my chest swelled. Liz took a Marks & Spencer bag from me and placed it on Becky's bedside cabinet beside a water jug.

"We brought you a few things, Becky," Liz said, her brown eyes shining under the neon lights.

"Aww thanks, Mum...Dad...does he seem OK?" I watched her open the bag, take out some items and shove most into a drawer.

The healthy new arrival with a ruddy complexion, blue eyes, and the evidence of sandy hair, stirred, kicking his tiny bare legs in the clear-walled cot, which he nearly filled.

"Well he does look like your father, I'm afraid." Liz peered into the cot. "But we'll have to live with that." Liz leaned over to place a kiss on Becky's brow. "Well done, sweetheart. Well done, he's lovely." She placed her fingers into the baby's tiny hand and I felt a sudden glow inside and an intoxicated grin spreading across my face.

I picked up the magazine on Becky's tray. "You have any thoughts on names yet?" I asked, swatting Liz for the remark about the baby's looks.

"Wesley John Morgan." Becky turned her brown eyes towards the baby. Goosebumps tingled on my neck. Hours later, family and friends gathered around the hospital bed, peering into the cot. I heard the populace proclaim that the new addition manifested the "spitting image" of his granddad.

"Why's he wearing gloves?" our son James asked, with a mischievous glint in his eyes.

"They're baby mittens," Liz said, "because he could scratch himself." James ducked as Liz playfully swiped at his ear. He clicked his camera phone several times and then retreated to the corner, examining his work with glee.

"You'd better delete that, James Morgan, if you've taken me!" Becky threw a magazine at him. "I don't want to be on your Facebook looking like a sweaty blimp!"

"OK, Sis, no probs." James smirked, busily pressing buttons.

"Oh, God, not another copper head," Sean said, looking at the baby and grinning all over his face. I felt slaps on my back and he offered a large brown cigar. "Don't worry, Boss, we can wet the baby's head with a Bud later."

"Just the one," I said with firmness, and returned his smile, placing the cigar in my breast pocket and pointing to the "No Smoking" sign.

A couple of days later, from the front steps, I watched Becky bringing Wesley home, her arms straining to heave the carry-cot indoors. Beaming smiles and hugs met her, congratulation banners stretched across the entrance hall, vocal celebrations filling the house.

Later the smell of talcum powder, and worse, seeped onto the landing amidst a baby's cries. A fuzzy feeling of being a granddad filled me with warmth; a flame ignited in my heart.

Liz, too, had a glow in her cheeks and a spring in her step, punching me on the arm for calling her Granny and laughing.

Every day was a learning experience for the infant – learning to walk and talk, finding bugs, collecting stones, learning the names of things, eating with hands or a spoon – every moment opened a new lesson to life's apprentice student.

Christmas made me euphoric. It was made for granddads. But I had a strange premonition that it could change.

A Dark Cloud Settles

The darkness appeared in 2008, like a suffocating cloak, when my grandson, Wesley John, then a two-year-old, became seriously ill.

With the family, I sat with him through test after test until a doctor at Great Ormond Street Hospital in London called us into his office on the fourth floor. I sat in an uncomfortable plastic chair studying the certificates on his wall, attesting to the skill of the mild-mannered man before us. A stethoscope dangled from the pocket of his checked shirt, strong aftershave filled the air: such a contrast from hospital disinfectant assaulting my nostrils. His crestfallen countenance and quiet whisper indicated "bad news" to me even before the bombshell he dropped. I felt Liz grab my arm tightly and heard Becky swallow.

"I'm afraid it's not good news," he said, lifting a brown manila folder from his desk and extracting notes from it. "Wesley has neuroblastoma – a cancer – already at stage four: treatment must start immediately." The room became dark.

Becky, leaning forward with hands trembling, said, "Are you sure? Can there be a mistake?"

"The results are undeniable I'm afraid," the paediatrician said. "I'm so sorry."

'It's not his fault,' I thought, anger and resentment flooding my soul. My fist clenched, I asked myself, 'Why Wesley, why us?'

Collecting Wesley from the playroom, we thanked the nurse and slowly trudged to the elevator. I felt feeble before our caved-in world. Our little family stood silently while the machinery hummed down to the ground floor. Wesley was cuddled in his mother's arms, as we looked for the exit. The buoyant but pale toddler asked, using two words that he could put together, "Home, Mummy?"

"Yes, darling, for a few days," Becky said in a weak voice. "But then the hospital wants to do some more tests."

More tests, more needles and vomit-inducing chemotherapy to come, but our little soldier trustingly replied, "OK."

London blurred lifelessly by, as if numbed by our news. I drove home on autopilot. The traffic on the motorway seemed unreal as I weaved in and out, dodging vehicles. Speeding home, I raged with anger. Becky sat in the back of my BMW, holding Wesley's hand. He seemed bewildered by the fuss, pointing out the passing vehicles from his booster seat.

"Big truck, Mummy," he strained in his seat belt to watch the overtaking HGV, black smoke spurting from its exhaust.

"Yes, darling, it's a really big truck."

Becky caught my eyes in the rear-view mirror as I accelerated. I swallowed a lump in my throat. I turned the steering wheel rapidly as if it was to blame. Sweeping past blue road signs, I hurried home. Liz opened the glove box, wiped her eyes with a tissue and stared hypnotically from the passenger seat. We exchanged few words.

Over the months, Kirmingsham Hall and our family entered a confusing universe we didn't know existed.

"I feel that we're lost in a maze," Liz said. I agreed, as tests, treatments and anxiety were waiting like spectres around every corner.

Slumped on a stool at the kitchen counter, Sean and I shared a coffee.

Sipping from my cup I said, "You know, we've both seen suffering in Afghanistan when we helped injured military, or wounded civilians caught in crossfire. Bloodied clothes, ragged bandages on limbs and a sense of helplessness in the hospitals. The grief. You know that, Sean, right?"

"Yeah, Boss, I know what you're talking about," he placed a strong tattooed arm around my shoulder. Our minds were often in sync. "But this is different, isn't it? When it's one of your own it's different."

"You're right, Sean." I placed my mug down. "The awfulness of watching children – especially your own – undergoing chemotherapy and suffering daily bouts of sickness is like a rack of torment; it's such a contrast to his happy birth."

By 2011, the years of romps and play with Wesley John seemed a distant memory. A maelstrom of hospitalisation and treatments pulled him in. Hair lost through the chemo, his body little more than a skeleton. From his weary torso, thin arms protruded, wrists bruised and pin-cushioned where needles had been inserted. For almost four years, he'd undergone chemotherapy, radiotherapy and two surgeries. Yet, after each course of treatment, the tumours returned, always aggressively. Slowly the light of our lives faced being extinguished, and we felt helpless.

Great Ormond Street Hospital, or GOSH, London's renowned hospital for sick children, famous for breakthroughs and medical excellence, gave Wesley the very best treatment and care.

"I'm afraid it's not good," the paediatrician and head of children's oncology sombrely announced. Looking into each of our faces, speaking quietly, he said, "Without further radical treatment his life expectancy is two to three months."

"And with it…what hope does he have?" Becky's lips quivered as she gripped my hand. I gazed around the familiar office. We had sat here many times over the years of Wesley's illness. Had we reached the end? I wondered, feeling a hole in my heart.

"It won't be good," he said. "We'll do our best." He placed his glasses in a pocket and stood to shake our hands. Clive

Thomas: a caring man with such a burden. I guessed he found it difficult to say more; he'd walked this path with others.

Travelling back to Cheshire for a brief respite, we were silent. I crossed the hall, forcing my legs to move. Becky conveyed Wesley to his room and an eerie silence pervaded the house.

In the lounge, the second hand of a silver wall clock twitched uncaringly. I poured Liz and me a drink, spilling clear golden liquid on a tray. I gulped it down, the burning sensation making me cough. I poured another, the smell stinging my eyes when I forced down another swallow. James was in his room and I called him down, and I rang Sean asking him to come over so we could tell him the news. James gripped the edge of the lounge table with whitened knuckles. Gazing at the carpet, he shed no tears.

"James shows his feelings differently," Liz said to me quietly. "But he does care." I nodded and finished my drink with a gasp.

Rising from a leather recliner chair, Sean hugged Liz and me, and I heard the front door close. Through the patio window, I could see him at the far edge of the lawn, kicking some trees and bushes, throwing rocks into the lake. I like to get it out of my system by work or doing something. Sean's coping mechanism differed: his was more violent. Coping with the black cumulus, I clung to the hope that fate would give us a chance. We needed a miracle.

Holmes Chapel 2011

I parked Liz's white Nissan in a two-hour spot and strode across the pavement towards the stalls, walking and thinking. I heard traders announce their wares in loud jovial voices.

"Come on, darling, two for a fiver," a female vendor, muffled in a scarf tucked into a woollen cardigan, called out loudly. She pointed out pink bed sheets wrapped in cellophane to shoppers. Christmas earrings dangled from her ear lobes as she repeated her sales pitch.

I bumped into someone. "Sorry."

"You're dreaming, mate," the man said with a frown. 'It's true,' I thought. I dreamed and I walked. Not contemplating my fate or reason for being I looked forward to visiting the market thoroughfare, just walking and thinking.

I had told Liz before I left home, "I just need some happy memories from my childhood to give us strength and resolve for what we face. As a boy, I worked at my granddad's market stall. Maybe I'll feel the joy of those times." I think Liz understood. She was one of the few who "got me".

On Saturday February 11th 2011, a few days before my 61st birthday, I braced myself against the cold wind. The farmers' market in Holmes Chapel was only a few miles from where Liz and I lived at Kirmingsham Hall.

Buffeted by jostling crowds buying vegetables, shoes, clothes, knick-knacks, and all sorts of wares I strode on. With a hint of pleasure, my eyes focused on a flower stall 100 feet away. An assortment of coloured blooms spilled out of buckets. Customers happily carried bunches away dripping with water. A cold breeze chilled my cheeks as I slowly made my way. The aroma of bacon caught my attention; it circulated the air and directed me to a cafe near the flower stall. Combing my fingers through my hair, I walked on with a plan: 'kill two birds with one stone,' I thought. I slowed my walk to an amble, my hands deep in my trouser pockets.

A market trader nodded to me as I passed and spoke. "From round here are we, Sir?"

"Yes," I said, "my brothers and I splashed in the waters of the River Dane, and we danced to Elvis and the Beatles in the town hall." The man nodded knowingly and weighed some tomatoes for a customer.

"Time flies, doesn't it?" the man said, serving dripping lettuces to another customer. "But we can't turn the clock back, can we?"

"Well my school motto, at a school not far from here," I said, "was, 'what a man sows he will reap', so let's hope we don't reap everything we deserve, huh?" The man nodded but looked mystified. He moved further down his stall. I felt foolish.

I did wonder if I had brought a harvest of pain because of my misdeeds. When I'd asked Sean months before about my concerns, he'd said "bollocks", that I was one of the best blokes he knew. And then he joked, "Mind you, I know some right buggers."

Confident that not every decision I had made had turned out bad, I recalled meeting Liz and asking her to marry me.

Thinking of Liz, my mind continued to wander while I walked. I moved sluggishly, hardly aware of the stalls around me.

*

I had met Liz Davies in 1984 at her dad's haulage business at Ebbw Vale. I thought of our first meeting. Liz worked in her father's office, a brown porta cabin in their vehicle yard. Typing invoices and worksheets, she flicked her black shoulder length hair back as she worked. I noticed her perfect neck and coughed. A soft-featured face with naturally rosy cheeks turned towards me as I stood in the doorway.

"Oh, hello," she said, piercing brown eyes surveying me. "Dad will be back in a sec…he's in the yard somewhere."

"It's OK," I said, "I'll wait if that's no problem. I'm John Morgan by the way."

"Nice to meet you, John", she said, standing and pushing back her chair. "I'm Liz, Bill's daughter."

Her hourglass figure was snug in Levi jeans and white tee-shirt. She extended a warm hand and shook mine. My cheeks flushed when her perfume drifted towards me. My ears grew hot as I became aware of her closeness, aware of her body in the confines of the porta cabin. On my trips to Ebbw Vale I couldn't resist popping into Davies Transport to stand at the door watching her shuffle papers, type or answer the phone. I watched the way she moved, confident but not arrogant, the way she solved problems by doodling creatively.

One day, noticing Liz had gone out in her white Renault, I spotted Bill, his sleeves rolled up, near an HGV. I called, "Bill, can I have a word?" He strolled over to me, splashing through dark muddy puddles in his steel-capped boots.

"OK, John, you happy with our service?" Bill replied, rubbing his hands on his overalls. His boots squeaked as he walked closer.

"Yeah, it's not that…it's personal." I think I wanted to gain his approval.

"Oh…OK…let's wash this oil off, boyo, and we can have a drink." Bill dried his arms and hands on a checked towel. We slurped from beer cans and I outlined my intention. I felt my cheeks growing hotter.

"You'd better ask her, John my boy," he said. "Not up to me." We had another cold beer.

Later that day I combed my hair with my fingers until it felt orderly, stroked my tie and plucked up the courage to ask her out. I added, "You OK about me being 34?"

"What, and me only 24?" she laughed, punching me on my shoulder. "Of course I will go out with you. Are you OK about me being Labour, and my dad racing pigeons?" she said, her dark eyebrows rising in friendly mockery.

"Sure, I can't have everything!" I was relieved that she giggled.

Going out meant the cinema or a restaurant. Sometimes, after his retirement, we took Bill out too. We grew serious, and Liz took a job with a fashion chain in Manchester and bought a flat. We married in August 1986.

A month after we married, as we lay in bed reading, Liz said, "John, what do you feel about us having a family?"

"I think that'd be great." I rubbed my eyes and continued to read.

Placing her book on her bedside cabinet, Liz said, "Oh, that's good, 'cos I'm pregnant." Her cheeks glowed under the hue of bedside light.

"We're going to have a baby?" I sat up fully alert. "We'd better get a bigger house." My immediate reaction was to make plans.

Liz laughed, her voice echoing around the bedroom, "Well, he or she is very tiny at the moment so won't need much space." Her eyes sought mine. "You are glad, aren't you?"

"Yes, wife of mine, I'm over the moon", I said, and tossed and turned all night. We needed a home. We needed a decision.

Kirmingsham Hall

The day after Liz's shock announcement was a Saturday and Liz and I were sitting in the offices of Barlowe's in Holmes Chapel.

A woman in her mid-thirties with bobbed hair sat opposite us at a teak computer desk. She shook our hands and handed us her business card: "Miriam Davenport, Sales Consultant". Glass displays stood proudly in the shop window and full-colour A4 property descriptions furnished the blue painted walls behind me. An assistant placed a wooden tray with steaming cups in front of Miriam's nameplate.

"Please call me Mim," she said, and spoke crisply, "where are you looking and what sort of property? Do you have one to sell?" Her quick-fire questions startled me. The vacuum stood in the corner; the smell of polished desks tickled my nose. 'OK,' I thought, 'if she is heading home and isn't interested we'll try another.' An expectant pause stilled the room.

"It seems to make sense," I said coldly, "to look within a stone's-throw of here." I sipped my drink, balancing cup, saucer and brochures. "We need a family house. We've a flat in Manchester and our semi here to sell." I felt I had exactly articulated our position. I weighed the pros and cons in my head as I gazed around.

Mim's eyes lit up as if she had just woken up. I could almost hear her brain cogs whirring: "kerrching!"

"Mmm, I do have one property. Just got instructions this week." Spinning around in her chair, she stretched her hand into a filing cabinet drawer and extracted the details, sliding a pack across the teak desk to Liz with a smile. "Kirmingsham Hall: a 17th century period house in 22 acres of attractive gardens and with three lakes."

"It looks amazing." Liz's polished fingernail pointed out the photos. "When can we see it?" I noticed Liz had a glow about her cheeks and she looked more radiant than ever.

"Hang on, Liz, let's get the details on a few more too," I said.

With a loud clunk, Mim passed more folders to Liz with a sigh as she looked at her sympathetically.

"I can arrange a viewing of Kirmingsham Hall on Monday," Mim said, her eyes fastened on Liz. "The owners have moved overseas."

I saw with astonishment that Liz had not even glanced at the other property details. I picked them up.

"Oh good." Liz's eyes were sparkling like a teenager's when she opened her Filofax to make the appointment. "What about ten?"

In the car, I pressed the start button. "You're supposed to be the cautious one." The engine fired and the BMW gently purred into life.

"It must be my hormones," Liz giggled, holding the Kirmingsham Hall folder against her chest above her little bump. Details of other properties littered the back seat, discarded like junk mail.

"Come on, John," she said, "you know you're the calculating one...I don't mean that in a bad way," Liz quickly added. "You're the forward thinker...the strategist...*my* strategist."

"And you?" my hand rested on the gear stick.

"John, you know I'm the creative one. Designer...clever...gifted...original..."

"Original is right...you're unique." I felt defeated but secretly enjoyed it.

Liz continued, "Wife…housekeeper…cook…and soon-to-be mother…" Mother: the ace in her pack.

"All right, all right, I get the picture. You want us to look at the house," I said, feigning a crestfallen expression, my bottom lip pouting.

"Yes please," she gave me a peck on the cheek.

On Monday, my car snaked up the driveway and Kirmingsham Hall appeared. In my side mirror, the lakes sparkled in the morning sunlight, waves lapping towards the gravel path around the lawns. Pulling up at the front of the property, gravel crunched under my feet as I walked and a strange warmth settled within me. Mim waved at the door. 'Miriam Davenport, Sales Consultant', I thought.

Inside, Liz's heels clicked across the red-tiled hallway. I saw her take a considered look at the kitchen and heard her gasp. Mim escorted Liz and me up balconied stairs, which spiralled upwards from the ground floor. Morning sunlight filtered through a balcony window and created a warm glow as we opened bedroom doors and peered in.

We returned to the ground floor, Mim and Liz walking arm-in-arm.

Mim said, "Plenty of rooms, huh?" Gently patting Liz's tummy, she added, "You'll soon need a nursery for baby. There's a guest room with en-suite. It's brilliant, isn't it?"

'Why don't you buy it, Miriam?' I thought. But the house was growing on me.

"The vendors are leaving some landscape framed prints and some furniture, adding to the purchase price." Mim steered Liz firmly towards the lounge. "All the grounds you can see belong to the property as far as the fields and fence on the other side of the lakes. The three garages have workshop potential, and plans have been approved for a conversion to a spacious bedsit above."

"Fantastic!" Liz said. I felt hooked and reeled in.

"What do you think of the view?" Mim asked, her hands like a conductor, sweeping towards the panoramic scenes through patio windows. I thought, 'My three-piece and Liz's two easy chairs will look lost in this lounge, and what do we need for a baby? A cot and…I've no idea.'

Liz clasped her hands together and caught my eye, her face saying, "Well?"

We took a walk around the house – without Mim – and studied the sheer size. The three manicured lawns soft under our feet, Liz hooked her arm in mine as we watched ducks skimming across the dark water.

"Can we do it, darling?" Liz drew me closer to her. "Maybe my dad and your parents should see it first? Perhaps they'll help too?"

I agreed, and we made an offer a few weeks later. Kirmingsham Hall came with a £295,000 mortgage from Lloyds TSB Bank and wiped out our savings.

Liz had Rebecca in June 1987, nearly a honeymoon baby. Liz's father and my parents brought armfuls of presents into the hospital, staying a few days at our home. They also helped us to furnish it.

A Flower Stall

My mind returned to the market place. I had made little progress through the crowds. I stopped walking, took a breath and thought of my family – my family and its storm-clouded times.

Heedless to my surroundings I had passed stalls and shoppers while I sauntered on through the market and reflected upon my roots and my family.

A voice interrupted my stupor. With a jolt I stopped, daydreams evaporating like soap bubbles in the wind. Buckets of assorted flowers were at my feet; pot plants and tied bunches rested on a wooden trestle table. The scent of sweet pea, lilac, lavender, and roses filled the air. The voice brought me back from my world of thoughts to my present reality.

"Good morning, Sir, shalom," the stall-holder announced jovially, bowing his head. "What can I give you today?"

I said, "A bunch of red roses...oh, and a cure for cancer... if you have one."

It was an utterance that had surfaced with no premeditation, leaping out from a deep place in my soul. A verse in the Bible says, "Out of the abundance of the heart, the mouth speaks." I wanted to reel back in what I had said. I felt the colour rising to my cheeks. My jaw dropped at the visibly shaking foreigner. Before I could apologise, or the earth open up and swallow me, the foreigner took hold of my right hand.

With both of his hands, the stall-holder inspected mine carefully, shaking it repeatedly as if I was a long-lost friend. He stroked his beard, mesmerised.

"I knew you would come one day," he said. "This is why I'm here. Please come with me." He spoke with an interesting deep-voiced Yiddish accent.

My mind did somersaults. The stranger with his hand on my back gently ushered me around the side of his market stall towards the cafeteria patio, and bid me to take a seat. The aroma of frying bacon floated towards me with sounds of sizzling sausages. Customers were inside the cafe seated at tables.

'Am I dreaming?' I asked myself, combing my fingers through my hair.

The white plastic patio chair creaked when I sat down under the green and white striped awning flapping in the breeze. Nobody else was braving the outdoor climate. The flower seller said something to the cafe owner who minutes later brought toast and coffee. Sitting back in my chair, I looked carefully at the man. 'Don't suppose I'd better mention the sausages and bacon,' I thought.

Taking a deep breath, I tried to relax, sipping my coffee, not allowing my fevered brain to overload with thoughts of intrigue. The trader seemed genuine enough. 'But what an oddball,' I thought. 'What on earth did he mean about knowing I would come one day?'

"My name is Joseph," he said, brushing crumbs from his navy-blue business suit. His skullcap tottered amidst his black curly hair. His deep voice and accent fascinated me. "I am from Jaffa in Israel," he continued.

As I spread marmalade on my toast, the sun caused the gold watch chain on his waistcoat to shine. His crisply starched white shirt –he was also sporting a red bow tie with black spots – contrasted with his olive skin and curly black beard. I liked the twinkle in his eyes. Eccentric maybe, but growing on me.

"And I am John." We shook hands again. Two customers

passed us to enter the cafeteria looking surprised that we were sitting outside. He looked again at my hand.

Joseph drew his chair closer to the table and, glancing left and right, said, "My home and business is in the UK; my older brother remains in Israel. Do you know anything about Jaffa or its history, John?" He smelled of fresh soap and seemed like a man who thought about his words, but today his hands were restless.

Replying honestly, I said, "I know very little about Jaffa, except for Jaffa oranges and some disputes about land, which seems the norm in your part of the world." I hoped the last phrase didn't upset him; I still wanted those flowers.

Joseph seemed to be weighing up whether he could trust me. Looking right and left, he scrutinised my right hand again.

'What is it about my hand?' I thought. 'This is getting very weird.'

I was becoming fidgety and about to tell him to forget the bunch of roses, when he cleared his throat.

Turning towards me, his eyes locked on mine, he began his story.

The Tale of the Box

Wiping a tear from his cheek with the back of his hand, the flower seller spoke in a faltering voice, "Please don't be worried; I'm not insane. I am a *mentsh,* a man of honour. Years have passed while my brother and I waited for you. Today I'm so happy."

He looked cheery, which shocked me. I touched my wedding ring and scanned the area; my eyes roamed for a quick exit. Crowds shopped a few yards away; the cafeteria owner was within earshot.

"I know what I've said must sound strange," Joseph said, "and what I'm about to tell you will appear the ravings of a lunatic or the tale of a *schlemiel*...a fool. Please hear me out, John." I nodded and felt goosebumps all over.

'OK', I thought, 'John James Morgan, here comes the spiel.' With some reluctance, I decided to give him a chance, settled into the white chair, and chewed toast with butter sliding down my chin. The awning flapped in the breeze, which made me start.

Leaning forward, he lowered his voice, taking a deep breath. The fresh soap smell greeted me again.

"My elder brother, Simeon, and I were born and raised in Jaffa," he said. "As young men we worked in our family business, buying, clearing and renovating houses. Years rolled by. We bought the properties and chattels to rent or sell, making a good living. We were comfortable until fate pulled the rug from under us. *Oy vey!* What a day!" Joseph interrupted his narrative and wiped his curly beard with a paper serviette. I looked at my watch.

He persevered and said, "In a house in 1992 we made a remarkable discovery. The house had a cellar and there we found a hidden antique box. Inside the box were secreted very ancient manuscripts and parchments and a white cloth bag with drawstrings. When we opened the bag, it revealed a few ounces of a dark brown powder."

"Drugs! You must be kidding!" I rose from the chair, pushing it back roughly. "I thought this was some con." I felt my cheeks burning with indignation. From the corner of my eye, I noticed other shoppers had stopped and were watching us.

"No, no, please, John," he said. "Please listen to the rest of my story." The flower seller looked visibly hurt. He lowered his voice. "It has nothing to do with drugs, I promise." I sat down and indicated warily he could carry on as I pulled my jacket tighter.

"At the time, John, my brother and I were as astonished as you are. We took out the documents one by one, shining our torches on them. Our throats were dry like dust."

"Yes I can believe it," I said. "In fact I'm dry as a board now." I called to the cafeteria owner. "Do you have Mellow Birds?" He shook his head. "OK, decaf for me then please." Joseph also gave his order. The cafe owner returned minutes later.

We sipped our hot drinks and Joseph asked me if he could continue. I nodded and watched him.

He continued. "On the fragile scrolls were drawings and maps. Alongside the script were hieroglyphics and scrawled inscriptions. Devout Jews, we did recognise some of the words, but neither of us were experts in ancient Aramaic. We did understand the gist of some of the text, especially the phrase in the heading of the top page."

The flower seller paused. "John," he said. "It leaped out as a message from the gods. In first century Aramaic text it stated the scroll to be 'the last will and testament of Simon Peter', disciple of Jesus Christ of Nazareth.'"

"What?" I said. "Come on, my friend. First it's dark powder and now this! I wasn't born yesterday. I've read about stuff like this: Dead Sea Scrolls…Da Vinci Code…the Lost Ark, and all that. C'mon…pl…ease."

"Please, John. Your hand is the sign. Please listen," he said earnestly and urgently.

"OK. Carry on." I sipped my coffee, feeling mystified.

He continued. "Our hearts beat quickly. We were like drunken men, finding it difficult to believe our good fortune. Our immediate thoughts centred on selling the box. Museums and collectors would part with substantial sums for the rare artefacts. We agreed, however, we had urgently to get the whole text properly translated. The box and contents needed an expert's inspection. Our Uncle Caleb, in Cairo, lectured in mythology and archaic languages at the University of Egypt. We were sure he would help."

"And did he help?" I asked, hoping the preposterous lunatic would hurry up. I looked at my watch again.

Joseph nodded and narrated the rest of his tale about the visit to Caleb Weingart, Professor of Ancient Languages and Artefacts at Cairo University.

I sat back and rocked in the flimsy cafeteria chair and laughed, nearly splitting my sides. 'I needed a laugh,' I thought, 'and this is it.'

At the nearby café, several diners were staring at us. Stretching my hands above my head and yawning, I told the stall-holder that I swallowed none of his tale.

I said, "Two thousand years ago St Peter's box and sacred maps were hidden in a box with magical leaves? I've seen some tricksters in my time. What an unbelievable tale!"

"But the sign," Joseph said, with a puzzled and desperate look.

Rising to leave, I said, "I'm sorry, my friend, but you must be deranged! What made you assume I would believe you? And what do you want?"

"The sign," he pointed to the tattoo on my right hand. "It is kosher. You are the one. The tattoo is identical to the box lid. The rabbi said in the parchments that what is depicted on your tattoo would be a sign." Lifting my hand, he held it before my eyes. People around the flower stall and cafe must have assumed a lovers' tiff. I felt the heat rise to my ears.

"It's OK," I said to our audience, "flower prices, huh?" They dispersed gossiping, looking mystified.

Looking at the golden angels surrounded by green leaves tattooed on my right hand, I saw and felt I understood his predicament. Shivers went down my spine before I slumped down again. My mind went back to the day Sean and I had got our tattoos.

*

I remembered that one night in Afghanistan, in 1990, when Sean decided we would each get a tattoo. He had several, including the SAS insignia. I had none.

"Come on, John, it'll be fun." Sean placed his arm around me and steered me towards a tattoo parlour in downtown Kabul. A moment of madness at a mad time.

Every day, Soviet military commanders ferried me to harvest roadside graveyards of tanks, APCs, jeeps, and mortars. The tough Afghan people were a hard nut to crack, as Mother Russia had discovered, leaving behind enough scrap to keep Morgan Steel very busy.

Sean was busy too. He had told me something of his history. He had been a soldier as an 18-year-old, later a paratrooper, then he'd served in the Falklands in 1982, on his 20th birthday. He'd joined the SAS, where he gained promotion to captain. With the Mujahedeen in Afghanistan, acting secretly as an advisor, he met with tribal elders in their villages and hills. When I met him, he was a civilian and worked in personal protection.

I recalled saying, "Look Sean, I know you like a drink, but you must get it under control. I'm missing my family and I have a pregnant wife, so try soda or juice, huh?"

"Jesus! Going into a bar for soda? That's like winning a blind date with The Corrs and getting the brother!" he said, referring to the Irish band consisting of the Corrs siblings.

Gradually he cut down his drinking and we became great friends. I returned home to the UK with Sean and a tattoo.

"I quite like him," said Liz, stroking her hair behind her ears. "He's tough and sometimes over funny, and he's mixed up and hard like concrete."

"Yes, and he's permanently set: we won't change him."

Liz shivered. "Yes, but do you think he'll be OK with Becky when you take me to maternity?"

Holding her close, I patted her bump. "Yes, she'll be safe in his hands; even the tattooed one. He can stay in the guest room."

After our visit to the tattoo parlour in Kabul, an image of a golden angel amidst green leaves gleamed on my right hand. A yellow serpent wrapped around a crimson devil shone on Sean's left hand: a matching pair. My first and last tattoo.

Someone speaking brought me back from my memories. The flower seller was repeating, "The sign is on your hand, and also in what you said. You asked if I had a cure for cancer. It all fits. I'm not a pharmacy; I sell flowers! Everything the rabbi told Peter. My brother and I have waited 20 years." Beads of perspiration moistened his beard.

After two hours of Joseph's persuasion and pleadings, I trekked home with a bunch of flowers, a photo of Joseph's brother Simeon and a phone number in Tel Aviv. I had promised Joseph I would discuss the matter with my family, and then call his brother. I never break a promise.

I could hardly wait to see the reaction at home when I rehearsed my tale. They were used to my daydreams and imagination but this story, I sensed, would beat them all.

John Tells the Family about the Box

Despite my mind being in turmoil, we needed a miracle and maybe, just possibly, this box could give us one.

On the driveway, James' bike was leaning against the wall alongside Sean's Range Rover. I was tense.

"Sean," I said aloud. "Bloody Irishman; bloody tattoo." Then I felt guilty. "Supposing it's true?"

I paused at James' bike and remembered our last acrimonious words. I had accused him of being immature and needing a job.

I pushed the front door open carefully. It creaked. 'Crap,' I thought, 'the dogs...no time to think strategy...ah, to hell with it.' I walked boldly in. Sure enough, Bourne came barking with tail and backside wagging. He jumped up and I patted his head. He licked my hand with a warm tongue – my right hand.

Walking along the tiled hallway towards the kitchen, I swallowed and pushed the white swing door. As I entered with a confident stride, the kitchen warmed me. I gave Liz the bunch of red roses, received a loving hug, a peck on the cheek, and a plate of sandwiches.

"You're late. But you're forgiven." Liz lifted the roses, inhaled their scent and clutched them to her chest.

Rebecca – Becky – came around the kitchen counter and embraced me. A smooth-skinned raven-haired young woman with sparking green eyes, a younger model of her mother. But tiredness and worry clouded her face. Sean Casey popped his head through the doorway and gave his customary thumbs up. TV sounds came from the lounge.

"Everything OK, Boss?" he asked. "And where's my flowers?" His military-style buzz cut and jovial style reassured me. I knew – at least I hoped – that he and my family would stand by me.

"Yes, thanks, I'm fine," I said. "Sorry I'm late, everybody. I met somebody and got talking."

I looked at the faces surrounding the maroon kitchen units and there seemed nobody taken aback at the news that I'd been distracted. I saw myself similar to Joseph in the Bible: a dreamer *and* a planner. 'OK, here goes,' I thought. 'The dream and the plan.'

Taking a bite at my sandwich, I took a deep breath and announced, "But I've important news, and I'd like to talk with you all."

Like a traffic cop, I beckoned everyone towards the lounge doorway. Raising her dark eyebrows, Liz looked fractionally cross with the interruption to her planned respite day with her daughter. Becky shrugged her shoulders and walked into the lounge. Sean saluted and followed militarily.

The morning room or main lounge at Kirmingsham Hall was comfortably spacious. The northern and southern walls were papered with an "ahoy" design of white yachts on a sea-blue background. East from wall to wall and ceiling to floor several double-glazed aluminium windows and sliding doors opened onto the patio and overlooked the lawns. Our western wall consisted of polished oak panelling with a Tudor stone fireplace.

I stood at the fireplace while my audience took their seats on dark blue leather couches and two matching recliner chairs. I continued to eat my sandwich, some crumbs floating to the hearth. Everyone seemed mystified and nonplussed. Sean switched off the TV.

"Please hear me out first before I answer any questions or we discuss what I have to say." I placed my sandwich plate on the mantelpiece. 'So far so good,' I thought. Sean edged forwards on the recliner, hands squarely on his knees. Liz and Becky looked questioningly at each other, seated together on one of the leather sofas. Liz still held the flowers, a few red petals coming loose and floating down.

It took an agonising 30 minutes to explain every detail of the meeting in the market. I recounted the story of the brothers, the box, the Saviour's words, and the healing leaves. The heat rose in my face and my palms went sweaty. I held up my right hand. Sean lifted his own hand, studied it, and scratched his head.

A hushed silence followed what I'd said. Bourne came and sat by me, his paws on the stone hearth. I patted his head. He nudged my hand and licked it. The tattoo glistened with his saliva. Across the room, Sean's husky, Aunty, turned her eyes towards me as if to say, 'What have you done now, human?'

Sean finally broke the ice. "Well I've heard few weirder stories than that, Boss. But if it was me I'd go to see this guy's brother. You've nothing to lose. Whatever you decide, Boss, you have my vote. Sorry, I gotta leave in ten. My plane to Nairobi is at 19.00 from Heathrow." I shook hands with Sean and he winked and left to pack his holdall. It would only take him ten minutes. His packing was simple and efficient.

Liz spoke up next. She could cut through falsity with precision. Her words were often gentle but her perception razor sharp. "It sounds like a very clever con. I think we should tread very carefully. Maybe this stall-holder saw your hand before he spoke to you and worked his tale around it."

My mind said: 'I'd never thought of that; maybe I am naive. But how would Joseph benefit?'

"I agree with Mum, Dad," Becky said. "Maybe they design the box lids once they spot a victim, like all those Ark of the Covenant boxes in Raiders of the Lost Ark." Becky had done a few months of a psychology degree some years before when her studies were put on hold. But clearly, she still read the books.

I had faced the Morgan family interrogation several times in my life so I knew how things went.

My wife's eyes were fixed on me. Still holding the roses I had bought her, she said, "Are you sure it's wise to set off on your own? Couldn't this meeting wait?" Her brow furrowed as she wagged the flowers at me. "It could be a wild-goose chase." Rose petals dropped to the carpet contrasting with the blue Axminster and the scent of roses filled the air.

"I agree it's a shot in the dark," I took a deep breath, "but it seems to me we've no choice. This seems a risk worth taking. I've promised, so once I've phoned Tel Aviv, I'll make a decision: to go or not." I exhaled.

A tennis match of words then occupied the rest of the afternoon.

Finally, they relented. Even Bourne sensed it, wagging his tail. "OK, Daddy, we trust you." Becky crossed the lounge to touch my shoulder gently. "We know you want the best for Wesley; we're just afraid you'll get drawn into something. You know what you're like," she winked, and patted my back.

"So if we go with it, what next?" Liz asked.

The story of the box sounded far-fetched, I knew that. But a supernatural cord had already wrapped around my heart and was pulling me towards Jaffa.

John calls Simeon

Over the phone, Simeon's daughter, who told me her name was Esther, announced his unavailability until Monday morning, two days away. The Morgan family had hours to reflect on the situation.

For Wesley, though, the sands of time were seeping away: Wesley John was deteriorating.

A call from GOSH had brought the distressing news. Becky had left the hospital on Friday night for a few days' rare rest.

"Listen, Daddy," she said, "do whatever you feel is right. You're usually right. Go with your gut."

Becky and Liz travelled to London on Sunday morning to be with Wesley. Our family friend Tony and his son Alan, Wesley's best friend, had been keeping Wesley company, but he needed his mother.

I dreaded facing James and his million questions once news of the magic box reached him on the family grapevine. Taking a deep breath, I rapped on the door to his room. James moved in a world that I did not understand, but he knew more about IT and programmes than anyone I knew. His main interests consisted of chatting online with fellow computer buffs, and playing online games.

"Dad, you have to go with the feeling in your water," he said with a glint in his eyes. "How many guys with that tattoo have met this Jew? Answer: NONE. You may be 'the chosen one' like he says. But I'll do some research. I'd like to help."

It had been years since I had entered his inner sanctum.

His fingers whizzed across the keyboard, typing white code onto a blue screen. "I'll print off the search results about the two brothers."

After some time, the printer spluttered and spat out several A4 sheets with images and text.

"They do seem legit, Dad." James showed me the details of the brothers' business. "We'll look inside their computers if we can, and see if there's anything dodgy."

I felt a chill. Did he say we? "But isn't that in itself 'dodgy', James? Won't they know that you've accessed their details? I don't want to upset them, especially if this is genuine and it could offer us hope. It could be our last hope." My stomach churned.

"Look, Dad," he passed me the papers. "What my friends and I do may sometimes be on the boundaries, but we're circumventing a government body having to do the same. Let me do my stuff. If UK citizens are being conned – like with the Nigerian letters – we're saving the British taxpayer millions." He turned almost inquiringly, his eyebrows raised like his mother's.

"Yeah…OK…Just be careful, thanks anyway," I said, stuffing the information gathered so far into my pocket. "I'll have a look at this. Thanks, James."

He smiled. His fingers tapped across his keyboard with lightning speed. Screens changed and brought yellow envelope icons.

"By the way, Dad, this could be something to do with supreme intelligence," James said. "This tree and stuff…I bet in Area 51 *and* the CIA they know all about it." James looked exhilarated.

"James, you must stop this nonsense about conspiracy and superior intelligence. Get some friends in the real world."

He grimaced and turned to his screen, and I left the room.

On Monday, I got through to Simeon at 10:30 GMT, 12:30 in Tel Aviv. We talked at length. He gave the same history and persuasive argument and convinced me I should see him. I felt, though, that he sounded less spiritual than Joseph.

I sat in my office while Jenny, my personal assistant, made plans for me to travel to Tel Aviv. On my desk sat a pile of paperwork. I picked up notes left by Sean, which were amongst my main concerns. On yellow Post-It Notes® I read, "Two civil servants were kidnapped by terrorists on the Kenya/Somalia border area. The hostages worked for the Kenyan Prison Service." The Morgan Group had negotiated our prototype with the Kenyan government for floating prisons and so we considered it necessary to respond to their call for help. Sean travelled to Nairobi.

Liz and Becky were staying overnight in flats for new parents above the chapel. I would be travelling to Tel Aviv alone.

*

Tel Aviv. I had followed my destiny. Now alone in a strange place, I was on a Holy Land journey, although instead of following a star I was pursuing a box.

The taxi driver slotted the gear in drive and moved the green and white Volvo forwards; my body jerked right to left. Bright lights from the windows of Ben Gurion International Airport blinded me. Cars honked sharply and alien sights greeted me through misted windows as we drove the 12 miles to the metropolitan area.

The city of Tel Aviv – modern-day Jaffa – is known as the city that never sleeps. Jaffa, an ancient port city, is a part of southern Tel Aviv in the old part of the city. When the taxi braked suddenly and my body was thrown to the opposite side of the seat, the bearded driver apologised over his shoulder. "Sorry, Sir, the other drivers do not observe my signals."

Scanning the flapping identity card attached to the steering column by a black cord, I said, "That's OK, Ahmed. We're in no hurry."

In my mind, I reasoned, 'I've crossed the globe to fulfil my destiny, not to become a traffic casualty. So take it easy, Ahmed.' White smoke trailed from a car that sped past us.

"This is our harbour, Sir," the driver spoke again, interrupting my thoughts. "Over four thousand years she remains. Much blood has been shed."

My spine tingled. My fingertips wiped the misted windows and with my nose pressed against the glass, I could make out the Mediterranean lapping gently against the steps of the stone esplanade. There stretched before the taxi headlights a mammoth lake of black ink streaked by moonlight. Circumnavigating the old area of Jaffa, I noticed silvery-white waves splashing against the eroded harbour wall, with worn grey stone steps snaking down to the ocean. Over his shoulder, the taxi driver gave me a potted history. Perhaps he did the same for all tourists. I appreciated his effort. He had a job to do. "That is the clock tower built by Sultan Abed-el-Hamid II. The famous Abulafia bakery and Yoezer wine bar are in the square. You must visit them while you are here."

Not here for the tour, I reached for the photo in my jacket pocket and asked myself the same questions I'd asked on the plane. 'Will he be as amiable as his brother? Is the story true?' When we went through a traffic island with an ancient clock tower, I looked at my watch. Holding the passport-sized black and white photo, I gazed at it for the hundredth time. Would this man lead me to my destiny? My stomach fluttered.

I looked again at my watch and then settled on the back seat concentrating on the task ahead. 'Come on, John, stay sharp', I thought, 'be firm and clear.' I heard Liz's voice in my head say, 'and no daydreaming.'

Directing a silent prayer, I said, 'God, I hope you can help. Time is running out.' Looking again at the photo made my hands clammy. I put it away. Soon I would meet a man who could change our lives forever.

"We'll be there in a few minutes, Sir," Ahmed said.

We exited at a sign indicating Arlozorov and kept right. After a few minutes, there was another sign, Hilton Hotel 1km. A few jerks and gear changes later we arrived at 205 HaYarkon Street, Independence Park.

"Thanks, Ahmed." I opened my wallet and placed the fare and a tip in Ahmed's hand. Exiting the taxi, I took a deep breath. I was here. What would the next few hours bring?

The large stainless steel "H" of the Hilton caught my eye, the familiar cheering me miles from home. Palm trees shone in the foyer lights. Stars danced above the brown-tiled roof. Outside the hotel forecourt, a smart-uniformed porter quickly approached the Volvo taxi. I smiled, amused that hotel porters around the world always mysteriously appeared when a taxi arrived, as if they had been tipped off. The smell of a gratuity drew them out of their lairs like hyenas.

The porter bundled my blue and white metal suitcase and flight bag onto a luggage trolley, seeming surprised at their lightness. I waved bye to Ahmed and followed the porter. I hoped I would be taking home one more item than I had brought. If I left everything else behind, I had determined that if there was a box, I had to bring it home. Except for my flight bag containing my passport and travel documents, I had only a toilet bag and a change of shirt, socks and boxer shorts in my suitcase. I was not expecting to stay more than a few hours. It would either go well or not.

The hotel deputy manager gave me a room card and the porter disappeared with my luggage. Despite being eager to get the evening over, I enjoyed a Budweiser Light in the bar to slake my nervously dry throat.

"Do you want a snack, Sir?" a barman asked, shuffling glasses around.

"No thanks, just the Bud. I want an early night."

It felt late. A digital clock behind the bar displayed midnight local time. There were several people at the bar. I nodded, trying to avoid conversation. With so much on my mind, I didn't fancy being drained listening to others' problems.

There was only one voice I wanted to hear. Reaching for my mobile, I called my wife, Liz. I didn't have any news, it was just an excuse to hear her voice. I imagined her rubbing her eyes. Raven-black hair falling across her soft cheeks, billowing soft strands on her neck, not cascading softly on my pillow that night. I would miss her shapely warmth and voluptuous curves nestling against me.

"What's the hotel like, darling? Is it comfortable?"

"Yes, it seems very pleasant. I've just arrived. How is he?"

"Not good. Becky and I are staying in London. Let's hope you find good news." I heard Liz's voice breaking.

"Yes, I hope so too, something spectacular. Love you. I'll see you soon." I closed my phone and went upstairs to my room to sleep.

Caleb's Diary

Caleb Weingart, Professor of Ancient Languages and Artefacts at Cairo University, enjoyed happily married bliss with Miryam, his soulmate. He looked back and recalled the obstacles to their happiness, especially in their early courting.

Thirty years before, Caleb's family had been anxious that he might marry beneath himself: beneath their expectations. They had held high hopes that their son would marry an academic with similar interests to his own. To their dismay, they had discovered that he had fallen in love with Miryam Latchman, information they had gleaned from his diary under his mattress. Blushing at the intimate details of their secret meetings, they had finally confronted him.

"Caleb! Your father and I are very upset that you have been seeing this...this Miryam behind our backs!" His mother waved his diary at him. "It must stop immediately. We've made plans. Your father and I want you to have a *baleboste*, a homemaker for your wife," his mother continued. His father nodded; easier to agree when Mrs Weingart reached full flow.

"But we love each other..." Caleb protested in frustration.

His mother interrupted, as she often did, "*Oy vey iz Mir.* There are other considerations than love, Caleb! Isn't that right, Papa?" and she assailed Caleb with other pleadings and arguments. Caleb's father nodded.

"Anyway," Caleb said when his mother drew breath, "how did you find my diary? I had it *hidden* in *my* bedroom."

"No good son keeps things from his mama," Mrs Weingart said, folding her arms around the diary to her ample bosom. Mr. Weingart nodded; he kept nothing from his wife, an impossible quest. He winked at Caleb and looked proud of his son.

*

Caleb did one day marry Miryam. But he had learned from the experience with his parents that keeping his diary from prying eyes was vital. So whenever he left his study at Cairo University, he locked his diary in his desk drawer, and carried the only keys in his jacket pocket. He believed his secrets were safe.

*

Eitan Dreyfuss did not know or care what the 'stupid professor' had in his study: he just wanted to find something he could sell. Eitan worked as a cleaner at the university and he knew that he would not be under suspicion if he was spotted in the corridor with his cleaning trolley. He had tried a few doors and found with frustration that his master key didn't open them, but his heart raced when old man Weingart's door clicked open.

"Ha ha," Eitan whispered to himself, "that old goat has slipped up. What a *klots,* block of wood." Glancing left and right and feeling safe, Eitan entered the sanctuary of the professor, pushing his cleaning trolley. Taking a can of pine polish, he quickly sprayed the desk, making himself look busy, his eyes and ears alert.

He scanned the shelves and desk and quickly placed whatever looked valuable into his refuse sack. He secreted a clock, a silver trophy, some expensive-looking pens, and a few silver photo frames. "The old *shmendrik* has nothing of value. What a jerk. He even takes his laptop home," Eitan spat with disgust.

Grabbing a letter-opener from the desktop, he levered the drawer catch with a loud "crack!" and glanced inside. He stopped, listening carefully for any noise in the corridor. A diary rested atop papers, pens and a magnifying glass. He threw it all in with his other loot, and dragged the trolley backwards through the door. The door closed with a gentle 'clunk'. Eitan smirked and wheeled his trolley onwards to complete his shift. 'A few more hours to go,' he thought.

Hours later, his right arm above his head, he said, "What a boring old toad," and breathed a disappointed sigh as he lay in bed reading Caleb's diary. Page after page he turned over impatiently. Arriving at one page, however, the hairs on the back of his neck tingled as he read of an "ancient box with treasure". He read on, his heart pounding. He came to the last entries about the professor's nephews talking with an Englishman who would be flying over to Israel to collect the box. Eitan swallowed and checked the dates.

He rubbed his hands together. "Well, well. Perhaps there is something in this." The next morning, he spoke with some people that he often did business with, careful not to give too much away. Eitan and two others made plans to stake out the Hilton.

Liz and Becky at GOSH

In the midst of the usual night-time noises rebounding across the car park, there came cries. Cries, calls and sometimes screams. Little people were in pain; small children were suffering in another world.

Above the chapel in the parents' block, two women craned their heads to listen. Nature recognises the calls of its own. Amidst the cries, the women could discern one.

"It's him, isn't it?" Liz inquired. Becky, in an adjacent single bed, sat up and strained to hear through the thick chapel walls and stained-glass windows. She looked tired, as if her vibrant youth had been drained away like sand through an hourglass.

"Yes, Mum. It is. It's him." She slid out of the check-patterned quilted cover and sat on the edge of the bed, the steel springs creaking. The cold metal frame pressed against her legs when she slipped her feet into red slip-ons. She picked her pink bracelet watch from a white bedside cabinet and looked at the digital face: 4:00 a.m. She pushed off the bed and took two steps to the door. The dark polished oak floor creaked. She lifted a white terry-cloth bathrobe from a hook. It had a blue "H" over the breast pocket. Its softness gave some comforting memories of happier times. She snuggled it around her.

"Pass me mine, Becky," Liz said gently, running her fingers through her hair. She was also sitting on the edge of her bed.

She put on her plum-coloured Clark's slippers. "I'll come with you." Becky passed Liz a brightly coloured kimono. The trees, birds and pagodas stood out against a black and scarlet background. The silk rustled as she tied the belt.

The wooden door closed gently behind them and their steps sounded on the metal spiral staircase. Wood polish and the aroma of flowers met them in the dimly lit chapel interior. Candles flickered, lit by praying parents.

Becky's mum put a gentle hand on her shoulder, "I read somewhere that 'Gethsemane' means wine-press: the last few years have felt like that." Liz steered Becky between pews to an oak door. They said their prayers, although their hopes were in a box.

Becky pushed open the heavy dark oak chapel door. The two women walked through the doorway to the lift, Becky's flip-flops slapping against the tiled floor.

The lift jerked downwards to the upper ground floor and the doors swished open.

Cold air met the women in the corridor, harshly lit by strip lighting that blinked and hissed. The brick walls were painted white. It smelled of metal and heat.

"I don't think we'd ever find our way through this maze without this," Liz nodded towards a glossy red line, about six inches in width, stretching into the distance.

They walked past huge metal boxes with dials and flashing lights. Steel heating ducts about two feet in diameter pulsated and groaned above their heads. An underground world, whilst 30 feet above, most of London remained asleep, unaware of worried wakeful parents. Another world.

It became warmer as they approached the boilers, and Becky screwed up her nose at the strong smell of disinfectant.

Becky pushed apart two opaque charcoal-coloured plastic doors and they stepped through. The doors closed with a loud 'slap'. Maps, charts and various instructions were affixed to a cream wall facing them. In the brightly lit corridor, another pair of lift doors faced them.

Liz pressed "4"and when the lift doors opened on the fourth floor they were in a world of noises, smells and suffering. Children attached to drips tossed and turned in their beds. Some, like Wesley, were seriously ill, the seconds and minutes of his life fleeting away like a vapour.

The Kenya/Somalia Border

Sean Casey stood clothed in black: black beret, black tee-shirt, black zipped-up jacket, black pants, and black lace-up boots. His face was camouflaged with green and black paint. His four companions were likewise attired in black, but their faces needed no camouflage. They were as black as the night. The time for negotiation was over.

Sean had responded to a call for help from the Commissioner of Prisons of Nairobi. Two prison officials, a magistrate and a charity worker had been taken hostage on the Kenya/Somalia border. The Kenyans wanted Sean to work with the armed police and free the four of them.

The two Land Rovers bounced past a massive football stadium and Sean said, "Why the lights and music? Soccer match?"

"No, Boss," his driver said, "it's a gospel crusade with Christ for All Nations. It will be full every night." Sean shrugged and said, "Takes all sorts, I guess. Good luck to 'em. The world needs something."

Twenty minutes later, the vehicles drove with lights out and parked after a few hundred yards. Sean and the Kenyans moved stealthily through the terrain and reached a clearing.

Sean elbowed forward through the African bush, a 22-mm handgun in his right hand. He poked the silencer through the tall grass and signed for his companions to go two left and two right. The Kenyans had AK47 automatic machine guns, against Sean's advice.

"You'll spray those bloody things everywhere and be empty in two seconds," he had argued vehemently. The police commander, adamant that his men would only shoot when shot at, insisted they would act professionally.

"OK," Sean said. "But wait till I give the signal. They may be a ragtag bunch of guerrillas but I'll use a whistle. I don't want you bastards peppering my behind."

Intelligence, such as it existed, had informed the party of at least a dozen Somali hostage takers. Sean had coughed when he'd heard. The data was clearly wrong about the number of hostages that had been taken, originally two and then four, and so he did not feel hopeful. He used his own intel, his eyes.

"Anyone with a gun is a bad guy," Sean said. "Anyone tied up is not. Are we clear?"

"Yes, Boss," they whispered with nods. Sean suspected they were providers of large families and the last thing on their minds would be getting shot. They would shoot first from a safe distance and duck.

It turned out six "bad guys" guarded the compound. At least that was how many corpses were left after Sean crept forward, his right hand delivering a "phutt" periodically as another body crumpled. In the darkness, illuminated by a campfire, the hostage-takers tried to flee and the explosions of blood, flesh and brain matter were lost in the confusion as one body after another slumped over the campfire or on the ground in the bush: four head shots and two body shots.

Sean crept forwards silently and put another head shot into the bodies as he passed, rolling them over with his foot. Six dead before anyone had blinked.

He kicked in each hut door and jumped to the side each time, gun at the ready. Only one hut was occupied, and they were all tied up. By Sean's definition, these were the "good guys". He lifted a whistle to his lips and gave two shrill signals. Several pairs of white eyes appeared in the bush. Spinning the gun around his finger, he placed it in his belt and waved his four companions forwards. He was not a savage brute, unfeeling about fatalities, but his clear mantra affirmed "them or us".

Slapping his back in awe and celebration, his companions helped four hostages out, overwhelmed to be free. Two prison officials, one magistrate, and a Save the Children worker joined the Kenyan soldiers. The stunning blonde charity worker called Rachel came from Bristol, as Sean discovered when she hugged him. She clung to Sean like a limpet while the party walked through the bush to two green army vehicles.

The engine roared and diesel fumes filled the air as the army Land Rover bounced through the darkness, throwing them against one another.

"Oops, sorry," the blonde said.

"You're called Rachel, huh?" Sean said, looking at the vivacious 30-something blonde charity worker. "That's a nice name." She smiled. Sean smiled.

The Hilton Hotel: Tel Aviv

Mark Twain said, "The two most important days in your life are the day you are born, and the day you find out why." I awoke early on the morning of Tuesday 14th February 2011. I should have been with my family on my birthday, enjoying a Valentine kiss. Was I about to find out why I had been born?

I stared out of my hotel window at a 6:25 a.m. Mediterranean sunrise. The spectacular panoramic blues, greens and whites of the ocean were made brilliant by the rising orb of a golden sun. I yawned. Sleep had avoided me like a phantom pursued all night. A jack-in-the-box chased me in my dreams.

As I closed my door, other residents were walking ahead of me towards the sign "Reception and Restaurant". The plush red carpet felt springy as I descended the stairs, my hand chilled by the metallic stair rail. I caught my image in the glass of frames with glossy photos of Israel adorning the plush maroon wallpaper, and finger-combed my hair. Hilton stairs, Hilton carpet, Hilton signs: comfortable, familiar memories.

Enticing smells ascended from the breakfast bar. At the spacious bar/restaurant area, the deputy hotel manager caught my eye.

"Good morning, Mr Morgan. Did you sleep well? Is there anything I can do for you?"

"I'm fine thanks. I'm expecting a guest. If they inquire at

reception, can you send them into the restaurant please? A *Daily Express* too, that'd be appreciated…if you have one."

The small man with a tiny moustache withdrew a newspaper from the racks and passed it to me. His part black, part grey toupee looked flat and dry. I tucked the paper under my arm and wondered if underneath the toupee his head was like a billiard ball.

"Thanks again, I'm missing home and it's my birthday." I felt a blush and wished I could take the words back.

"Happy birthday, Mr. Morgan," the man said. A smell of garlic reached me as his bushy eyebrows rose sympathetically, "So far from your loved ones on your birthday."

"Thank you. My first time in your city — only here for a meeting today."

"Well, I hope your meeting goes well and you enjoy your stay with us," he said. "There are menus on the tables." He picked up some papers from his desk and bent down to make a phone call. Conversation over.

I strode on towards the eating area, hearing fresh cutlery being arranged, the aroma of coffee wafting to my nostrils. The smell of freshly baked croissants reminded me of my grandma's oven in my childhood.

In the breakfast bar, I nodded to a cluster of hotel staff at the serving area, signalling to a waiter in matching maroon bow tie and waistcoat. He came swiftly over.

"A table by the window please."

"Certainly, Sir," he replied, busying himself collecting redundant cutlery and going to locate seating. I noticed the restaurant had a modern appearance: three walls painted a grey mushroom colour, one papered with an embossed silver and gold paper. A mosaic of black and white ceramic tiles gave the restaurant floor a chess-board impression. Some had dared their move. I boldly stepped onto white king's four: my opening gambit.

My Blackberry bleeped, the ID flashing my friend Sean's name. Diners stared at me as if talking was forbidden. 'OK,' I thought, 'I'll tone it down. But come on, it's not a library!'

"How's it going, Boss?" the Irishman inquired.

"OK, Simeon hasn't arrived yet."

"I hope it goes well. I'll pray to the saints for ya."

"Speaking of saints…what's the situation in Somalia?" I was eager to know about the attempted rescue of the hostages.

"Tell ya later, I gotta dash." Sean hung up.

"Bloody hell, Sean. Could you be quicker?" I mouthed under my breath.

I closed my phone.

Diners were enjoying their breakfast and browsing daily papers. I glanced at my daily, scanning the headlines, deciding I would read it later. Most of the guests appeared European. Nobody matched the description of the photo in my jacket pocket.

"Is that one suitable, Sir?" the waiter asked, pointing to a table by the clear glass window overlooking the street.

"That's fine, thank you."

Making little eye contact with other guests, I edged my six-foot-one frame forwards. With my left hand, I combed my mass of hair: my Boris look according to my wife. I looked at the tattooed hand holding the newspaper. Freckles were appearing, lured out by the sun. From my table I could observe people coming and going if I kept alert. The waiter placed a card menu on the snow-white tablecloth.

I placed my order, "Buttered toast, marmalade and a decaf coffee, please."

"Yes, Sir, thank you."

He went towards the bar. I continued looking out of the window at people hurrying to work. My guest would be arriving soon, I hoped. Trying to relax until my coffee or guest arrived I picked up the paper, but failed to concentrate. I spread my fingers in my hair, trying to bring some order to the sandy thatch. Foot traffic hurried by outside, drawn into a spider's web of exhibit shop windows designed to hypnotise shoppers into a euphoria of spending. Could my expected visitor be pushing through the window-shoppers at that moment?

Pressing a number from my contacts list, I waited for an answer, knowing it would be approaching lunchtime in the UK.

The voice spoke quietly, "This is Joseph. Who's speaking?"

"Hello Joseph, it's John. I'm here, at the hotel, waiting for Simeon."

"Shall I call him for you, John?" he offered.

"No, it's fine thanks. I just wanted to be sure." I felt my cheeks getting hot.

"He will definitely come as we promised. You will not be disappointed."

"OK, thanks Joseph." Relieved, I closed my mobile and concentrated on meeting a man about a box.

As I sat at my table waiting for Simeon, moving the cutlery back and forth and organising the condiments for the umpteenth time, the waiter returned with my toast, butter and a small pot of marmalade along with a welcome decaf coffee. Outside grew warm with the sun's first blush, but air-conditioning cooled the diners inside. Scanning the restaurant area, I ate my breakfast and sipped my decaffeinated coffee. I waited for a man in his mid to late 50s, the brother of a market trader I'd met four days before, hoping he would be on time.

My fellow hotel guests looked towards my table. Sympathetic stares seemed to imply, "only Johnny-no-mates would be dining alone". 'Little do you know,' I thought. All eyes would have looked jealously towards me if my wife had graced my table. Liz was a huge strength to me. Her support over the years had anchored me in safe and familiar harbours. The kindness she emitted wherever she went left a summery atmosphere, warmly encircling me and our two children. Liz, my best friend.

My nerves told me the most important meeting of my life approached. Vinegar bitterness rolled around my stomach, but I fortified myself. Our whole world depended on one encounter. I felt convinced we had been presented with a chance, a naked flame flickering in the darkness, our only glimmer of hope.

In a daydream, staring through the hotel window, I was unaware that someone was standing at my table until he spoke. I turned my head to see a short, stocky, bearded man in his mid-50s, dressed in a long white sort of nightshirt and a poncho-like garment with a hole for his head, wearing a skull-cap on his greying hair.

"Are you Mr Morgan?" the stranger asked. "May I sit down?" I nodded and he took a seat opposite. He offered me his hand and I shook it nervously, while he carefully examined the tattoo on my hand. He took his time, looking into my eyes: an investigation.

"I'm so glad you came, Mr Morgan," he finally said. "My brother told me all about you before you rang, and I've also made my own inquiries. You seem an honest and caring man, and you must be courageous to travel alone all this way."

He spoke with an accent similar to his brother's. I noticed an identical black curly beard and the same twinkle in his brown eyes, but his were harder, more severe. His comment about my honesty made me feel a bit queasy. 'Hope James and his friends don't blow it,' I thought, remembering James' computer investigations. His eyes continued to search me and look at my hand. Stirring myself, I decided to grasp the nettle.

"Well I must admit, Simeon, that I had serious reservations when your brother related your story to me," I said. "But if you can help my grandson in any way we would be extremely grateful." The family had stressed that I must not build up my hopes or offer money before undeniable evidence was produced.

"Ah yes. Wesley John, your grandson. I understand that he is quite ill. It must be a difficult time for you and your family." I wondered how he knew about my family, and if he knew people like James did, who could "find out things".

"Please do not be worried, Mr Morgan. We've not been prying," he said, as if he'd read my mind. "My brother asked a few people around the market area and the locality where you live whether they knew you. It's amazing what people will tell you over a cup of coffee."

He looked at my coffee cup. I apologised for my lack of common courtesy and called over the waiter, who took Simeon's order and refilled my cup.

"It's an Eastern tradition, I suppose, Mr Morgan," he said, "that we like to discuss matters over food and refreshments. Now let's get down to why you came here." He paused when the waiter came over with toasted teacakes and coffee, and then continued.

"Let me assure you that my brother and I are not asking for any payment for the box or its contents. Whilst we are, of course, businessmen and we recognise things of value, we believe by the way the box came into our possession, and its clear instructions, that we are obliged to give it to you. My brother and I have made far more money than we will ever need. The stereotype of Jewish people being like Shylock is not accurate. We are kindly souls. Joseph travels Europe selling flowers, whilst I restore antiques. So do not worry, Mr Morgan, no money will change hands when I give you the box."

When Simeon had finished I felt overwhelmed, and I was about to say something when Sean called again.

"Please excuse me, Simeon, I really must take this."

"How much do they want, Boss?" I walked a few feet from the table and held the mobile phone closely to my mouth.

"Nothing", I whispered, "absolutely nothing. I'm as gob-smacked as you. Either they're balmy, or we've some genuine altruists. By the way, what's happening in Somalia?"

"Holy Mary Mother of God…nothing?" Sean said. I looked at other diners to see if they'd heard him. "That's a surprise," he continued. "Oh, and in Somalia there are six dead bad guys and four hostages recovered alive and well. I'm flying back in a Kenyan general's jet in an hour."

"Four hostages did you say?" I held the mouthpiece to my lips, my voice a whisper. "I thought there were only two?"

"It's a long story, Boss. One's a pretty missionary, and you know me and a pretty face. Plus, she's a Catholic. Gotta go." He hung up.

I placed the mobile back into my pocket and returned to the table, apologising again to Simeon for the interruption, although he appeared to have been occupied with his snack. He wiped the remnants of his breakfast from his beard.

'OK, to business,' I thought, castle to king's rook eight, CHECK.'

Strangers and the Box

"Is that him?" one of Eitan's friends asked, speaking in whispers with his hand over his mouth. The group of three friends looked out of place in the armchairs surrounding the bar. Their scruffy shorts and tops were frayed, their battered trainers stained.

"Yes, now shut up and let's see what happens. Stop blathering," Eitan replied curtly.

An older looking man joined them. "I see no box. You sure this isn't a hoax?"

The deputy manager of the Hilton in Tel Aviv didn't seem to me the cleverest of men. But it seemed he could smell trouble. I saw him wave a porter over and whisper in his ear. The two spoke with the security chief and surreptitiously nodded towards three young men sitting at the bar. The chief waved over another of the porters and they crossed the bar area with the deputy manager. The young men looked annoyed. The deputy manager said something to them, and pointed to the door. Then he and the porters escorted the complaining youths and their companion to the main entrance, the large security chief standing guard. The deputy manager called something after them and the teenagers walked away slouching, one of them raising his index finger to the deputy manager.

Simeon's voice brought me back to our own business.

"When you have finished your coffee, Mr Morgan, I suggest

we get a taxi to my bank and we can…conclude our business?"
Trusting myself in the stranger's hands, and eager to see the
box, I agreed.

Simeon seemed surprised when Ahmed wound down his
taxi window and called, "Hello again, Mr John."

"I took Ahmed's cab from the airport."

"Yes, he did," Ahmed said as he steered the Volvo away from
the kerb. "My brother is looking after my fish business today,
so I'm doing a shift."

Simeon gave instructions and sat silently in the back, while
I sat in the front with Ahmed. We passed through poor areas
in the densely populated city, and I noticed squalidly dressed
people living in the shantytowns. We skirted a conglomerate
of market stalls, their goods spilling into the road, and shop
fronts with wares of every kind. A hectic 20-minute journey
later, concrete and glass office blocks towered above us. The
sun warmed the inside of the taxi and cast rectangular shad-
ows on the sidewalk and road.

Our taxi pulled up outside the Bank of Syria in the financial sector of downtown Tel Aviv. I thought it a bit strange
that two Jewish brothers would have a safe-deposit box in a
Syrian bank.

"Wait here, please, Ahmed." I looked at the parking meters
and gave him a handful of coins.

"Thank you, Mr John." He placed coins in the meter and
pocketed the rest. "I will wait."

A portly man in navy blue uniform doffed his peaked
cap and pulled open the inscribed metal and glass doors of
the bank. He stood on the sidewalk, ushering in customers.
Business boomed in Tel Aviv. I hoped that business would be
the only boom.

Simeon and I walked past cash points, tellers and tills.
Security guards on each side of us held black semi-automatic
Uzi machine guns in their hands, the straps wrapped around
their shoulders. The round wall clock indicated after 9:30.
Black wall-mounted cameras above me flashed with red dots.

Plush carpeted stairs led to a secure basement area, entered through a gate of white cast-iron bars. A uniformed security woman looked at Simeon's identification and allowed him through the gate. The smell of metal polish filtered through the area. Through the bars, I watched Simeon approach an official behind a desk, fill in some forms and show his passport. I took a seat on a leather bench outside the safety deposit box area until Simeon returned with something: a cube-like structure wrapped in a white cloth, held tightly under his arm. As I looked at the parcel, I felt that like Frodo Baggins, I had stumbled onto my destiny.

"Let us go, and please be quick, but don't draw attention to us," Simeon said urgently.

I didn't understand but I obeyed, in a hurry too for my own reasons. So far, it had been easy. 'Maybe too easy,' I thought. Outside the bank, we found Ahmed waiting, his engine running, exhaust moisture dripping onto the road.

The Volvo snaked its way through busy morning traffic, narrowly missing other cars. Ahmed seemed to understand the road signals and road etiquette, lurching forwards at intersections, as everyone drove as a law unto themselves. Looking sideways at him from the front seat, I noticed the lines in his face around his unkempt beard. The photo identification card attached to the dashboard portrayed a younger man.

Outside the Hilton, I pressed notes into Ahmed's hand. Kissing me on both cheeks, he jumped back into the Volvo. Simeon looked up and down the street and entered the hotel foyer cagily.

Placing a "No Room Service" sign on my door, I entered with Simeon behind me and locked the door. Simeon reverently placed the box on my bed, on top of a dark blue quilt, and removed the white sheet. Placing my hand on top of the box, I looked at two sets of golden angels amidst green leaves. My mouth was dry, my hand was shaking. 'Could I really be the authentic box owner?' I wondered. 'It has to be true.' My heart was pounding when I thought that this could be the reason I'd been born, the reason I was on earth.

Simeon lifted the lid, showing me the contents.

"Look, we were not lying, John," he said. "It's exactly as we related. See the ancient manuscript scrolls, maps and drawings?" Holding up a small white cloth bag, he placed it on the bed and invited me to look inside.

I pulled the drawstrings and peeked inside, sniffing. It smelled unlike anything I'd ever come across. The dark brown powder resembled crushed and broken leaves but they sparkled. Taking one of the ancient maps, I saw drawings of rivers and a garden, in the midst of which were trees with strange writing underneath. Other maps were of an area with contour lines and places unknown to me. I held the bag again and could feel my heart beating fast. Carefully placing the bag on top of the parchments, I closed the lid with a sense of awe.

Simeon said, so abruptly that I stood bolt upright, "I have to go now. Please leave Jaffa quickly, and good luck!" The door opened and closed and like the genie of the lamp, he had vanished.

I called Liz's mobile and Becky's but both were switched off. I rang James and told him the news, bursting to tell someone.

"Dad, that's great. But get out of there quickly, I've a bad feeling about this. I'll tell you what I've discovered when you get home. I think others know about the box."

It took me only a few minutes. I paid, and the hotel receptionist called a taxi to take me to the airport. My driver was not Ahmed and I settled in the rear, without noticing the two men watching me at the hotel and calling a taxi to follow me.

By changing my ticket from Manchester to Heathrow, I could go straight to London and from there to the hospital. My departure for London was scheduled at 12:30 p.m. local time. I checked in my baggage, hoping that the miracle box would be safe in the plane's luggage hold. While waiting for the departure call, my mobile must have rung, but I missed it. Simeon had left a message on my voice mail: "It's dangerous to talk. Others know what you have...my uncle's diary...please be careful."

"Thanks, Simeon," I said to the air. "I'm about to board a plane with St Peter's last will and testament and you tell me to be careful." I felt consternation and elation, and mainly, I was relieved to be heading home with the box.

*

Biting the cellophane packaging to rip it open, I spread jam on my croissant and washed it down with coffee after enjoying the best in-flight meal I'd ever had.

I was relieved and euphoric to be heading home. I stretched out my legs and eased the seat back, relaxing and thinking of my family. I did not notice two other passengers watching me.

Excitement kept me awake for the comfortable four-and-a-half-hour flight until, with rapture, I heard the pilot announce landing, London time 4:30, and the usual protocols.

At the luggage carousel, my blue and white case made a bumpy circular journey on the steel conveyor amongst a handful of others. Flight bag slung across my shoulder, I moved forwards gratefully to collect my case, feeling a load off my mind.

Suddenly I felt a push. A scruffy young man had rudely pushed me out of the way, pointing to my luggage. He hurried to join an older, more menacing man as they made their way to the revolving carousel. I felt dazed when the other man grabbed my case and they ran.

"Oi stop! Those men are stealing my belongings!" I shouted. "Stop them!" Security guards standing in the corners started to move, but with a head start, the thieves had raced away. Seething anger erupted within me while I gave chase, my voice growing hoarse.

"STOP THOSE MEN!" I bellowed, pursuing them as fast as I could through the concourse. In the arrivals hallway, people jumped out of my way as I ran, breathing hard. Trolleys laden with cases spiralled away, striking walls and upturning chairs. I could see the two men even further ahead and dreaded that they were stealing our hope.

Suddenly a six-footer with a grey military buzz-cut leapt a security barrier to rugby tackle the man with my case. They tumbled along the hallway, scattering passengers and pot plants as they grappled, and my case fell from the man's clawing hands. The new arrival head-butted them and quickly stood to punch the younger man in the body. With a couple more karate kicks and punches, he despatched the two luggage thieves who ran away empty-handed, glancing back angrily, the guards in hot pursuit.

"I can't take you anywhere," said the grey-haired man with an Irish accent, his chest rising and falling. Wiping blood off his forehead, he said, "Don't worry, it's not mine. I bleed army."

"Sean, it's good to see you!" I said, puffing and panting. "You came in the nick of time!"

"What were those eejits after?" he said, "Not your Calvin Klein undies?"

I smiled with relief. Then I grew more sombre and said, "They must be after the box, Sean."

Sean handed me my case. "Come on, we'd better get out of here."

Minutes later, I strode through the "Nothing to Declare" customs line.

"How did you manage to be in the luggage area, Sean?" I asked.

The wind blew my hair as we walked to Sean's Range Rover. He said, "After I landed in the general's private jet…" I coughed. Sean continued, "I put my luggage in the boot and sorted a hire car for Rachel so she could journey straight to Great Ormond Street."

"Who's Rachel again, Sean?" I asked, amused.

"Ah, well, ya see, she's the other rescued hostage, Boss," he said, while we pushed the trolley with my case and flight bag. "Anyway, knowing you could get lost without me, and were arriving within the hour, I had a word with airport security.

I flashed my old SAS warrant card and used Irish charm, and they escorted me to luggage retrieval beyond the customs hall. They even gave me coffee."

I guessed he would fill me in on the way to GOSH. With the Range Rover door open, I placed my case and flight bag on the back seat.

As we sped past fields and buildings on the motorways, I opened the case. Laying the lid of the box aside, I put the drawstring bag in my pocket. At a service area, Sean looked at the box, took my hand, stared at the box lid, and slapped my back.

He locked the box and my luggage in his boot and said, "Well done, Boss, you did it!" Journeying through London traffic, he made a hands-free call to his new mates at Heathrow.

"Aye, it's me. No problem. Can ya email the Morgan Group the CCTV of the two bozos? Thanks."

With my head against the headrest, I fell asleep and then woke startled to Sean saying, "Wakey, wakey, Boss." Then, "Bloody English: Irish labour builds your roads and now I have to pay to park on 'em."

I laughed and rubbed my eyes. I had missed Sean's Irish wit. He dropped five £1 coins in the meter near Great Ormond Street Hospital.

The Fourth Floor at GOSH

In the GOSH foyer, standing before the marble statue of Jesus with a child in His arms and the caption "Suffer the little children to come unto me", I thought, 'With my hope for one little child those words are very appropriate.'

Sean sent a text message when we approached the lift. Making our way to the fourth floor as the lift jerked upwards, I struggled to put out of my mind all that could happen. Thoughts sought to gain entrance like uninvited guests: What did they know of cancer in St Peter's day? Did I trust in ground leaves from a tree? Did I believe in the Garden of Eden?

I felt Sean press his hand on my back. "OK, let's go."

The familiar metallic doors swished open and I steeled myself to follow the familiar arrows and grey flooring. I pushed swing doors and a vivacious young blonde woman ran towards us, linking arms with Sean.

Sean said, "John, Rachel...Rachel, John."

I could see Liz and Becky ahead of us sitting in hospital armchairs beside Wesley's bed. Two weary bodies rose to greet us, their tired eyes heavy.

After a warm embrace, Liz said, "I see you've met Rachel? She works with Save the Children." She looked at me knowingly. I hugged her again and held her for a few seconds.

I nodded. "It looks like Rachel has her own hostage."

Rachel giggled, "Hello again."

My gushing Irish friend fawned over her; a strong arm encircled her waist.

"Hi, Daddy," Becky pecked my cheek. I hugged her, struggling to keep my emotions in check.

"Hello, little man," I kissed Wesley's head, noticing his yellowing skin and gaunt frame.

He managed a smile. Becky told me, in a whisper, choking back the emotion, "His organs are gradually failing, Daddy." His little body was linked up to machines and intravenous drips, the beep-beep reminding me that time was slipping away, second by second.

"Well, come on, Boss," Sean said. "Do we make a brew with the magic powder and drink it like Typhoo, or do we just sprinkle the powder on his head?" He was trying to inject humour but was also being pragmatic.

"I must admit, getting the box and leaves is one thing, but I'm not sure how to use them," I said combing my fingers through my hair.

"Wesley can't eat the leaves; he would vomit them up straightaway," Becky said.

After a few silent moments, Rachel suggested helpfully, "In the Bible, Jesus made a mixture of soil and water and rubbed it on a blind man's eyes – like a poultice."

Sean beamed and gave the thumbs up.

Becky thought Rachel's idea to be a good one, so I followed her into the kitchen for patients' families and opened the white cloth bag. We mixed some of the contents with water in a paper sluice bowl. I placed the bag back into my pocket.

Back in the ward, Becky dipped her fingers in the dark brown gooey mixture and gently applied it to Wesley's forehead and chest. A smell of cinnamon, oranges and pine wafted from the dark patches. Within ten minutes, no visible trace could be seen on Wesley's skin. We didn't know what to expect or how long it might take.

"I guess now we just wait? Take turns at his bed?" I suggested.

The machines continued to beep. Children cried and nurses moved around.

Minutes turned to hours. Wesley slept comfortably while we slept intermittently in the waiting room on couches and chairs, taking turns by Wesley's bedside. The drinks machine was broken so Sean and I made trips to the ground floor, bringing back trays of drinks and sandwiches from the hospital cafeteria.

Night turned to day and the ward sounds increased. The hospital staff turned a blind eye to our numbers. The nurses had cared for Wesley throughout his illness and I surmised from their faces that they thought we were reaching the end.

*

At daybreak on Wednesday morning, I saw Wesley stretch his arms and yawn. I rubbed my eyes, then shook myself and finger-combed my hair.

"Morning, Mummy," he said, red rosy cheeks in contrast to his white pillow. "Can I have some toast?"

Liz looked at me, astonished.

Becky said, "Yes, of course, sweetheart. Are you sure?" He nodded, and Liz went to organise it. Sean and Rachel gathered around his bed. I just gazed in wonder.

"He looks amazingly healthy," I said to all within earshot. "The yellowness has gone." I couldn't stop smiling. I rang James.

"I've nursed children all over the world," Rachel said. "It looks to me like he's turned a corner."

Sean nodded and swirled her around, met by stares from the nurses' station.

Wesley chewed his toast, played on a Nintendo, and improved hour by hour. Nurses and doctors did tests and then repeated them, looking mystified. I understood their bafflement: they lived with pain and disappointment, their empathy and hope blunted by suffering.

At noon, Mr Thomas the specialist appeared with an entourage of student doctors, each holding clipboards and wearing stethoscopes around their necks. Hospital screens were pulled back to make room for a semi-circle of observers. Sean stood sentry-like.

"I've never seen anything quite so remarkable," Mr Thomas stated, glancing at the students one by one. "According to the ultrasound the tumours appear to have shrunk. The symptoms of disease have abated. The patient's blood count is approaching normal. Of course everything will need to be verified, but at the moment he should cease treatment and we will review his case and prognosis."

Silently I breathed a prayer of thanks as I felt inside my jacket pocket. Aware that others also knew and sought the leaves, I determined that I would guard the bag with my life. I emerged from my thoughts by the conversation between Becky and the doctor.

"You've done all you can, I know that," Becky said, looking directly at the consultant. "I'm not an expert like you. I know your word is law here. But you must admit, something unusual has happened, hasn't it?"

Mr Clive Thomas MRCP, appearing at a loss for words, said, "Err...yes, I agree Wesley's condition has improved. But, Miss Morgan..."

"Becky," she said.

The medical students gathered closer.

"Becky," Mr Thomas said, "it's too early to talk about a cure. We need to conduct more tests."

"You can do tests later," Becky was still looking the consultant firmly in the eye, "but in the meantime I'm taking him home."

Liz hugged Becky. Mr Thomas relented, finally agreeing with Becky's pleadings that we could take Wesley home temporarily.

A nurse came and removed the drips and test equipment.

As I lifted my grandson from his hospital bed, a beaming

little smile on his face, I knew I was carrying a miracle. My heart skipped with joy. Our family left the hospital in Liz's Nissan. Sean followed Rachel in his Range Rover to a nearby hire car drop-off point and soon caught up with us on the motorway. London looked a different place now. Traffic on the motorway appeared polite and friendly. Green fields sparkled with dew, birds sang in trees. The world had changed.

By early December 2011, Wesley had been home from hospital for almost ten months, his happy sounds echoing around the lawns while he played with the dogs. The house was filled with noisy clumping footsteps as he and his best friend Alan ran to and fro. We took turns driving Wesley to school every day. Rachel had moved in with Sean, in his flat above the garages, Sean's tree house.

The dark cloud once hovering over Kirmingsham Hall had dissipated. The true source of Wesley's healing was known only by an intimate few.

With the box and its contents locked in my safe, we made plans for Christmas and a special birthday party.

Long-Awaited Parties

Over Christmas 2011, pure joy permeated every nook and cranny of the Morgan household. Just as sunshine brings warmth to a chilled room, a sense of wellbeing radiated warmth to every corner.

"It's so wonderful to be singing carols, eating turkey, enjoying Christmas." Liz's glowing cheeks radiated warmth.

"Yes," I said, "it's like waking from a bad dream to have our little lad restored."

"And, of course, Sean is happy in his tree house with Rachel," James added with a wink.

Sean gave the thumbs up. Rachel encircled her arm in his.

"Well," I said, "if Bruce Lee here hadn't tackled those guys we could have lost the box and Wesley. Our family is indebted to him."

Sean saluted nonchalantly. Becky mouthed a thank you.

*

In 2012, Kirmingsham Hall was the ideal location for a party for the birthdays Wesley had missed during his illness. Over several months, the family had been meeting in huddles making plans.

Twenty-two spacious acres of lawns spread around the property like a huge green carpet. Three lakes met the grass, dark waters lapping against the gravel paths. Two rowing boats were moored adjacent to a wooden jetty stretched over the clear water. At the far side of the largest lake rose woodlands where birds called from their nests.

"We've erected the marquee and toilets blocks," Tony, our gardener and handyman said, "and heaters just in case. By the way, John, Liz, everyone is thrilled Wesley is well."

Liz said sombrely, "I don't know how any family can prepare to lose a child." Then brightening she added, "Just look at him opening presents. His eyes are popping out of his head!"

On Friday January 4th, on his seventh birthday, Wesley opened more and more presents, using both hands to rip the paper and parcel tape. A hill of wrapping paper grew in the lounge. Riding on a two-wheeled metallic blue bike with nine gears, he left the house tinkling the bell, a blue gift tag with "from Sean and Rachel" attached to the handlebars.

I noticed Wesley showing his bike to a small group of boys wearing Goostry Community School jumpers. Recognising two teachers from Wesley's junior school, I went over to make them feel welcome. They seemed at ease with the nurses from GOSH and were freely mixing with guests.

Shaking the hand of one special attendee, Mr Clive Thomas MRCP, I said, "I'm so glad you made it."

"I wouldn't have missed it for anything," the consultant from paediatric oncology said as he shook my hand warmly. "We had to juggle a few things around in my schedule, but I just had to come!" He appeared a remarkably humble man, given his knowledge in the field of childhood illnesses and his international reputation.

One story I knew he would never use as a case history was Wesley John Morgan: a healing that confounded the medical world. I hoped that we could keep the true story closed to all but a trusted few.

I saw James chatting in a corner to friends. Some were from his course in programming and network administration at Stockport College of Technology. James had been spasmodic in the pursuit of his studies but I knew he had abilities in IT, remarkable abilities. Others I guessed were people he had met online, cyber buffs like he was, either on social networks or playing online games like World of Warcraft®.

I watched Liz move in and out of the house and marquees, radiating warmth, shaking hands, hugging and kissing friends. Liz and Rachel were central to the chatter, almost as if they were mother and daughter.

I stood with Becky, watching the five-foot-eight attractive Save the Children worker, and Becky said, "I feel like she's an older sister. I'm so glad Sean saved her."

"Yes," I said, "she fits in well and she seems ideal for Sean."

I thought, 'She must have seen a darker side to Sean while they were in Somalia,' although she never mentioned it. Maybe she was so used to dealing with death that seeing Sean in action had not fazed her.

I noticed that as Liz, Becky and Rachel busily carried food on trays around to the guests, they spent a lot of time with a slender young girl from amongst James fellow students. She looked eastern European, with brown eyes, a slim nose and an olive complexion. However, drawing closer, I heard her speak in a North American accent with a Texan twang.

Her long legs in stonewashed ripped jeans were straddled either side of her chair, which she sat on backwards, like a cowboy. On her red tee-shirt a slogan read, "Computers suck but I don't". A dark-brown leather jacket emblazoned with a red and gold World of Warcraft® logo hung loosely. Her hair, braided to her waist and jet black like Liz's and Becky's, almost reached the floor. A zebra-striped woollen hat with earmuffs sat on her knee. On her feet she wore red lace-up Doc Martens. A uniquely dressed person, who seemed unafraid to be herself, which I admired. She looked to be in her early 20s.

Taking Becky aside, I sat her down. "Who is she?"

I didn't ask James, knowing I would only get a grunt. Obtaining personal information from James was as rare as hen's teeth.

"Her name's Alyana," Becky said. "She was born in Albania but adopted at six months by a couple from Austin, Texas, and she's on the second year of James' course at college. Her friends call her Aly. I think James likes her."

Not sure that I had heard correctly, I said, "Huh?"

"James is cool, Dad, honest," Becky said. She continued, "You guys just don't relate to the same stuff. His friends are awesome people once you get to chat to them. She's a smart cookie...so don't blow it!" Becky prodded me, "James really, *really* likes her."

I remained seated as Becky walked away. Scratching my head, I struggled to imagine James in a relationship. 'He's not shy,' I thought, 'he just doesn't seem interested in people, only cyber-people. Most of his time's spent in his room. I've no idea what he gets up to, in his hermit-like existence.' My eyes were being opened.

Some years before I had popped my head around his bedroom door and seen a bewildering array of computers and peripherals. Two desktop PCs with monitors on the work surface, two midi-tower systems on the floor, and cables stretching to a large black server standing in a corner. On his two pine desks there were hubs and modems, cables galore, peripherals, and two laptops. All the machines were whirring, glowing, flashing, and bleeping.

I asked James what he was doing and received a strange look. I didn't inquire again about what he did. Deciding at 23 that he should go to college was one small step for man, a giant leap for James, I thought.

But had I misjudged him? My thoughts were interrupted.

Out of the corner of my eye, my muscles tightened when I saw that Becky's ex turn up. Jason was Wesley's biological father so I determined to be civil. He had landed a good job, apparently, with a pharmaceutical company in Germany. He must have been doing well as he had parked a new red Porsche Carrera on our drive and was wearing designer clothes. Crossing the lawns, I gave him a quick acknowledgement and walked into the marquee, a nasty taste in my mouth which almost made me spit. He was as welcome as a skunk.

Nodding towards him, Sean asked if I wanted him to take Jason on a boat ride on our lake. He could sleep with the fishes, he said. I laughed, tempted because Jason worried me. He was always talking on his mobile phone and looking shifty and suspicious.

Wesley tugged my arm, breathing a sigh, "Come on, Granddad, come and see my presents. They're in my bedroom. Now pl…ease. Come on."

Whistling to Bourne, I lifted Wesley into the air with more difficulty than I expected, placed him on my shoulders and headed to the house.

"Careful," James called, holding hands with the girl with braided hair.

I wasn't sure if he meant Wesley or me. My burden had certainly put on weight.

Liz, Rachel and Becky were busy in the kitchen dishing out red and green jellies and creamy trifles into small dishes. The girls had been preparing the refreshments for days. A catering firm had delivered plates of various meat and vegetarian sandwiches, sausage rolls, salads, pickled onion and cheese on cocktail sticks, crisps, pork pies, pizza slices, tacos, chilli, and a variety of dips. Appetising smells filled my nostrils as we climbed the stairs, Wesley feeling heavier by the minute.

"Don't forget that we cut the cake in about ten minutes, Dad," Becky said, her cheeks glowing as she spooned more delicacies into the dishes.

I was intoxicated to be sitting on Wesley's bed, seeing him look so vibrant. How would we have felt if instead of a birthday party, we'd had a funeral? I could not imagine that sorrow and shuddered at the thought. Losing a child would be one of the most heart-rending experiences a family could endure. I had read somewhere that when you lost a child, you always remembered them as children; they never grew up in your mind. I preferred to see them live and mature.

Taking up books, clothes, games, robotic figures, model cars, and a host of electronic gadgets, he showed them to me one by one. Holding an iPad, Wesley said, "This can be loads of books, games, a camera, and a phone. It's amazing." He pressed some buttons on the iPad that Liz and I had given him and it bleeped and started spelling a word.

I noticed the baby posters were gone from his bedroom wall, replaced by Liverpool FC and some school mementoes. One of the new posters, *The Girl with the Dragon Tattoo*, was stuck to the wall with Sellotape.

Becky, understandably, would not let Wesley watch the 18+ millennium trilogies when we watched the Swedish versions on DVD, but James argued it was allowable to stick a picture of Lisbeth on Wesley's wall. It was difficult to disagree. I looked at my hand, noticing that one feature of his wall had remained from his nursery days: a mural of a tree, flowing outwards with spreading branches, assorted flowers and green drooping leaves in the wind, animals sheltering under its shadow.

I thought aloud, "That could be the Tree in Eden."

Hearing me, Wesley said, "That's what Mummy calls it, Granddad, the Eden Tree, and she says it has watched over me since I was a baby."

The drawing had been stencilled on the nursery wall by a friend of Becky's before Wesley was born. How could a link be possible? I looked at the mural and the tattoo on my hand and felt cold chills.

Gazing at Wesley with such pride, my heart bursting, I remembered how much he had been through and how incredibly brave he had been. I had never heard him complain. His sandy hair, lost through chemo, had returned like red fuzz. His weight had improved 80 percent of normal.

Sometimes we were tempted to treat him with kid gloves, given all that he had endured. It would not have been right, though, to wrap him in cotton wool, for him to miss out on life. He had been given his life back. It was *his* life to live, not ours. He was a miracle child.

An Unexpected Visitor

The party was in full swing, happy sounds reaching me from the marquee, when I heard a conversation at the front door.

Liz came upstairs to announce that someone was at the door, a man she didn't recognise.

"He's most insistent to see you, John," she added, "I think he knows you. Anyway, after you've spoken with your friend, come to the marquee as we're going to cut the cake. Send Wesley down and we'll walk him over."

I recognised Joseph immediately. February 2011 seemed centuries ago, but I would never forget the flower seller in Holmes Chapel on farmers' market day, that figure in the dark blue suit with white pinstripes, waistcoat, pressed white shirt, and red bow-tie with black dots. On his head he was wearing a skull cap similar to the one he'd worn at the market. Nothing had changed in his attire, but his countenance was different: downcast, sad and dejected.

I greeted him amiably, "Joseph, it's wonderful to see you. Come in...come in." I took him to the kitchen, inviting him to have something to eat or drink. He declined.

After a few moments I knew for sure that whatever the reasons for Joseph's visit, it was not good news. This was not a social visit and his mood was sombre. The confident face with bright eyes I had first seen was inscribed with worry and sleeplessness, his face wearied and pained.

"John…"

I said, "Please, Joseph, let me watch Wesley blow out his cake candles, then we can talk. I've waited so long for this moment."

Walking across the main lawn with Joseph at my side, heading towards the white walls of the marquee, its steel wire guy ropes stretching out like tentacles, our feet squelched on the moist green grass. Joseph's silence was ominous.

I caught Sean's eye and signalled him over with my hand. Introducing him to Joseph, I let him know he would be needed for a meeting after the cake cutting.

Nearby, in one corner of the large tent, I spied Jason, Becky's ex. "The prat is drunk," I said to Sean. We had not made a big issue of the drinks because the party was for a seven-year-old, however, we were obliged to diplomatically offer some alcohol. Jason appeared to have consumed his fair share, probably most of it.

Liz leaned forward, her raven-black hair falling across her face. She took the mike in her hands. Clearing her throat and tapping the microphone twice, she announced, "We'd like you all to sing happy birthday, then Wesley will blow out the candles."

"After I've made a wish," the seven-year-old piped up excitedly.

"Yes, of course," Liz said, "after you've made a wish, darling, then you can blow."

Becky patted Wesley's head and kissed it. He shrank away from her to avoid more shows of affection.

Family, friends, teachers, nurses, and doctors sang their hearts out, like a Wembley crowd. In this festive atmosphere, everyone celebrated Wesley's life together. Cake candles cast flickering images on the canvas, a gentle swirl of smoke rising. There was a faint smell of candle with the rising crescendo, "… dear Wesley, happy birthday to you!"

Wesley closed his eyes, silent for a few seconds, taking a big breath, then he blew out all seven candles with one puff.

He looked at his grandmother for reassurance that he'd done it properly. Liz gave him the thumbs up, wiping her eyes. His first time, but his little mission was a success. A year before, we had wondered if the next breath would be his last.

Liz smiled and started a clap. Other hands joined in, the sound resounding like running water spontaneously around the tent.

Out of the corner of my eye, I saw others wiping tears from their eyes, even my two older brothers. Andrew was a retired naval radio officer, Mike an HGV driver. I attempted to leave the marquee with Sean and Joseph when the mike spluttered and squawked.

"Excuse me, I have an announcement," a nervous voice sounded over the mike from behind us.

It sounded like James and I turned to see him at the mike. "What's he playing at?" I asked. I looked over to Liz who shrugged. Becky, though, winked, then whistled, hands behind her back.

"Aly and I are getting engaged," James continued, his hand shaking. "I called her parents in the USA for their blessing. It looks like we'll be married in May...on the 11th." James combed his fingers through his sandy hair and breathed out a sigh.

Applause erupted, followed by loud catcalls, cheers and shouts. I looked at Liz and Becky. Their hands were clasped together and they were mouthing, "Thank you, God." I felt struck with wonder. 'My son James engaged?' I thought. I had really misjudged him.

I gave a thumbs up to James and quickly kissed Aly's cheek. Once more, I attempted to leave the party when the mike crackled again. This time Jason swayed and tottered at the microphone, a few feet away from me. The hairs on the back of my neck rose. I made a fist. He stammered a few incoherent words and belched, but appeared to be building up steam for a speech. The party atmosphere changed and guests looked embarrassed and worried. Sean crept behind him and touched him, catching him as he collapsed like a redundant Guy Fawkes.

"It's OK, friends," Sean loudly announced. "He's feeling a bit crook. I'll get him some air."

Sean picked Jason up under the arms, manhandling him through the canvas flap, the exit for the mobile toilets. A muffled thump broke the silence. The tarpaulin bulked and moved as if a heavy object had buffeted it. I heard someone vomit. Sean returned moments later supporting Jason with one arm and sat him down, slumped on an empty metal beer barrel. Sean then poured ice cubes down his shirt.

"Rachel," Sean called, "get some strong black coffee please." Rachel ran through the tent flap.

Sean placed his fingers in his mouth, whistling for Aunty, who came running into the tent, panting. "WATCH!" Sean addressed the husky, pointing to Jason. Aunty sat on her haunches with her fierce eyes fixed on Jason, her teeth bared while she snarled. People slowly backed away.

Sean eyed Jason menacingly. "Now sit the frigg there. Move, and the dog will eat ya." The guests moved even further away, leaving a perimeter in the trampled grass surrounding Jason and Aunty.

Walking through the guests, nodding politely and smirking, Sean joined us.

"What did you do to him?" I asked.

"Ahh, it's just the Vulcan neck hold. I learnt it from Mr Spock."

Amused, I walked the three of us into the house, periodically looking sideways at my Jewish friend, my concern increasing. Liz, Becky and the children raced gleefully past us to the house.

*

Joseph, Sean and I entered the hall and wiped our feet. I called Liz, who came from the kitchen. Her cheeks were flushed with joy. I needed her tact and diplomacy. She was good at pouring oil on troubled waters.

Drawing her to one side in the hallway, I said quietly, "Can you make sure we aren't disturbed, Liz?"

Puzzlement on her face, she smoothed her hair behind her ears. "OK," she said. Opening the lounge door, she addressed a group of children beginning to watch a DVD, "Can you guys play in Wesley's room please?"

"Aww Gran, it's *Toy Story*," Wesley pleaded.

"You can watch it later, hun," Liz the diplomat replied, "come on, let's go. I haven't seen your toys yet."

Like the Pied Piper, Liz herded a party of boys and a few girls up the stairs. The noise of chattering and laughter continued until a door closed.

We took our seats in the lounge. The pressure in the room built up like somebody inflating a tyre. Even Bourne seemed to understand the tension; he curled up on the hearth, his head low.

Joseph edged forwards on the blue leather couch, which made a soft squelching noise. He cleared his throat and stated the reason for his anxiety.

"My niece Esther called me in great distress from Jaffa yesterday," Joseph said. "She sounded overwrought. Nobody has heard from Simeon in several days. Since New Year's Day he has vanished."

Shocked, I repeated, "Vanished? Nobody just vanishes." I indicated with my palm that Joseph should continue. Sean looked at him expectantly.

Joseph swallowed, wiping his eyes with a white handkerchief. "A phone call the day before had instructed her to get the box to her house if she wanted to see her father again. She insisted she didn't know about a box but they hung up."

I looked across at Sean questioningly. 'Who else knew about the box?' I wondered.

Sean's face muscles tensed. He gritted his teeth, then stood and placed his back against the fireplace, moving Bourne with his foot. The Labrador looked back with questioning eyes and slunk down on the carpet, stretching out his paws.

"Please carry on, Joseph." I was increasingly nervous.

"She called me with her concern. Who took her father and why? What was this box? she asked me. I called friends in Tel Aviv, where I thought Simeon would visit. It soon became clear to me that Simeon had been…kidnapped."

At this phrase, Joseph broke down sobbing and his shoulders slumped. He continued after some time, his voice becoming hoarse, and his hands shaking. "I assured Esther I would help, and warned her that she must not contact the police yet, because that could result in danger to her and Simeon."

"You did the right thing saying that," Sean said, "let's find out what they want."

"It's the box," Joseph cupped his hands in prayer.

"We share your worry, Joseph," I stood to place my hand on his shoulder. "We'll do whatever is necessary."

"Aye we will," Sean added, "don't worry, we'll find your brother…and deal with those who took him."

I felt dark claws reaching across the globe, dragging me back to Israel. The box and its contents were linked mysteriously to both good and evil.

My head spinning with the news, I said, "Joseph, you must stay in our guest room. You're welcome. We'll call the family together tonight and make plans."

"I'm afraid that I cannot make this evening. I'm celebrating our Sabbath with friends. I believe we need our God's help. Please, we must call Esther now. Then, maybe we can meet on Sunday?"

"OK. Sunday it is then. Meet at 10:00?" I looked at Sean and Joseph and they nodded.

I took Joseph by the arm into the kitchen, put the kettle on, and offered him the phone from the wall. Sean and I opened cupboards while our friend held a conversation in his native tongue. I poured boiling water into mugs, adding milk and sugar to Mellow Birds.

Joseph said, "No milk please, John." Sean had his coffee black too.

Placing the phone in its cradle, Joseph said, "Esther is comforted to hear we'll do something. She says it's like a cloud has lifted. She is trying to busy herself with her job as a staff nurse."

After our coffee, I asked Becky to drop Joseph at the railway station. Joseph shook our hands and embraced us, kissing us all on both cheeks. I felt a chill as we stood on the doorstep waving to him seated in Becky's car. Was it the wind or some ominous feeling of dread? At the same time, James and Aly squeezed into the back of Becky's purple Ford Ka, eager to share their news with friends in Aly's college digs in Stockport. The car, looking cramped, crunched over the gravel and eased to the gateway.

Amidst the discomfort over Joseph's news, I had forgotten James' engagement. 'Engaged,' I thought, 'my lad is engaged!'

A Villain in the Midst

After Joseph had left, Sean and I returned to the lounge to a subdued atmosphere. Children's voices still echoed down the stairs, but our world had changed.

Sean eased himself back into the recliner and sprang the footrest. "These are not the same clowns who were at the airport," he said definitively. "It doesn't feel the same. This is more professional, more threatening." He patted Aunty, returned from Jason guard duty, and she growled.

"I agree. This is someone who knows about us, and understands the box and its value."

I lifted a crystal glass decanter and poured us both a tumbler of whiskey. The amber fluid burned my throat as I sipped. "They know the brothers' involvement too."

Sean nodded.

I ruminated for a few minutes as I swilled and then swallowed the alcohol. "Just have the one, Sean," I emphasised, as he downed his drink in one with a satisfied gasp. "Let's take the dogs for a walk to the lakes. I need a break and some air."

At the words "dogs" and "walk", Bourne jumped up, his tail thrashing to and fro. Maybe fresh air would clear my mind. I was deeply disturbed and worried about my two Jewish friends.

*

Over the months of Becky's pregnancy and throughout Wesley's illness, Jason had hardly showed his face. He'd appeared once Wesley returned from Great Ormond Street – for a brief respite – just to assure himself that a "cancerous gene" did not threaten him. He worried about no one, cared for no one apart from Jason Gould.

The remarkable recovery of Wesley had intrigued him. He'd wondered what had resulted in his son's amazing cure. Jason did not believe in God. His god was money: money and success. His commercial antennae were twitching. He needed data. He tried to get close again to Becky, after all, they had been lovers, but she rejected his charm.

"OK. The bitch won't talk. I'll try the hospital, and if that fails, I will talk to the kid," Jason reasoned to himself, "after all, he is mine." Once Jason had a goal, very little could hinder his pursuit.

The doctors and nurses at GOSH were tight-lipped. "Confidentiality crap," Jason mouthed, feeling that they were thwarting him personally. But Jason always bounced back.

On a business trip to London well before Wesley's seventh birthday party (his father had entrusted the negotiating to him) he'd decided to have another try at the nurses on the fourth floor. Jason's father and mother had never met their grandson and had only heard rumours. Consumed with "the bottom line", they had pushed their "boy" into making money in their antique business.

Jason sat on a plastic chair in the parents' waiting room on the fourth floor, sipping coffee from a vending machine. "Tasteless shit," he muttered under his breath, his face etched with displeasure. His face lightened when an attractive nurse entered the room. Her crisp red and white striped outfit showed off her figure. As she bent to fill a cup with water from the cooler, she noticed Jason eyeing up her legs, and smiled to herself.

"You want a coffee?" Jason asked. "Or would you like something stronger?"

"Not on duty," she giggled. She was six weeks into her new job but she was not new to a pick-up line, although it had been a while since she'd heard one.

"Maybe after work then?" Jason said, with predatory ease. Bold, arrogant and tireless in the chase when he smelled blood.

"Err...OK...Meet me here at five?" she replied. Then when she pushed the door open, she asked awkwardly, "You're not a parent, are you?"

"No. Not in the way you mean anyway." Jason reeled in his prey. "My boy was here some time ago." His eyes searched hers for sympathy.

"Oh I see. Well I gotta go. See ya at five," she called and left the room.

"Result!" Jason said aloud, a grin spreading from ear to ear.

Later that night, the nurse told Jason everything she knew about the "miracle boy". Cured, it seemed, by something his family had brought back from Israel.

The circle of people who knew about the leaves grew by one. Later, it was to grow by several more when Jason made a phone call and began a new job with Leitz, a huge pharmaceutical firm in Strasbourg. His starting bonus was a brand new red Porsche Carrera. He had pieced together bits of information and used them subtly to open a door at Leitz.

The Party Winds Down

"God, what's that smell?" Becky asked. After dropping Joseph at the railway station at Holmes Chapel, she was now visiting Aly's college friends' digs.

"It's probably last night's pizza," one of Aly's housemates called from the kitchen.

"POOH! It smells like last year's!" Becky chided. Paper plates, empty coke tins and cigarette butts festered on the threadbare carpet. An assortment of discarded clothes, socks and trainers occupied a corner. Moving the debris of late-night meals aside, she sat on a couch.

More of Aly's housemates appeared, slapping James' back and hugging Aly. Some presented her with cards.

"Aww, thanks ya'll," Aly said, "that's awesome."

Becky soon relaxed with the group as everyone toasted the couple with beer and lager. "What's the college like?" Becky asked Aly and her friends.

"Right fine," Aly said, her friends nodding. "It's where I met James," she added.

James went beetroot red to whistles and calls of, "Oooh, lover boy!"

*

I returned to the party with Sean and threw myself into the remainder of the birthday celebrations. I noticed no red Porsche on our drive, and felt some relief.

"I hope Aunty didn't eat him," Sean joked. "That bastard will give her gas."

I chuckled.

Guests inside the tent were enjoying the music and games, led by Rachel. Wesley and his friends had rejoined the party. Grabbing his mum's hand, he took his friends to the lake, running breathlessly across the lawn, eager to show them the fish and the ducks.

Most of the Koi carp were hiding at the bottom of the water; the occasional splash and plop broke the surface. I saw Sean, slyly hiding behind a bush, throwing stones into the water. The children leapt up and down, looking into the swirls of water, shouting, "There's one!"

Taking Tony, our gardener and odd-job man, by the arm while his lad Alan played with the other children, I invited him to the family meeting on Sunday morning.

"I would really like you to come, Tony. We're making some changes and I value your input." He could not hide his surprise and enthusiasm when I explained what I had in mind. The change would give him independence and the work would help him take his mind off his marriage problems.

I took Liz and Becky aside and told them about Joseph and the reason for his visit. Telling them my intentions for a family meeting, they agreed with some consternation. Sometime later, Sean returned from the lake in a mood as sour as vinegar. He moped about in the kitchen, clattering pans and dishes.

"Come on, for goodness sake, tell me what's troubling you, Grumpy."

Sean smiled half-heartedly, "It's the engagement, John, I don't know what to do." His face looked pained and serious. I struggled, perplexed, and asked was it James and Aly? "No, it's not about that...it's Rachel. What do I do?"

"I don't see the problem, Sean. You like Rachel and Rachel likes you."

"OK. One, I'm 48 and she's 29." He showed a thumb. "Two, I'm independent and a loner, while she's a caring person who loves people." His index finger pointed. "Three, I take lives, she saves them." He used his middle finger. "Four, she's sweet, and I'm a right bastard at times." His fourth finger joined the others. "And there's more," he said, looking more troubled than I had ever seen him.

I breathed a sigh of relief when Wesley came over and rescued me by his innocent intervention. Relationships were important, I knew that well. Luckily, I had stumbled upon Liz in her dad's office in south Wales, otherwise I'd now most likely be a lonely bachelor. Advice from me on relationships? It was the blind leading the blind.

Wesley wanted to show his friends how dogs chased sticks. I whistled for Bourne. Aunty joined too. I headed out of the house, with children following me, and quickly whispered to Liz, "Have a word with Romeo," pointing my thumb to Sean. She raised her dark eyebrows and shrugged her shoulders with a querying look.

Later that evening, when Liz and I were sitting in bed reading, I happened to say, "Our chicks are leaving the nest."

I immediately sensed it was a bad idea. Liz said, "What do you mean leaving? We can all live here. The house is big enough or we can make it bigger."

She turned her back to me and switched off her bedside light. I realised someone else felt insecure.

Following an old adage my mum lived by, 'Don't let the sun go down on your wrath.', I put my arms around her, feeling her body shake with sobs.

I whispered, "It's OK. We're getting older; life grows and changes. Our children are becoming independent but they will always be our children. They will still need us, and if they want to live here, that's fine. We'll make room, I promise."

Liz turned to me and said softly, "Hold me." I did. It felt good.

Relationships and Plans
in Cheshire

Through the kitchen window on Saturday morning, I watched men from the hire company collecting the marquee, mobile toilets, chairs, tables, and heaters. Sean stood at the toaster singing along to the radio.

At the best of times, Sean was tuneless and tone deaf, but annoyingly he carried on, smug when happy. He had clearly made a decision.

"Rachel and I are going to Hereford after breakfast," he announced, buttering the toast. "I'm taking her to the regiment to meet the lads, at least those in active service or who are in the TA. I'll chat with my old major about our situation. I'll try to get a contact too, for ordnance. We wouldn't even get a peashooter through customs," he added with a wink. He carefully placed toast, marmalade and a cup of tea on a tray and walked towards the front door whistling.

Sean had my utmost confidence. Whatever he shared with his service friends would remain confidential. I also guessed that he wanted to travel to Hereford to allow his girlfriend Rachel into his world: a disciplined tough world.

Our destiny was rolling like a ball in a pinball machine, the goal to rescue a kidnapped friend.

Liz came into the kitchen just as Sean left through the front door.

"What did you tell Romeo?" I asked, perplexed.

With a flourish, she flicked back her hair. "Sean felt a bit insecure because of their differences. I told him Rachel really loves him and he should talk with her."

"That's just what I told him." I raised my hands in surrender.

Liz smiled wickedly, "Yes, but you're a man and you don't know women. Men are from Mars, and women are from Venus, don't you know that?" she chuckled. "By the way did you know that Rachel has a degree in business management?"

"No I didn't. Why?"

"Well I thought it may be handy to our business, especially with the charity plans. Anyway, I asked Sean if that was a problem," Liz said. "Guess what he said."

"Go on, enlighten me."

"'It's OK, Liz,' he said. 'I've about a thousand degrees... centigrade for this little lady.'"

'Relationships,' I thought, and heard James enter.

"God. And here comes another lover boy." James came into the kitchen alone. "No Aly?" I asked.

"We aren't sleeping together until we're married," he said, his face growing red." Her adoptive dad – Rev Wickham – is a minister of a church in Austin, Texas. They believe in the virtues of abstinence so Alyana goes along with it."

I choked on my toast. Liz hugged James, and whispered a quick word in his ear. His red cheeks met the edge of his sandy hair. Like me, his freckles grew larger in the sun and he blushed to his socks when embarrassed.

"That's a great idea, Mum", he said. "Thanks. I'll tell her when I see her later today. By the way, can she come for dinner?"

"Aly is welcome anytime, James," I said, and then stated emphatically, "it's imperative that you're both at our family meeting on Sunday morning at 10:00. Don't be late."

"OK, Dad, will do. Thanks."

I saw my main role to be the strategist. I had in my head the blueprints that could change the Morgan circle of family and friends.

*

After breakfast, the dogs bounded down the lawn towards the lakes and I sauntered behind. I needed fresh air to help me think.

Bourne chased ducks until they flapped into the lake, wings creating a trough of water, their noisy shouts directed at the Labrador yapping on the shore. They appeared to mock him: "Come and get us!" Aunty scratched the earth near some hyacinths, staring condescendingly at Bourne.

At Morrison's half an hour later, our weekly shopping was interrupted by people stopping to talk to Liz. The model of politeness, she parked her trolley and I overheard the conversations about James' engagement and Wesley's health. Beaming shoppers patted Wesley's head. He grimaced and ducked his head, trying to avoid the attention. Standing next to me, he looked the picture of health.

While I enjoyed my Morrison's "Flying Start" breakfast, Wesley sitting next to me asked, "Granddad, what's klestrel?"

I chewed my toast and said, "Cholesterol is like a build-up of fat in your blood vessels. What makes you ask?" I suspected that I knew the answer.

"Granny says that if you have too many Flying Starts your klestrel will be bad," he replied innocently, slurping his orange juice.

"Mmm, OK, I get the point. Thanks, Granny Liz." 'Better stick to toast and marmalade from now on,' I thought.

Just as I thought of toast, the manageress, Jan, came over with two assistants, looking rather pleased. She placed a coloured sheet labelled "All the colours of toast" on my table. Thirty plus shades of toast met my eyes, from white to burnt charcoal.

"It's for that awkward bloke, the one who's never happy with his toast," Jan and the girls giggled. "We'll tell him, OK, pick one!"

I laughed with them. 'God, what's wrong with people? If you're not happy, put some jam on it!' I thought.

At 10:00, I intended to drop into our office complex for a couple of hours. Turning off the ring road in my BMW, I drove past industrial units on the estate, a former milk-processing plant. The landscaped grassland and trees ahead gave a bright and relaxing appearance as I approached the modern five-storey block.

I walked towards the double-glazed doors and pressed the intercom. A voice said, "Morning, Mr Morgan," and the doors clicked. A concierge in maroon jacket and black pants with a crease that could cut nodded, passing me the register to sign. He placed a pile of assorted mail, held together with an elastic band, on the reception desk.

"How are you, Steve? Anything happening today?" I stood with envelopes and some magazines under my arm.

"Not really, Sir. Just the usual," he replied. "Saturdays... you know."

My post, emails and messages showed nothing urgent that morning. I could relax and think. The smell of furniture polish made me sneeze. I stacked the mail in the wire in-tray for Jenny to sort and wiped my mahogany desktop with my palm. It glistened in the reflected neon light.

I leaned back in my chair. Liz, Sean, James, Becky, and apparently Rachel all had their unique abilities. I believed mine to be the ability to view a challenge without being restricted by emotion, along with listing scenarios and making a plan.

I tugged a drawer open and finding the right folder, drew out our articles of memoranda, placing the A4 sheets into my briefcase. Dialling a number listed on speed-dial, I held the handset to my ear and waited.

Mike, our company and family solicitor, said, "Hello, John." He listened and accepted my invite to the family meeting. The plans had just taken a step forward.

The Queen's Diamond Jubilee

By Saturday evening, Sean and Rachel had returned. They walked into the kitchen holding hands, a couple in love.

James and Aly had been inspecting the bed-settee in the study: Liz's suggestion. Aly would be comfortable in the study. I suspected it was roomier and more hygienic than her student bedsit.

A few days before, I'd said to Becky, "It makes sense, Becky, now that Wesley is better and back at school, you can get some of your old life back." I thrilled to see the vital bounce in her steps. At 26, she could have the world at her feet. Hopefully, there would be no more slobbering Jason-like suitors.

I asked Liz how she thought Becky was faring.

"Becky," Liz answered, "is shopping in Manchester with some school and uni friends. She'll be home soon I guess. She's enrolling again to restart her psychology degree." Liz looked overjoyed.

During the news on Central TV, a report announced the forthcoming Queen's Diamond Jubilee in the summer of 2012. I could hear Sean say, "Tosh." Those of us closest to Sean knew him to be no royalist.

The Morgan family always watched the Queen's Speech on Christmas day, a heart-warming way to let the Christmas dinner go down and something I'd done since childhood with my mum and dad.

Sean, however, stood and announced, "What a load of cobblers. I'm going for a walk."

By the look on Rachel's face, she clearly did not understand. "But didn't he fight for king and country?"

"Sean would say that he fought for the men of his troop: the men of his regiment."

Children are remarkably good listeners and Wesley had overheard.

When Sean returned and sat down comfortably next to Rachel in one of our two-seater couches, Wesley asked him whether he liked our queen. I indicated with my eyes that Sean must be careful with his answer. Sean looked through the panoramic window towards the lawn before answering.

"Well, little man, I don't like any toffs who sit in ivory palaces while good men and women bleed, crying for their mammy," he said. "But don't misunderstand me. I'm loyal to HM, and respect Prince William and Prince Harry for serving."

"Uncle Sean, did you ever kill anyone?" Wesley asked, innocently playing with a new Buzz Lightyear. I felt an intake of breath around the room. Sean stroked Aunty and sat forwards on the couch, his hands on his knees.

"I did take the lives of some bad people, Wesley," he said. "I helped them to Heaven because they were hurting boys and girls and their mums and dads. But I promise you: I never shot anyone who wasn't shooting at me."

Wesley seemed satisfied with the answer and gave the thumbs up. Sean smiled and returned the thumbs up and Rachel gave him a hug and a tender peck on the cheek, and we settled down to Saturday night TV.

I thought, 'She witnessed Sean take lives in Somalia. Were they evil men who deserved to die?' I guessed she didn't know, nor could she judge. And neither should we.

Without Sean, she knew she might not be alive today to enjoy another Christmas dinner, and our grandson would probably not be with us either.

Official Family Meeting

Sunday morning. January 6th 2012

I hoped the meeting would be one to change lives.

Liz as company secretary took the minutes of the special meeting of the shareholders of Morgan Steel and the Morgan Group. She began by reading out, "There are no absences. The invited guests present and noted are Rachel Wright, Alyana Wickham, Joseph Latchman, Tony Bullock, and Mike Steward. The time and date of this meeting is 10:00 a.m. on Sunday January 6th at Kirmingsham Hall, Kirmingsham Green, Holmes Chapel, Cheshire."

I cleared my throat, "Liz and I are joint 50/50 shareholders of Morgan Steel Limited. We own a depot and smelting works in Ebbw Vale South Wales, a scrap metal yard in Brierley Hill, and we lease one in Crewe specifically for rail freight. Within the company, we have six employees including Sean. We use sub-contractors for some of our work. Sean engages security and personnel for all the properties and invoices us."

The main reason for the meeting, I outlined, was not about Morgan Steel. It concerned the Morgan Group PLC, an entity created in 2007 following legal advice. Morgan Steel had struggled for a decade, trying to compete with cheaper imports. We had hoped and planned to enter new business areas. However, the new umbrella PLC had remained an unused shell.

"Diversification is essential for us," I said, "implementing the vision has been on the back-boiler. Family demands and other pressures have delayed the realisation of our goals."

"Aye…and you're a lazy sod," Sean said.

We all laughed. Rachel punched his arm, "Sshh." Her arm linked through his.

"I'll cover each item in turn. Anyone can contribute at any time. Our future requires an open discussion needing everyone's opinion, guests included," I emphasised.

Liz motioned with her hand for me to hurry up. Bourne placed his paws over his ears.

"The shareholding of the Morgan Group PLC is split. I have 51%, Liz 20%, Becky 10%, James 10%, and Sean 9%. Correct, Mike?" I paused.

"Yes, John, that's correct," Mike our solicitor said.

At this point, James chipped in, "Boring, can I go and play with Wesley and Alan upstairs?"

I felt my brow furrow and resumed where I had left off. "The Morgan Group uses the same offices and can use the identical staff and premises as Morgan Steel. But they are two separate entities. I have several important proposals to make today." I cleared my throat. Silence pervaded the room.

"Firstly, I make the proposal that as part of the Morgan Group, we establish Morgan Security officially. Sean is brilliant at the coalface but he's not a finance or administration person."

"You're not wrong there, boyo," Sean said. "Like an Irishman would say."

"Boyo is Welsh, you goon," James said.

I coughed and resumed. "Morgan Security Limited will have Sean as an 80% shareholder and managing director, with Liz and me holding the other shares. He can allocate his shares as he sees fit. He'll install the floating prison off the coast of Kenya, manage the personnel and build up the business."

"More friggin' work," Sean said, his eyes twinkling with mischief. "And who's the goon now, Jamie lad?"

James guffawed.

Speaking louder, I said, "I propose that James and Aly join Sean at Morgan Security as employees or consultants. Their role will be – under Sean's guidance and using his contacts – to approach public and corporate bodies about IT network security. They'll accept commissions to attack and infiltrate systems, repair them and give a report to the IT directors. We have no intention of becoming private eyes, but we will offer protection and consultancy to large corporate or public bodies."

James' cheeks went bright red. Aly smiled and kissed his hand. Liz also smiled radiantly and blew me a kiss. We had talked with Sean and Rachel over the last few days about our plans. Our conversations were now becoming a reality.

Blushing, I started again, "My second proposal is that we establish Morgan Development and Property Partnership. I've outlined the idea to Tony and would like him to be my other partner: 50/50. Tony has been a loyal friend of the Morgan household for several years, also maintaining our 22-acre site. He has converted the space above our three garages into living accommodation or 'Sean's tree house'."

Everyone chuckled at that.

James banged his chest and did a Tarzan impression. Aunty walked over, fixing her eyes on him. Bourne stirred, tail wagging.

"Down!" Sean commanded. "He's an eejit, Aunty. Leave him."

"Oops," James said. Aly moved to pat Aunty. Sean shook his head. Aly withdrew her hand quickly.

I said, "Tony will continue to maintain Kirmingsham Hall and the grounds, approaching other potential clients for landscaping and maintenance contracts. We'll look at possible investment on redundant sites or properties for development. Tony and Sean will work together regarding conversions of other liners into floating prisons."

"Thank you, John and Liz," Tony said, "I hope I don't let you down." The room went quiet.

"No. Thank you, Tony," Liz said. "It can't have been easy for you with the family tensions you have experienced over the last few months."

"My third proposal," I said, "is that the Morgan Group found a charitable wing called the Morgan Foundation." Nodding to Rachel, I continued, "I propose Rachel to become chief executive. She has a business degree and heaps of experience. She has to travel to the Philippines with Save the Children, after James' and Aly's wedding in May, so I suggest that she plan to begin with us full-time in June."

Sean kissed Rachel on her head. James said, "Uh huh."

Turning to Aly, Sean said, "I'd think long and hard about hitching your wagon to that..." Seconds ticked by before Sean added "...fine example of a young man...the perfect marrying kind. Why, I'd marry him myself if he'd have me."

Aly spoke for the first time, "Yes, he's a fine example ya'll. And he IS taken." James' cheeks turned beetroot red.

Spontaneous applause erupted. Sean whistled and rose to shake James' hand.

"My fourth proposal is that Liz and Becky find premises ideal for their fashion ideas. Tony will conduct a survey giving advice when they've located a property. The wholesale and retail arm will be Morgan Fashion. Liz and Becky will be joint owners."

Liz jumped up and shouted, "Yes!" She then gave me a long kiss on the lips. "Thank you, darling. You're definitely on a promise tonight." Everyone laughed. James blushed further and I felt hot. Becky and Liz hugged and remained standing in a huddle, like girls in a playground.

"My final proposal, certainly the most critical one today," I said, "relates to Joseph's situation." I briefly outlined the history of the box again and how it had come to me. Presenting them with the latest news, I suggested strongly we do everything possible to assist Joseph and Simeon, considering Wesley's miraculous recovery. My plan outlined that Sean, James and I would travel with Joseph to Jaffa. James would give us IT support, whilst Aly kept us up to date from the UK.

"There is vast potential in the healing leaves. Any company that can analyse the constituents and formulate a drug will make billions. If we sell the leaves and maps to a buyer – which we will never do – we could virtually name our price. Someone has found out about the box and attempted to steal it. They need to be found and Simeon freed – without giving those scoundrels a thing."

"We'll just give them a little headache," Sean said.

"Let's hope it doesn't come to that," Liz cautioned.

"I could not possibly condone or be party to any violent or criminal act," Mike stated unreservedly. "So don't tell me about it", he added, and looked at Sean who just shrugged his shoulders and winked at him.

"No, Aunty, leave him alone, he's a friend," Sean addressed the grey and white husky at his feet, who growled, fixing her eyes on Mike. We all laughed.

"We have no intention of selling the box or its contents," I said. "It would be a better goal to use the Morgan Foundation in some way and offer healing to the desperate."

"It's about time you recognised the importance of information, Dad," James said. "How you run all your businesses with only a Blackberry and a crap computer I don't know."

I took the hint, asking Aly to acquire the latest laptops and other mobile paraphernalia the key personnel and I would need, so it would be ready when we returned.

James said, "And some 'silver surfer' training," cheekily alluding to my age.

Aly laughed.

I summarised, asking for a vote on each proposal. Loud 'Ayes' resounded after each item. Mike took the information down and assured us everything was in order, while he kept his eyes focused on Aunty and his hands tucked away.

Bourneville padded over and nudged his hand until Mike patted him. The solicitor was clearly relieved to have one four-footed friend in the room.

Inviting further comment, I asked if anyone wanted to speak. Mike said that before any of the newly formed companies became employers, we needed to familiarise ourselves with legislation such as health and safety, the Equality & Diversity Act and the Briberies Act.

Everyone in the room agreed that we wanted to comply with the law. As we grew, the Morgan Group needed a secure basis for each facet of the business. Any section that became a risk would become defunct.

Joseph said, "Would I be allowed the courtesy to speak?"

"Of course, Joseph," I said, "please do. You're one of us."

"I would like to thank you for your kindness," he said, looking at each of us in turn. "I'm relieved that some of you will accompany me to Jaffa. I hope my brother will be found safe and well, preferably without yielding the box. Now I have two questions for Sean."

Sean and I indicated that he should ask.

"Why is the husky called Aunty?"

"She's just like my aunty in Ireland," Sean quipped, "strong-willed, ruthless and a bitch."

"But how did you come to own her?" Joseph asked.

"Well I'm not sure that anyone 'owns' Aunty, she's her own lady," Sean said. "But a military friend gave me Aunty. The sergeant had been in the Falklands with me romping to Port Stanley with the paras. He'd joined the SAS two months later than me and later joined the SAS TA. During exercises in Sweden, the sergeant adopted a bitch husky, little realising her pregnancy. He pleaded with me to have the most boisterous and snappy puppy of the litter. I agreed if the Red Caps would train it. Eight months later in 2007, Aunty the husky joined the household here. John, you want to add anything?"

"We were not overjoyed, to be honest. Bourneville was not impressed and neither was Becky, who had an 18-month-old toddler. But Wesley broke the ice. He patted, played with and tugged Aunty's hair and I think she knew the boy was no threat. Bourne got used to playing with Aunty. For the first three weeks that Wesley endured hospitalisation, Aunty moped around the house. Some nights she would be in Wesley's bedroom whimpering. We knew she would defend his life with hers."

"Thank you. My second question," Joseph said. "Would she really have eaten that young man in the tent?"

Whether he meant it in jest or whether he had only seen pampered toy poodles on leashes or wild feral street dogs in Tel Aviv I was not sure. I thought I detected a smile and a twinkle in his eyes. 'Joseph is back!' I thought.

Sean replied, "Well now, Aunty is a bitch, and she'll eat anything, just like my aunty in Cork. I think, though, that Jason is unclean meat. She would spit him out."

Uproarious laughter lasted several minutes. Joseph laughed longer and louder than anyone, his girth shaking. He acknowledged that in the Torah, the Jewish Law, "There are unclean meats. But they have four legs."

"OK," I asked, "is there any other item before I close the meeting? Then we can eat."

Becky stood, "I have one. I've agreed with Mr Thomas, the GOSH paediatrician, that all of us except Mum and Dad will run in the 2014 London Marathon to raise funds for the GOSH baby unit. Dad and Mum can stand in the crowd cheering, dispensing bottles of water and meet us at the finish tape."

Sean and I looked at each other in mock amusement. We knew that he would train hard. He would make it a competition. He had yomped miles across the Falklands.

I formally closed the meeting and signed the forms necessary to make the changes. Mike placed the paperwork in his briefcase and excused himself. The clock showed 1:00 p.m., time for dinner. Sean and Mike shook hands. "I was joshing ya, me bucko. No harm done."

We all went to the local harvester pub and had a Sunday lunch from the carvery. Tony excused himself and headed home with Alan in tow.

Back at the house, we all watched Liverpool FC live against Spurs. Joseph was as excited as any of us when Stephen Gerrard scored a goal: the only goal. We would have gone to the game at the Spurs ground but the next day would be a very big day for all of us.

Preparations for a Journey

Monday January 7th 2012

James appeared at breakfast with untidy hair, his shirttails hanging out.

A few minutes later, Aly came into the kitchen, combing her long black hair with a comb. Her black tee-shirt stated in white lettering, "It wasn't me...I didn't do it...I know nothing...NOW SOD OFF."

"Aly didn't sleep well?" my eyebrows rose.

Sean guffawed and nearly choked on his shredded wheat. Rachel hit him playfully on his arm.

"Behave," she said, and then announced that she was going with Liz and Becky to look at possible premises for Morgan Fashion.

I knew Aly had not slept in the study. I'd seen her enter James' room in the night.

"OK, OK, I get it," James said, his colour rising. "It's OK if we keep our clothes on," he added meekly.

"They sure look creased," Sean mocked.

After breakfast, Joseph arrived and James and Aly gathered us around his laptop to show us what they had discovered so far. He made the information onscreen intelligible. Aly's fingers moved across the keyboard like a pianist's. "Caleb's hard drive has been mirrored on James' laptop," Aly said.

"We needed to look at what started this off," James said, showing us images as he clicked on "notes" and "diary". I saw that anyone with access to Caleb's PC would have known all about his meeting with his nephews and the box. "There's no record of an intrusion on the PC but..."

"...we think what kicked this off, Joseph," Aly said, "is the theft of his desk diary last year."

Our Jewish friend looked over our shoulders. Aly continued, "Your uncle made extensive notes about the Tree of Life and the Garden of Eden, making drawings from his memory of the parchments. He also noted conversations with Simeon and detailed the arrangements with John on Feb 14th. We think the diary is the key."

"We have the images of the guys from Heathrow," James said.

"OK." Aly scrolled to another folder and images appeared.

Placing his finger on the images on screen, Sean said, "Here are the CCTV photos that Heathrow security emailed me. These are the bozos we tussled with."

"Yes, that's them. They tried to steal my case and the box," I said.

"The younger one is just a punk," Sean said. "But this older guy is a nasty piece of work. We know from Interpol he worked as a security guard for Leitz, a huge pharmaceutical firm in Strasbourg. He was fired because of his drug use. Interpol are not interested in finding him for attempting to steal a suitcase. But his drug peddling may get him extradited."

Joseph recounted his uncle telling them about the robbery in the university.

He said, "Simeon tried to warn you. Caleb's desk diary was stolen. Some clues must have been in it. Since that desk diary theft the conspirators must be working with dangerous people, John, and they have my brother." Joseph sobbed, his shoulders quivering. "But my uncle lives in a plush retirement complex overlooking the Mediterranean. His laptop is next to him at all times."

"But that doesn't prevent cyber-theft," James said. "Industrial espionage is huge business. It's likely the man from the pharmaceutical company called in a few favours and is now working with others."

Sean agreed. "The two men at the airport luggage island were pushovers. They're not the sort to resort to kidnapping unless they're ordered to do so. Things have changed in the chain of command," Sean's voice grew with menace, "now we're dealing with some very bad people." Aunty growled.

An action plan was formed. Sean would have St Peter's box in his in-flight bag. The white cloth bag with the crushed leaves would be in my jacket, hopefully immune to sniffer dogs. James would bring his laptop, working from the hotel and liaising with Aly from our home.

"I've given Aly all my user names and passwords," James said. "It's better that she stays in my room. Mum, you OK with that?" Liz nodded enthusiastically. She seemed glad of the chance to spend time with her future daughter-in-law.

"You've given Aly your user names and passwords and she is sleeping in your bedroom?" I asked. "Without torture?"

Sean and I sang in unison, "It must be love, love, love."

The Team Travels to Israel

We pushed our holdalls and flight bags into the boot of Sean's car. The car shook as we slammed down the lid. The sun was setting over the lakes in a grey sky as the family waved to us and shivered on the steps in the wintry chill.

James hugged his black laptop case on the back seat and Joseph got in beside him. I eased into the passenger seat, a cubic shape under my feet inside Sean's flight bag. Sean slid in, looked at each of us and turned the ignition key.

"Let's rock 'n roll," he said. The engine gave some splutters and we rolled forwards to the wrought-iron gates.

Sean looked right and turned towards the Chester Road. James was busily tapping on his laptop. Joseph sat soberly until the large white dish of Jodrell Bank telescope appeared in the distance.

"Have you ever visited it, John?" Joseph asked, pointing at it through his window.

"Couple of times I've been as a boy and with the family. I must take Wesley now they've the planetarium," I said, "it sounds amazing."

Blue motorway signs dripping with moisture directed us to the M6.

Sean's satellite navigation interrupted our thoughts with, "Take the motorway."

"OK, my darling, I will," Sean joked. His humour lightened our mood.

The vehicle moved through light traffic. A few minutes later, the airport sign on our left directed us up the slip road. Joseph tapped Sean on the shoulder and cupped his hands together in a prayer. We were getting nearer. We passed brightly lit hotels as we skirted Ringway Airport and pulled into the carpark nearest to terminal two. We grabbed a trolley, filled it with our luggage and made our way to check-in.

Sean took his flight bag from me, swinging it over his shoulder. Typically, he relieved the tension by asking, "Why are those men in orange nightshirts singing to hairy Christians?"

James was the first to retort, "It's Hare Krishna, and it's a Hindu god!"

Sean winked at me. Our holdalls vanished through plastic strips on a conveyor belt behind the BA check-in. A smart navy-suited lady wearing a blue and white striped blouse gave us boarding passes. I detected the faint scent of her perfume.

The flight to Tel Aviv was similar to the one I had taken on Feb 13th 2011: scheduled for 17:00 GMT, boarding half an hour before take-off. At the security scanners, an official inquired about the item in Sean's flight bag showing up on her X-ray.

Joseph quickly interjected, "It's a box with my mother's ashes. We're returning to Tel Aviv to scatter them." He bowed his head. She waved us through.

We sat in the departure lounge and I nudged Joseph with a warm smile, "Didn't the commandment say 'Thou shalt not lie?'"

"No, no, John, you are mistaken, "Joseph said. "The Torah commands that we do not 'bear false witness', which I have not done. But have you never heard that 'God helps those who help themselves'?"

"I've heard of that one," Sean said. I smiled at my two friends and we laughed.

Our tickets, passports and boarding passes were scrutinised. I felt a chill as we walked through the metal and glass mobile tunnel and boarded. The seats were soft and roomy. To my left, I could hear James tapping on his laptop on the meal tray.

"I've left a message for Aly."

Sean felt the flight bag, which prompted me to pat my jacket pocket. The window revealed scenes of crisscrossed fields and then sea while we devoured tasty in-flight meals washed down with refreshing iced coke.

"Look, Dad, here's our flight plan, weight, current location, weather, and ETA," James said, nodding to his laptop screen where a white plane icon blinked and moved slowly. I was fascinated.

Annoyed about exhaust emissions, my son reaffirmed his belief that climate change law was essential. Looking exasperated, he said, "Our carbon footprint from this journey alone wipes out Kirmingsham's recycling efforts."

*

The nightlife of Tel Aviv provided a kaleidoscope of colour as the plane taxied at 11:30 p.m. local time. Joseph took a taxi to his brother's house to check on his niece, despite our warning against it. Leaving the arrivals area, I pushed the clattering trolley towards the car hire firms. The first was the red and white Avis.

"Rule Britannia," broke into the night and Sean opened his mobile. He mouthed into his phone, "Yeah, just got here. OK, matey…Avis rental in five." He hung up.

Placing our luggage in a white Audi, I drove the few feet to collect James and Sean, who were leaning against the Avis wall. A man with a military stride and bearing approached and conferred with Sean. He swung over to him a heavy black holdall and then walked away. Sean popped the boot and pushed his new luggage in to the sound of metal clunked together.

The Audi took us on modern concrete roads with brilliant streetlights, following in the steps of the Old and New Testament periods, the Romans, Saladin, the Ottoman and many other empires. We passed Christian churches and mosques, ancient and modern buildings. Circling the clock tower, brightly illuminated by spotlights, I remembered my first visit and thought of Ahmed, my taxi driver friend. I remembered praying a desperate plea.

At the Hilton in the room I was sharing with James, I opened the door to a rap and Sean entered the room. James was staring at a screen on the dresser, while I was relaxing in a chair.

"Rachel wants to say goodnight, Sean," James said.

Sean peered at the laptop screen and gasped. An onscreen Rachel sat in James' bedroom at home. Aly and Liz were peering over her shoulder.

"You can see and hear them and vice-versa," James said. "I don't trust any hotel's Wi-Fi."

"So how…?" I asked.

"See that stick in the USB?" He pointed, "Never mind. Anyway, I've a 3G connection. Aly and I don't use Internet Explorer openly; we ping each other's ISP tags direct."

"Huh?" I said.

James tapped his head with his palm. "OK, so I'm using Skype's free video conferencing. Aly and I recommend everyone at Morgan use it. Much cheaper to hold a meeting over a phone line than fly across the world with airfare, cab fares, meals, hotels, etc. Plus, cutting down on exhaust emissions will save the world."

"Jesus, I gotta get me one of them Skypes. I could look at Rachel in her PJs," Sean said.

Laughter erupted from the screen as the girls at home giggled like a girls' hockey team in a changing room. Sean exchanged pleasantries with Rachel, flexing his biceps to the titter of his audience. Liz and I had a chat too. My cheeks and ears felt hot. 'Like father, like son,' I thought.

"G'night ya'll," Aly said, leaving the screen.

I brushed my teeth and stripped to my boxers.

"Point that away from my bed," I said. "I don't want my family to see my mortal frame, and I *don't* want their friends on Facebook laughing at me for years to come. Night James. Night all," I said, pulling the quilt over me.

Becky, who had joined the female trio, piped up with, "Night John boy."

I growled, then smiled at the reference to *The Walton's*. A family joke.

Exhausted, we arranged to meet at 8:00 a.m. the next day in the Hilton's bar restaurant. I sent Joseph a message to let him know. The plan had worked almost a year before; I hoped it would work again.

*

Jason Gould relaxed in a Jacuzzi in a five-star hotel in Germany. Extinguishing a panatela cigar in the bubbling water, he chuckled. He swatted bath foam across the gleaming mirrored tiles and grinned.

"I could get used to this," he said to his reflection. "Here's to you, Jason Gould. If the old Jew has done his job, I'll be rolling in it soon." He sank under the bubbles and spat out water like a whale.

*

Simeon Latchman groaned. His hands and feet were tied with strong plastic tape. In the dark, he heard men talking. He lay quietly, trying not to make the camp bed creak.

"I hope Joseph and some help will come," he prayed. "God of Abraham, Isaac and Jacob, I need thee."

*

Tuesday morning 7:45

Hungry, James and I knocked on Sean's hotel door. It swung open rapidly and we entered, with Sean standing to the left of the door.

James said, "If you're worried about who's knocking why don't you look through the spy-hole?"

Sean looked at me and then at James. "Eejit! Easiest hit in the world," Sean said. "The spy-hole darkens with a shape and BLAM! Your brains are blasted across the room. Game over."

Clearly shocked, James said, "What kind of people...oh, never mind." He went pale.

Sean inserted a commando knife into a sheath that was Velcro-strapped to his right leg, and meticulously covered it with his sock. An automatic weapon was sitting on the bed. Sean picked it up and placed the pistol into a light brown shoulder holster over his right shoulder with the straps around his back. I suspected he could draw the weapon quicker than any gunslinger, aim and fire with deadly accuracy.

James, mouth agape, continued to stare at the pistol.

Sean said, "It's a SIG Sauer Tactical P226. It has a 15-round magazine. It's the favourite weapon of US Navy Seals – but don't worry I'm only gonna tickle 'em with it. I've also some extra friends – flash grenades – in my flight bag, around St Peter's box. They'll see the light quick enough and meet him at the pearly gates before they know what's happened."

I whispered to James, "He's like steel wool: OK to touch gently with fingers, but those who make an enemy of him by rubbing him up the wrong way experience severe pain."

"GOD!" James said. "You're serious, Sean, right?"

"Too right, kiddo," Sean said, "it's them or us. They've made that clear. They've messed with the wrong marine...or whatever."

Sean put on his jacket, covering his weapons. He pulled on and laced his combat boots. I realised he was preparing for war.

We descended the carpeted stairs that I had used 11 months before. Very little had changed; the velvet wallpaper, the photos of Israel, the same orange plants in the lounge and bar. I smiled, reflecting on Jaffa oranges.

Whilst little had changed in the hotel, we had enjoyed

momentous changes in the Morgan family. Our grandson Wesley fully recovered from cancer, thanks to the intervention of two Jewish brothers, an Apostle's box, and the Saviour of the world; it was time to return the favour.

Sean pointed to a vacant table adjacent to the restaurant window. Crossing the black and white tiles, I felt the hairs on the back of my neck bristle. Once again, I was walking the chessboard. Making moves. We took our seats and ordered from the menu as James visited the food island.

"Once again I'm sitting in the Hilton Restaurant in Jaffa waiting for a Jewish man," I said, "but this time I'll be helping him."

General hubbub filled my ears. The smell of beverages and cooked food drifted towards me.

Sean pointed and I saw Joseph enter the hotel foyer, slowly making his way towards us and avoiding pot plants. Sean nonchalantly sipped steaming black coffee, his eyes scoping the area. Joseph acknowledged each in turn, helping himself to a croissant and coffee. As we busily caught up with his situation and discussed his brother and niece, my Blackberry bleeped.

"Excuse me, it's Liz." I stood up to take her call.

It became clear to my audience that Liz and I were not having a loving chat. I grew increasingly irate while I listened, finally sitting down with a "buggeration!" Other diners stared.

Sipping my coffee, I gathered my emotional control and took some deep breaths.

"There's good news and bad news," I said. "The good news is that the girls have found some premises they feel are perfect. James will get the details by email." I paused. "The bad news is that some local journalist called late on Monday evening and left a message on the answerphone while the girls were chatting to us on Skype. The *Cheshire Gazette* is planning to run a story about Wesley's healing." The mood at the table became troubled.

I continued. "The paper has an 'unknown source'. They know that a Middle-Eastern man attended Wesley's party and that since February 2011, Wesley has been in remission. They've invented a story. It's a compilation of guesswork, yet remarkably close to the truth. Truths we prefer remain hidden."

"I'll get Aly to access the paper's servers, Dad." James patted my shoulder.

"Thanks, son, that could help."

"Aye, we gotta nail the bastard who leaked the story," Sean said.

"Liz and Becky called Tuesday and denied that the report was true. Liz told the reporter he had an unsubstantiated patchwork of innuendo. We're certain that few at GOSH had information or that they'd support the story even if they knew anything."

"This could be bad, Dad," James said. "If a daily like *The Manchester Evening News* or worse, the tabloid press gets hold of the story..."

Whoever had snatched Simeon and held him would learn more about us. It would be dangerous for Simeon and it would make our mission harder. We all pushed our food around our plates.

The rays of the sun fell on our white tablecloth while we continued to toy with our food, looking at passers-by through the restaurant window. James placed his laptop on the table, pushing aside remnants of croissants, butter and jam. He pressed keys and Aly's face appeared on the screen. It was 11:00 a.m. in Holmes Chapel.

James said, "Aly, I want you to contact our friends and find out who leaked this story to the paper." I felt so proud that my son was more 'together' than I'd thought.

"And gidday to you too," Aly said. "Morning ya'll."

"Oops, soz babe," James said, his ears turning bright red, "you know how I am with relationship thingies."

I leaned over to James' side of the table and said, "Will it be possible to have an online advance copy of the paper before it's printed, Aly?"

"I'll check," she said. "We think the story will be finally edited and printed on Wednesday. Circulation to wholesale distribution centres will be on Thursday evening. It's a free paper, so we can expect it dropping through letterboxes on Friday and Saturday. Don't worry, John. If all else fails, we will plant a mail bomb."

James rubbed his hands together.

Joseph's ears seemed to prick up at the word "bomb".

"It's not a detonation device, Joseph," James explained. "But we can swamp their media files with junk: Viagra, Nigerian millions, bingo, puzzles, Russian brides. Their heads will be spinning by the time we've finished."

I patted James on his back and passed him a croissant. He took a bite and continued typing on his keyboard.

"I want you to look at this." James clicked on a yellow envelope icon on his screen. Pulling our chairs closer, we huddled around his screen. "This is Caleb's computer contents. Look at his latest diary and notes."

"But how...?" Joseph caught his breath and we studied the pages.

"You can see Caleb made entries last night," James said. "The good news is we've found no Trojans. Just a few small viruses, but no keyloggers."

Sean scratched his head, "Keyloggers, huh? Err...is that good or bad?"

"It's good there's none, Gunny Highway," James said, referring to Clint Eastwood's character in the movie *Heartbreak Ridge*. "We don't think the bad guys have infiltrated his laptop. There's no sign of a hostile takeover or of any malware."

"Thanks, James," I said, "that's a relief. So they're basing their information on his old desk diary and this informer, right?"

"And anything they've got from Simeon," Sean turned sympathetically to Joseph.

"My brother will not talk," Joseph said, "he's different from me: he's as stubborn as a mule."

"Even so," I said, "we need to make Caleb's laptop safe, and warn him."

We debated for a while what our strategy should be, particularly to locate and rescue Simeon. The waiter refilled our coffee cups several times. Using the back of the menu, I penned our plan.

"OK. This is what has been in my head since I heard about Simeon," I said. "James will remain here, keeping in touch with home and also, crucially, guarding the box."

"Keep the door locked," Sean said. "Keep away from that friggin' spy-hole unless you hear *me*. Don't use room service. Grab stuff from the downstairs shop on ya way up."

James saluted, "Yes, Sir!" Sean roughed James' hair and they play fought.

"OK, settle down, people are watching," I said. "Joseph and I'll visit Caleb to collect his laptop so that James can make it secure. Sean has a meeting at 12:00 in the city centre at Mossad – courtesy of his Hereford visit. He can drop us at the airport for our flight to Cairo and meet us later at Simeon's house. OK everyone?"

James had chatted with people on the Lonely Planet Travel Forum and planned our route. We were flying from Ben Gurion Airport to Sharm El Sheikh International Airport on EL AL Airlines. As James swung his laptop over his shoulder and walked towards the shop, I realised that I had misjudged him. He had demonstrated himself to be a real asset, a valued member of our team. I believed I was the tactician, Sean the fearless warrior, and James the plodding Intel gatherer.

Flight EA 125 would arrive at Sharm at 1:00 p.m. local time, a 60-minute flight. Sharm was Egypt's second largest airport, second to Cairo, the favourite destination of tourists to some of the world's best scuba diving.

Our plan moved on. I hoped Simeon could hold on.

Colonel Balak

Crossing a carriageway, Sean steered the hire car north. The location of Mossad's headquarters was deemed a secret, but Sean knew that "was bullshit". Across large intersections, he looked for signs for a country club – in particular a 12-storey office block adjacent to the club.

He flashed his warrant card to a security guard, drove under a yellow barrier and pulled into a parking space.

Works of sculpture by some renowned artists adorned the landscape around the entrance. The 12-storey complex housed local Tel Aviv police, their logo displayed in white letters attached to the grey marble foyer wall. No sign for Mossad.

Mossad's motto had changed from Proverbs 24:6 "For by wise guidance you can wage your war" to Proverbs 11:14 "Where there is no guidance, a nation falls, but in an abundance of counsellors there is safety".

Sean approached the reception desk, his warrant card extended towards the desk sergeant. She followed entries in a desk diary with her finger. "Friggin' diaries," Sean said to no one in particular. The woman pressed a button on her phone keypad and spoke privately into it, cradling it to her ear. After a few minutes, the lift doors swished open and two soldiers in camouflage gear stepped out: muscular men with jet-black hair and olive skin. Their boots resounded across the tiled foyer. The soldiers conducted a quick body search on Sean.

The desk sergeant wagged her finger and tutted while Sean's gun and knife were removed. A hand scanner bleeped and Sean's survival kit was placed in a plastic bag with his other weapons.

"I want that back," Sean pointed to his kit. "I got it from Mothercare."

The tough soldiers made no comment and escorted Sean to the elevator. On the console, one soldier pressed the button with an UP arrow and Sean stretched. A ding announced the 11th floor.

Sean said to himself quietly, "Here we go." The guards remained in stand-easy position until a matronly woman appeared dressed in a charcoal-grey skirt and jacket along with a white frilled blouse and black shoes. She showed him into a small lounge area; the soldiers stood outside.

"Coffee, Mr Casey?" she asked in slightly accented English.

"Yes please. Black, no sugar would be great." A clock on the wall ticked the seconds away: 11:50.

The woman brought a silver metal tray with steaming coffee. "The colonel will see you in a few minutes, Mr Casey."

Sean sipped his coffee and paced to and fro, studying landscape photos of Israel. The woman walked back into the lounge like a soldier on parade.

"The colonel will see you now. Please follow me." The two soldiers left.

The couple marched in tandem through a room with dozens of people sitting at computer screens. Sean nodded at a few but received no acknowledgments. At the colonel's door, a burly male figure in navy blue uniform frisked him once more.

"Oi, be careful, that's my willy," Sean said, the humour lost on the soldier.

The guard escorted Sean into an office, smartly saluted, and closed the door. Sean sat on a padded office chair facing the back of a broad-shouldered man with a shaved head and tough leathery sun-tanned skin. The five-foot six-inch man's hardened back tensed and he continued to gaze through a window. Though not tall, he was solidly built.

He turned, his dark eyes focused, and assumed a seat behind a mahogany desk. He was a soldier who had seen some action, the sort of man you didn't want as an enemy. The highly polished desk contained stacks of books and magazines, a phone with an intercom, an open laptop, and a pile of brown manila folders. The colonel drew the top folder and opened it, slowly leafing methodically through the papers.

Then he looked up at Sean and asked in perfect but accented English, "You are Sean Casey?" Sean noticed a scar on the man's right cheek. His hairless head glistened in the sun.

"I think you have my photo in the papers that you're scanning."

"Yes, of course," he said, "and I can see the famous SAS tattoo in your details. I see you have one on your hand too? Please bear with me. This is a very interesting conundrum. Allow me to introduce myself. My name is Balak, which means 'lightning' in your language."

Sean nodded and extended his hand. The two shook hands, still measuring each other.

The man continued, "I am a colonel in Israel's Defence Force who has the pleasure of knowing your Major Edwards at Hereford. He gave me some details concerning your problem and I offered to help, especially as it involves rescuing an Israeli citizen and recovering national artefacts. Please feel free to talk. Sergeant Joshua Federman will be joining us. Would you like more coffee?"

Sean relaxed, taking in his surroundings. He knew it would be a monumental error to underestimate Colonel Balak. Concern about his intimation that the box, parchments and healing leaves were Jewish heirlooms occupied Sean's mind.

More coffee arrived with the sergeant, a 30-something, muscular, hard-looking, six-foot-tall soldier with short-cropped black hair. Dressed in camouflage combat gear and polished black boots, he gripped Sean's hand strongly. Studying each other, they took their seats.

Colonel Balak gestured to Sean with his hand, "Please recount your story, Mr Casey. Your major's details were sketchy."

Sean took a deep breath and narrated the story, from John's meeting with Joseph to the current situation. He omitted telling about Wesley's healing: a mistake.

The colonel interrupted: "The boy recovered and celebrated his 7th birthday. It appears that the leaves have healing power." He fixed his eyes on Sean like X-rays.

"Yes, I'm getting round to that," Sean lied. "Wesley is well now. But there are no more ground leaves in the bag." He lied again. "Why Jesus only inserted a few leaves we don't know, maybe one day we'll find out, when we meet St Peter." Sean's attempt to deceive his audience with humour fell flat.

The colonel stood and turned his back, staring out of the window. Balak was a tough man, not easily fooled.

In a gruff commanding voice, he said, "We'll see about that when you bring the box to us. I am instructed from the highest authority that the manuscripts found in Jaffa are part of our national heritage. In the meantime, my sergeant will assist you with the search and rescue of our citizen. The family must also be protected. A family support officer from the local police is being sent. Thank you for coming, Mr Casey. We will meet again soon."

No salute. The meeting was over and the colonel did not turn around from the window as Sean left.

Sergeant Federman spoke. "Let's go up to the 12th floor. We can have lunch and a chat in the staff cafeteria."

"Phew," Sean said, "I thought you were gonna throw me off."

"No, the sun patio and swimming pool are on the roof. That's where we throw people off." Joshua laughed.

Sean laughed, "The only swimming pool at Hereford is for training...and it's bloody cold!"

They took the concrete stairs two at a time and entered a well-lit restaurant where two or three hundred plastic-backed chairs were set around tables in groups of two, four or eight. Panoramic windows stretched from ceiling to floor, surrounding the room. The central island housed a modern buffet and food area. Dining staff in starched white aprons served diners from the rectangular metal hot and cold containers.

Tops of office blocks, the minarets of mosques, church crosses, and modern financial buildings complete with helipads filled the horizon. Shoppers and workers in the street below resembled ants scurrying about. The place was only half-full. Joshua led Sean to the buffet area.

The sergeant said, "The menu today is schnitzel, salads, hummus, tahini, rice, mashed potatoes, and assorted vegetables."

"Can't be worse than the greasy goat meals I endured with the Mujahideen." Sean helped himself to a plate and ate with gusto.

Joshua was called away and Sean used the opportunity to make a call. Parts of the plan were coming together.

Sharm el-Maya Bay

My Blackberry rang vibrated in my jacket pocket. Pleased to hear the familiar voice of my closest friend, Sean, second only to Liz, I was with Joseph as our taxi was pulling up outside Caleb's retirement apartment in the town of Ofira overlooking the Sharm el-Maya Bay.

"Yeah, we just got here," I said. "We haven't seen Caleb yet." Seagulls soared in a clear blue sky, cawing. Wooden and straw beach shelters stretched for miles along the sandy beach. Waves battered granite cliffs beneath us.

"How are you getting on? You made contact yet?" I asked Sean.

"This colonel is something else, John," Sean said. "A small man made of rock. He knows almost everything so I can't bullshit him. You know me, John, I'm no diplomat."

I smiled. 'Sean the diplomat?' I thought. "But will he help, do you think?"

"Yeah, I feel in my gut he will, John. He's given me a sergeant babysitter called Joshua, but I think Mossad's onside. The colonel is interested in the box. I think that could be bad news, John. We may have to give it up."

"OK," I said. "We'll cross that bridge when we come to it."

"But the sergeant seems eager to help us with finding Simeon," Sean said, "so that's a bonus. I'm just surprised they're working alone, with no police involvement...oh...and you may find a family support officer at Simeon's."

"That's good. Esther will need that. I think the young thug's seen to be a local problem, and the drug dealer I guess. But maybe the box is viewed as a national issue."

"OK. Gotta go, Boss, Joshua is back." Sean hung up before I could wish him good luck.

The news that Colonel Balak had an interest in St Peter's box and the scrolls was no surprise, although it was disconcerting. I knew that others suspected the box had important details. When I'd first seen the maps and parchments, I'd realised they contained information about finding the mysterious place called Eden. Whilst the healing leaves were effective in healing Wesley, the cloth bag's contents had lessened by a third. What if during some crisis we needed more? I had hoped Mossad would offer assistance in the rescue of one of their citizens, without conditions.

Joseph greeted his Uncle Caleb at the door and waved me up the steps towards a ground floor apartment. The complex was built on the rock and overlooked the bay. A portly jovial man kissed me on both cheeks and introduced us to Miryam, his wife of many years.

"Joseph, you must visit us more often," she chided. Then she directed herself to me, obviously thinking I must be here as a tourist. "The famous old market is within easy walking distance. There's a network of streets, shops and vendors selling everything from tourist tat to delicious Egyptian spices. By the way, how is Simeon? Why hasn't he come?" she asked Joseph. It was clear that neither Miryam nor Caleb knew anything about what was happening.

"Please, Uncle, Aunt, let me start at the beginning," Joseph said.

While he narrated the recent events, there were gasps, looks of astonishment and the words "my diary" repeated. Miryam sobbed into a white tissue.

Blowing her nose, she proclaimed loudly, "You must do something, Caleb!"

It struck me that Caleb was otherworldly and naïve. He

appeared to live in a cocoon of antiques, languages and arte-facts. He listened to us both but it did not appear to compute in his brain.

"You hear what they're saying, you *dreykop*! You're always facing both ways!" Miryam said. "Caleb, fetch your laptop now!"

Like a scolded dog, Caleb left us and returned holding a black carry case marked Toshiba.

"Thank you, Uncle," Joseph said, "the people who have Simeon are very dangerous. Please be careful."

"I'll drive you to the airport," Miryam said, "I can see you're in a hurry."

Sean gets a Licence

Sean closed his mobile phone and examined his plate at the dining table, while Joshua resumed his seat and placed a box on the table.

"I apologise for my colonel's seemingly curt manner. He's a hardened soldier, Captain Casey," Joshua said, "as you would say, 'a man's man'. He does not bullshit."

Sean picked up a forkful of mashed potato and nodded. He smiled when the sergeant addressed him as "Captain". Chewing mouthfuls of salad and rice, the two talked.

"What's the way forwards, Sergeant?"

"Please call me Joshua. I have some ideas but first we eat. It's an Israeli custom."

"OK. Sure, thanks Sarg...err, Joshua. And you can call me Sean."

"Coffee?"

"Please, black no sugar," Sean said. Joshua waved a waiter over. After a few minutes, the waiter returned with a tray with coffee, cream, sugar, and iced buns. As they sipped, Joshua pushed the box across the table. Sean looked inside at two mobile phones still in their packaging.

"For Joseph and Esther, the niece," Joshua explained. "We're not sure how good these terrorists are. But it's better to have secure comms."

"I think 'gangsters' covers it better than 'terrorists'," Sean said, but he now realised how Mossad were justifying their involvement. The sergeant passed across a document showing a golden seal in the shape of a candlestick with seven bowls.

"This authorisation," Joshua pointed to the document, "is a licence to carry firearms within Israel. I made strong representations to my colonel that you're a trained, experienced and responsible former officer of the UK military." Joshua sat back and looked amused.

Sean coughed at the term "responsible". But he appreciated that his teeth were not being pulled by Mossad and his admiration for the young sergeant grew. He gave a thumbs up.

"I'm assigned with an operational mandate to accompany your group," Joshua said. "I'm allocated resources and a team of four in Tel Aviv, enlisting the support of the local police if needed." Joshua swallowed and hesitated. "Though you outrank me, Sean, Mossad are in command. As far as my government is concerned I'm working with some civilians to locate and rescue a Jewish businessman, and recover an antique housing several scrolls of national significance."

He looked into Sean's eyes. "I know you tried to deceive us about the healing leaves, Captain Casey, and so does my colonel. He is not a man to deceive. We are eager to help, and anxious that the media is kept in the dark. However," Joshua paused, "you must not exclude us from any information that's in your possession. Any further deviation will lead to your group's arrest and deportation."

A tense atmosphere fell upon both men, who finished their iced buns and coffee in silence. Sean wiped his mouth and gave a humbling apology, and assured his new colleague he had a chastened obedient recruit, confirming it with a salute. Both men laughed.

"I'll call John," Sean said. "He'll give us an update."

Walking to the elevator, Sean talked into his mobile. Reaching the ground floor, he collected his weapons and equipment from the reception guards, who smartly saluted. He left the Mossad building in the hire car; Joshua followed in a sleek black 320D 3-series BMW. The vehicles were soon parking at Simeon's house in Me Ragusa street, adjacent to the Ha-Pisga gardens.

Tel Aviv and Strasbourg

After a further brief exchange, Miryam returned us to the airport to catch the earliest return flight. Through the 747's passenger window I took my first look at Jaffa's setting sun. I pulled up the shade to see a resplendent blazing orb sinking below a blue horizon.

Joseph, in an adjacent seat, pointed to scenes below us. "Many believe, John, that the name 'Jaffa' originates from the name of Noah's son Japheth. Jaffa is mentioned several times in the Bible, even in your Christian Bible when St Peter raised a widow from death."

'St Peter, in Jaffa, and it's in the Bible,' I thought. I wondered when he'd decided to bury the box.

My mind returned to hear Joseph saying, "Jaffa has been extremely important militarily. Tel Yafo, Jaffa Hill, rose to 40 feet and gave commanding views of the coast."

I looked through the window again and felt my stomach lurch when the plane banked. The wing tip appeared to touch buildings, and I heard the "clunk" of wheels.

A red sign blinked on and the pilot announced that we were to fasten seat belts. We were landing. The flight had been so quick I had hardly noticed it.

In the arrivals area, Sean called me to give an update.

"Hiya, Sean. We've just touched down at Ben Gurion." Looking at my watch I continued, "It's 16:00 here. We'll hail a cab and head to Simeon's house." I told him about our meeting with Caleb. "Yes, he's in his mid-70s. He's very upset that his stolen desk diary opened the door for the attempted theft of my case at Heathrow Airport and resulted in the abduction of his nephew. How are you getting on?" I asked.

Sean gave me a brief summary of his conversation with Joshua.

"Get this, John, I am, and I quote, 'a trained, experienced, and responsible former officer of the UK military'. What do ya think about that?"

"What do you want, a cub scout good deeds award?" I gave a spluttered laugh. "Anyway, about Caleb. He thrust his laptop at us as if it had leprosy. We sympathised with the old man and tried to placate his guilt and worry, told him it wasn't his fault that there were evil people."

"Listen, John, before I set off," Sean said. "We've some extra personnel. Working under Joshua we've four Mossad people. My instinct is they're computer and telecom buffs. How about they hook up with James?"

"Let me chat to James and Aly," I said. "They work on the edge…if you know what I mean. They may not want official recognition. I'll call him now and let you know when we get to Simeon's." I ended the call and looked up James in my contacts.

*

During the day, Simeon was taped to a plastic chair. He winced; the chair was hard and uncomfortable. His captors brought him lukewarm microwaved meals and cups of water. During meals his hands were freed, but cruel eyes watched him closely, the fierce eyes of hardened men. Through the broken slatted windows, he could see trees and fields through gaps. He remembered being forced up some stairs, blindfolded, but he had no idea where he was. He thought he recalled hearing crowds cheering as he journeyed. Did they pass a stadium of some sort? Would help come soon?

*

Jason Gould, seated in a plush chair, stretched his legs under a huge mahogany table. The executive boardroom table. Neon lights reflected in its highly polished sheen. Jason's jacket draped the back of his velvet-cushioned seat, but he felt uncomfortable.

"Look, I don't know any more about it than you do," Jason said. A man with grey hair and bushy eyebrows whispered to a younger man who was doodling on a pad.

The older man suddenly jumped up and slammed his fist on the table. "*Du Hurensohn*! You son of a bitch!" he yelled.

The doodler stopped and smiled. Speaking in English for the benefit of Jason, he said, "The box is in Tel Aviv as we speak. Morgan and the other Latchman brother are staying at the Hilton."

The grey-haired man slumped into his chair and stroked his goatee. "Why so long?" he spoke in broken English.

"Don't worry, Granddad," the doodler said. "We'll hear from our guys soon. They still have the brother."

The grey-haired man, called Karl Leitz, leaned on his walking cane and left the room.

"Horst, you know this is not my fault, don't you?" Jason said to the young man on his left.

Horst Leitz replied, "Yah, yah. But we'd better get to Tel Aviv and find out what these *miststücks* are doing. Bastards! The old man will blow a gasket if we don't get that powder soon."

Simeon's House

Sean and Joshua were met at the door by a female police officer in a navy blue uniform. Joshua showed her his ID.

"I'm Sarah," she said in accented English. "I'm family support officer, to support and if so protect Esther." Turning to Sean, she asked, "And you are?"

"The cavalry, ma'am," Sean bowed. "Captain Casey, a trained, experienced and responsible former officer of the UK military." He winked at Joshua.

The policewoman smiled, nodding. "The Englishman."

"No ma'am, the Irishman," Sean said. "Do you have any mace in that handbag? I've always wanted to see that."

"I hope we won't need," she tapped the handgun resting underneath a Kevlar vest in her belt.

A 40-something woman in a green nurse's uniform entered the room.

"Hello, I am Joseph's niece, Esther," she said, kissing Joshua on both cheeks and nervously doing the same with Sean. "I have flapjacks and cold drinks." A kettle whistled in the kitchen, "And coffee," she added. "We're overcome that my nation's authorities are offering such overwhelming assistance. Thank you."

"Have you heard anything since the telephone call?" Joshua asked.

"No, nothing at all," she said, "is that bad?"

Joshua and Sean were silent. "Your landline and mobiles may not be secure," Joshua said. "Please only use them sparingly, and speak of nothing personal. Try to use them for misinformation if you can."

"Tell lies, you mean?" Esther said. Joshua looked uncomfortable.

"Aye, for the greater good, sometimes that's important," Sean said, "even your uncle, Esther, said recently that 'God helps those who help themselves', so it must be right." Sean smiled.

"Your laptop at home, Esther, and your computers at work will need to be monitored," Joshua said. Sean ate a flapjack, holding his hand under it to catch the crumbs.

"At the hospital?" Esther said, her voice quavering.

"Our government is fully behind these measures," Joshua said. "Use your IT equipment normally; we don't want to warn these people. But avoid sensitive information. The defence minister has asked me to personally assure you that we'll do the utmost to rescue your father safely, and recover the stolen Jewish heirlooms."

*

A female police officer opened Simeon's door and patted us down as Joseph and I entered. Another woman wearing a nurse's uniform kissed Joseph on both cheeks, then turning to me she said, "Oh, you must be John. I'm Esther, Simeon's daughter. Thank you so much for helping us. Please come in."

Kissing me on both cheeks, she swept her hands indicating the refreshments. We joined the small gathering. Esther appeared relieved to see her uncle and took it upon herself to introduce Joshua and Sarah the policewoman.

Joseph tore open the package like a toddler at Christmas unwrapping presents. His face beamed as he examined the new phone, but periodically his eyes grew moist. Teardrops ran down his cheeks. Esther too started to weep.

"Thank you so much," he addressed to us all. "Please find my brother and bring him home."

"We'll do our utmost," Joshua said. "A substantial team is involved: the Tel Aviv local police, Israeli security services and Interpol. My team is triangulating the signal from Simeon's mobile phone. We hope its location can be pinpointed."

He addressed the policewoman, "We'll be at the Hilton, if you need us."

*

Back at the hotel, Sean and Joshua joined James and me for a debriefing session in our bedroom. Introduced to Joshua, 'Josh' to James, he updated us with news from home.

I moved crisp packets, Mars Bars wrappers and empty coke bottles from the duvet. The room was morphing into James' bedroom. We had told him to stay put, but James had been living like a hermit.

"Sorry about the mess, guys," James said, clearing space around him. Pointing at Sean and smirking, he said, "He told me not to leave the room."

"Aye but you have bins, you eejit," Sean said. James held his hands up.

Aly appeared on James' laptop screen on the dresser, just as if she was in the room.

"Hi ya'll. We've made some progress," she said, "Thudd is in the *Gazette* server and now has administer rights."

"Who is Thudd?" I asked.

"A friend," James said, "you'll meet him at the wedding, plus a few other guys. It'll be ace!"

Aly looked at James, "DUH... Anyway, the *Cheshire Gazette* reporter requested payment to a 'GJ' from his news editor."

James continued, "We scratched our heads trying to figure out who the hell the source could be but came up blank. But then bingo, the same initials are in Human Resources at Leitz Pharmaceuticals. Someone called GJ joined the payroll and...

listen to this: GJ received a 'relocation bonus' of 115,600 Euros; £85,000!"

Sean whistled, "That's some bonus!"

"Why are you making a hostile takeover of Leitz?" Joshua asked with a furrowed brow.

"One of the guys who attacked me at Heathrow used to work for them," I said. "We wonder if they're searching for the leaves."

"That's some serious money," Sean said. "GJ has sold us out to the newspaper and Leitz."

"Aly, we agree that to crash the paper or delete the print will sound alarm bells and give credence to the story," I said. "For the time being we'll track the source and offer denials."

The Mossad sergeant seemed impressed, asked some questions about their knowledge of the dark web, and offered Aly and James a job. Aly and James looked embarrassed.

Aly's voice went quieter. "John, Liz wants a word later on Skype."

"OK…sounds ominous," I said. Aly said nothing.

The Jaffa hotel arranged a room for Josh. The manager's face showed delight when he viewed Josh's identification. He offered the wedding suite immediately.

"Meet in the restaurant at 20:00?" I asked. "We can freshen up first."

Joseph returned to his brother's house to spend an evening with Esther. "Esther is working from 6:00, so I'll be here at 8:00 on Wednesday morning."

We ate heartily from our table loaded with plates of food carried from the serving area. James made up for hours of takeaways. I tugged at my belt, loosening it another notch, and walked the familiar stairs past photos of Israel, smoothing my hair in the reflection.

Josh opened the door smiling and said, "The Jaffa Hilton has 'donated their most luxurious suite to the work of the Israeli Government' to quote the manager." We examined the many rooms of the suite and felt like kings.

Sean said, "It's better than that piss-hole in Afghanistan, John". Agreeing with a nod, I observed Josh raise his eyebrows. I clarified that in Afghanistan my company recycled scrap Soviet armaments and that Sean was not at that time in the military.

Josh said, "There is much scrap metal around the globe. Conflicts destroy mans' war machines leaving behind monumental graveyards."

I felt our camaraderie was loosening his tongue. I agreed with him that most war seemed pointless once it had ended and the impact assessed. Some plans, it seemed to me, were made and implemented without counting the cost. I hoped the outcome of my plan would be better.

*

The bleep of James' laptop on a desk in Josh's room caught my attention, snapping me out of a pensive and philosophical mood. My wife, daughter and soon-to-be daughter-in-law were lighting up the screen. I had been daydreaming in a spacious recliner.

A worried mother inquired, "Where's James?"

"He's trying the hot tub. He'll be out in a minute," I said, placating her.

Becky came on and teased, "You have a hot tub?"

"It's not ours," I said. "It's his. *He* is Joshua, or Josh." I pushed him towards the screen.

I heard Liz and Becky squeal with delight, "What a hunk!" At that point, James appeared in a white Hilton hotel bathrobe and took a bow, his damp ginger hair dripping everywhere.

Sean uttered, "Not you, James, it's the rabbi here. By the way, where's Rachel?" Sean inquired.

Becky came onscreen and said, "Rachel is in Berne for a conference with Save the Children."

"She texted me about that, but isn't she back yet?"

"Aww don't worry, lover boy, she'll be OK for the fitting,"

Becky said. She could see we were confused and explained that Rachel and Becky were going to be chief bridesmaids at James' and Aly's wedding in May.

Beaming with pride, she announced, "And Wesley will be a page boy."

I asked about him and tingled to hear that he was growing stronger by the day.

Not knowing the full story, Josh inquired about Wesley. He seemed disappointed that Becky had a child, but when we clarified the domestic situation, a glowing smile reached from ear to ear.

"Miss Morgan, I think you've pulled," Sean mocked. "That was quick!"

Becky blushed and twirled her black hair. I rarely saw her blush.

The young Israeli soldier seemed amused as he stroked his chin and stared at the screen, seeming to maintain eye contact with Becky.

James sat at the laptop. "OK, that's enough comedy."

"If you don't pull that robe together we'll all be ROFL," Sean said. "See? I'm not the technophobic Neanderthal you say I am."

I laughed.

James drew the bathrobe together, blushing furiously.

Aly's face came to the front of screen. "What hairy legs ya'll have, James," she mocked.

Changing room guffaws broke out from both laptop screens. Neither group had had a revelation over the newspaper sneak with the initials GJ.

Josh said, "It's someone you all know."

We started sounding out possible names: John, James, Jack, Jethro, Jasper...

I stroked my chin and said, "Someone at Wesley's party... someone who saw Joseph, and invented a story."

"Someone with a grudge," Joshua added, "whose initials are JG or GJ." 'JG or GJ,' I thought.

Liz said, "I didn't think it might be the surname first. The only person that springs to mind is…"

"Yes, it's him," I said. "It's obvious. GJ, Gould Jason, aka Jason Gould!"

"Didn't that toad come to the party in a brand new Porsche?" Sean asked. "Of course. A friggin' 'relocation bonus'! That's what he spent it on!"

I nodded. James walked around the room, cursing.

We explained who he was and Josh hit his left palm with his right fist. "He *will* be stopped!"

Joshua and Becky shared a tender moment as she mouthed a "thank you".

Sean drew his first finger across his throat.

James took charge again. He invited his mother to clarify the problem she'd mentioned when we were having dinner.

I sat cross-legged on the bed watching the images on the laptop, eager to see my wife and hear her news. A bewitching face appeared, piercing green eyes that searched souls.

"Go ahead, Liz." My hands were clammy. I missed her warmth.

Carefully, Liz said, "We were in the kitchen with Tony. We had the plans, drawings and our notes spread out. We'd seen a place ideal for Morgan Fashion, a cafe and the charity offices above." Liz paused and continued, "Tony's lad, Alan, and Wesley were playing upstairs. Suddenly someone started banging violently on the front door. I hurried to open it and Maria, Tony's wife, was standing there ranting and raving."

"What's her problem?"

"Bloody Morgan this, bloody Morgan that," Liz said. "She shouted he was a puppet, that we were pulling his strings. She ridiculed his surname Bullock and mocked that it should be Bollock, insisting their lad went home…'NOW!' she hollered. She made my eardrums throb, John," Liz continued tearfully. "Alan was dragged away crying. Wesley was crying and shaking."

My wife looked to me for sympathy and support. I gazed

into her green eyes and told her how much we all missed home, that we were sorry we could do nothing about Tony tonight, and that we would discuss the matter when we were back home.

I mouthed, "I love you", and she did the same.

Aly's face came nearer on the screen, "I've a few things, ya'll. James and I've talked. We're fixing ta hire two marquees for the wedding reception and evening disco."

"Epic," James said.

"Also," Aly breathed, "James an' I'll need a place to live after the wedding. I've some details from local estate agents I can email, but we need guidance. We're nervous at the rising price of property."

"I've had an idea about that," Sean interjected. I drew my breath, waiting for some jocular punchline when he placed himself next to me to appear onscreen. "You kids can have my apartments above the garages," he said. "I can pack all my stuff into trunks and live in my workshop. Tony will make some alterations for me – like a toilet and a shower. We would all have our own private door and access so there wouldn't be a problem. But I don't want any rumpy-pumpy late at night 'cos my ceiling would be your bedroom floor." James again blushed bright red. It was becoming a habit.

I'd known my friend would send us to bed with a smile. Josh was scratching his head, no doubt wondering at the meaning of "rumpy-pumpy".

A Search and a Suspect

On Wednesday morning, our breakfast of apple pancakes, breakfast burritos and caramel kugel littered the table. Jugs of orange juice sparkled in the sunlight. Black coffee stewed in a percolator jug. We ate heartily and then Joseph arrived, pulling out a plush red velvet upholstered chair.

"Esther is feeling much better," he said. "The lady police officer is becoming a friend. She drew me aside though to say she's worried Simeon's kidnappers have not been in touch."

Joshua's mobile bleeped. I did not catch all the conversation but it sounded like optimistic news. Sipping his orange juice from a clear glass, he dabbed his mouth with a white paper napkin and moved slightly forward. "My team got a triangular fix on Simeon's mobile. Navy divers are on their way."

Joseph said, "*Oy vey*! Divers?"

In my ear, Josh whispered, "The signal is in the harbour area. It looks like it's in the Mediterranean."

Standing up and stretching, Sean said, "OK, let's party."

Sean and Josh returned to their rooms to equip for conflict. In my room, I fidgeted and then lifted the lid of the antique box. My spine tingled when I placed the bag of ground leaves into my jacket pocket. 'Just a hunch,' I thought.

"James, remain in the room with the door locked again," I said. "Maybe you don't feel part of the group, isolated up here," I placed my hand on his back, "but you're vital. We need to be kept up to date with news. I hear Josh's team have respect for you. But for God's sake keep it tidy!"

James sniggered. "Yeah, OK. Anyway, we're in the loop… and thanks, Dad." James gave me a hug. "Good luck, Dad. Be careful."

I struggled to remember a time when James and I had hugged since his childhood. Father and son had finally bonded. It had taken over 20 years.

Sean placed a black holdall on the back seat of Josh's BMW and climbed in. Joseph accompanied me in the hire car. The engines turned over and roared into life. The flower seller that I had first met in a farmers' market in the UK in 2011 seemed anxious.

"Joseph, just because his phone is in the sea, it doesn't mean anything," I said, "they probably threw it away."

"But why the divers?" Joseph stammered. "If anything has happened to him I'll never forgive myself." Then the dam broke and he sobbed uncontrollably.

*

Bubbles floated on the surface of the blue waters, broken intermittently by effervescent foaming white waves. Water darkened my jacket and drops cascaded to the floor. I shivered. Seagulls cawed above our heads. The launch was moored 20 feet from the jetty, and the divers were below us, black shapes visible through the crystal-clear waters. The tide jostled the police search-and-rescue vessel and water lapped against the sides.

Perched on the boat's side, Sean bobbed up and down, a large grin from ear to ear, oblivious to the splashes drenching him. 'He's at home parachuting from the sky or landing from a dingy in the moonlight,' I thought. Josh eagerly scanned the surface. The frogmen periodically broke through the surface, spurts of water from their mouthpieces like porpoises blowing through their air holes.

"Nothing yet," Joshua said.

I was struck by the memory of surveying the dock area and old steps months ago from the back of a Volvo.

A crowd gathered on the dock esplanade. News vans parked, with satellite antennae revolving on their roofs. Reporters tumbled across the cobblestone surfaces, desperate to be the first. My thoughts turned to the story back home. I knew what I'd like to do to Jason Gould, but I didn't know what to do about the newspaper. Fifty minutes of relentless searching finally brought heartening news.

A navy frogman appeared above the surface, handing to Josh the remainder of Simeon's phone.

"It may not have fingerprints or DNA, but we'll try." Josh placed the broken phone into an evidence bag and passed it to a colleague.

Josh ordered the police launch to return to the jetty, warning us to look straight ahead and say nothing to the gathered journalists. We were to make our way back to the vehicles quickly.

"Say *nothing*," Josh emphasised again, "not even 'no comment'."

We got the message.

A police cordon protected us from the pressing questions of the media while we pulled up our collars and turned our faces from the flashing bulbs. It was a relief to be ensconced in Josh's car, the hire car left behind for local police to return. Sean lifted the holdall from the back seat, which gave metallic clunking sounds as he placed it into Josh's trunk.

"Please wait a minute, Joshua," I said, answering my bleeping Blackberry. "It's James," I said. "OK, go ahead, son."

"Aly has some stuff, but she doesn't want our friends to get into trouble." I relayed the concern to Joshua. He gave the thumbs up and watched the reporters from the corner of his eye as we pulled away.

"OK, James," I said, "our lips are sealed."

"Well, our friend Petros has gained access to Leitz's

mainframe. He opened folders in their mail server, looking at emails and listening to voicemail files."

"What?" I said. "Never mind…carry on."

"One caller to Leitz said he 'had the package' and was awaiting further instructions."

"That could be innocent, James," I said.

"True. But we found this call in an HR folder of ex-employees. Want to see who made the call?" he asked, sounding smug. "Hang on, I'll send it to Josh's phone, he'll know how to open the message."

I huffed. "Josh, James is sending…"

"Got it," Josh said, stopping the car and showing us the image.

"Got ya, you bugger," Sean said. "It's the bozo who tried to steal John's case."

"So this man who used to work for Leitz is one of my brother's kidnappers," Joseph said.

Joshua rang his office to contact Interpol and the local police, asking them to bring the man in.

We headed back to the hotel to wait. By midday, we were increasingly frustrated. When Josh's phone buzzed, he smiled and nodded to us. A burden lifted.

"It's not the Leitz guy, but the kid," Josh said. "We gave details to the police of the cleaner who'd stolen Caleb's diary. A young thug. He's being brought to Tel Aviv police headquarters to be interviewed. Interpol have also traced the ex-employee – the lab technician – from Leitz Pharmaceuticals. There's an arrest warrant out on him."

Personally, I felt they had taken their time about it. He'd tried to steal my case almost a year before. But I didn't understand international diplomacy. We had two clear suspects at least, one in custody. Our net was closing in.

Tel Aviv District Police HQ

At 3:00 p.m. local time, three of us navigated works of sculpture, walked up stone steps and entered the Tel Aviv Police Headquarters in Salame Street. We had suggested that Joseph go to Simeon's and update Esther.

Despite occupying only half of the floors in the building, the Tel Aviv Police HQ presence was substantial. A desk sergeant gave me a multi-lingual leaflet in which I read that there were 3,100 members of the Tel Aviv District Police Force. They had responsibility for policing 1.2 million people. In addition to local criminals, including its share of young thugs, the area, being an urban centre and major port, also attracted villains from around the world.

Before we were permitted to take the escalator, we were escorted by the desk sergeant to two full body scanners. A screeching noise greeted Sean when he walked through it. Within seconds, several male and female uniformed officers appeared out of nowhere, like worker bees from a hive, their feet clattering to reception. A scuffle ensued and Sean was wrestled to the tiled floor by four officers. Handcuffs and batons swung in the air. Then Sean was manhandled, spread-eagled against a wall.

"STOP!" Josh yelled, flashing his Mossad badge, and then commanding Sean, "Show them your licence!"

The uniformed officers warily released Sean. Tucking in his

147

shirt and reaching into his pants pocket, he held up a paper. "This, I believe, is my 'get out of jail free card'."

The police formed a huddle, led by a burly sergeant, and examined the authorisation to carry arms. Josh translated the sergeant's apology while we followed him to the escalator. We stood single file on the escalator, like shoppers in a shopping centre.

With Josh translating for us, the sergeant explained, "We'll proceed to the second floor where an inspector will be waiting for us."

"I had 'em beat, Sergeant," Sean joked to Josh. "Tell him that."

An open plan area of grey metal desks met us. All eyes turned towards us before everyone resumed their work. Josh, Sean and I walked slowly past men and women, both uniformed and in civilian dress, sitting at desks, staring at computer screens. Maps, charts and photos of horrific scenes of crime covered the wall facing us. My stomach churned.

The sergeant and Josh were chatting as we turned left into a corridor.

"Good luck," he said in English, knocking and pushing open a door.

A dark-haired man of about five feet sat ensconced behind an immaculate polished desk. A metal nameplate, the only item on his desk apart from a phone, was inscribed with "Inspector Abraham Maier". He steepled his fingers, reminding me of a bank manager.

He said nothing but waved his hand, signalling that we could sit down in the three plastic stacking chairs pressed against a wall, but Josh preferred to stand. The small man had greasy hair with a middle parting. His ears protruded like two jug handles. He stroked his ruddy and pockmarked complexion, twirling a waxed moustache and speaking to Josh in his native tongue. He paused after each sentence so that Josh could translate for us.

"Inspector Maier, Chief of Detectives in Tel Aviv District,"

Josh said, "does not like it. He is not going to be ordered about in *his* city by spooks, government spies or foreigners."

With raised voices, the discussion between Josh and Maier grew more heated. The faces of officers from the open area were peering through the partitioned office window of their chief. We had not prepared for this hostility. The little man reminded me of a strutting cock in a farmyard. I sensed it was not going well for us.

Exasperated, Joshua, our hero, played his trump card. "I'll not be deviated from my mission. If necessary I'll appeal to the highest authority and get him on the phone," he said.

"Go ahead, Sergeant," Inspector Maier said, "but this is *my* city, *my* jurisdiction, and *my* office." Josh continued to interpret for us.

How Josh kept his cool I don't know. He opened his phone and dialled a number.

"Yes. I'm sorry. Please disturb him. It is *very* important." There was a pause and then Josh said, "Yes Sir, I'm so sorry. Yes, it *is* important. Yes, I know it's busy for you too. Yes, he *is* being obtrusive." Then Josh handed the open phone to Inspector Maier with the words, "The prime minister for you, Inspector."

Sean and I gaped. The inspector loosened his tie and smoothed his hair.

We didn't know what the PM was saying, nor did we understand the inspector's responses, but he grew redder and redder. Nodding and puffing, he looked like a chastened schoolboy. We all understood he was probably saying, "Yes, Sir. Yes, Sir of course. Yes, Sir. Yes, Sir I realise that. Yes, Sir. Thank you, Sir."

I watched and could sense his pain. I could not count the times he had winced during that phone call.

It appeared that we had friends in high places.

Inspector Abraham Maier sat like a man chastened, the wind knocked out of him. His manner towards us and Josh especially underwent a transformation. Not a broken man, by any means, but a humbler man. He knew he was no longer commanding the investigation.

Rising from his office chair, he seemed to have shrunk in the past 20 minutes – if that was possible for such a little man. Poking his head through the doorway, he called to his sergeant in a loud enough voice for all to hear, which Josh interpreted for us.

"These men are to be escorted to the detainee. The officer from Intelligence and his friends are to be shown every courtesy. We are no longer in charge of the investigations. It is now a matter of national security."

He slunk back into his office. The faces in the open plan area seemed smug. Their eyes had a new sparkle; their body language was more positive. 'Nobody likes a bully,' I thought.

As we took the escalator to the ground floor, I asked Josh if it had really been Israel's prime minister on the phone.

"No, I'm afraid not," Josh said, "one of my team does a really great impression of Prime Minister Benjamin Netanyahu. I made a serious mistake, though, when I commented on his busy afternoon. He's in Osaka at an international meeting about Syria and its nuclear intent. He would more than likely be in bed because it's 22:30 in Japan. I hope it doesn't come back and 'bite us in the arse', as you say."

Sean and I roared with laughter, hoping too that Detective Inspector Maier didn't watch the news on TV that night and smell a rat.

Arriving on the ground floor, we were pleasantly treated by the front desk officers. Those who had frisked Sean earlier lowered their eyes in embarrassment. One of the female detective sergeants appeared at the top of the stairs to the lower ground floor and beckoned us to follow.

Our footsteps echoed as if we were in a chamber as we followed the blue-uniformed police officer down neon-lit concrete stairs. A musty smell circulated throughout the area. She unlocked the security gate with her identification card and ushered us through. The heavy wrought-iron gate shut with a loud "clang".

Entering a bleak corridor with whitewashed walls, we

turned right, facing a door and a plate-glass screen. "Mirror," the police officer said, "please…my English." We understood.

Josh said, "Take a seat and I'll interpret. The interview's about to start, but don't worry, they can't hear or see us. Please don't knock on the glass."

Voices came through two Bosch speakers, attached to the wall by metal brackets.

"Yes, my name is Eitan Dreyfuss," the teenager in blue nylon overalls said. At his side sat a slightly older female who bore his resemblance. "Yes, I worked as a cleaner at Cairo University. Yes, I took some stuff from the old guy's study." Looking at the young woman next to him, he whispered to her and said, "Yes, we staked out the hotel and followed the European. Yes, I met the Leitz guy. Look, he sprang for my airfare, so I thought 'why not'. No, I know nothing about drugs. No, I didn't know he would snatch the old man." He slouched in the chair.

Josh took notes.

The male officer stopped the tape and video recorder and opened the door, inviting Josh to talk with the detainee. Josh entered the interview room and said for the benefit of his audience, "I shall be translating the conversation into English. The perpetrator has just said 'and who the hell are you?'"

Josh recapped on Eitan's statement. The young woman, whom we now understood was Eitan's sister, wiped her eyes.

"You'll face charges of criminal damage, breaking and entering into the professor's study," Josh said. "You'll also be charged with theft of personal property, which is a felony. This could mean a five-year prison term, however, there are implications in a kidnap, as well as possible accessory to murder. We're leaving you for a break. Think about it."

Eitan's sister was shaking and sobbing. Eitan said something and she slapped him across the head, saying, "*Schmutz!*"

The interviewing police officers invited us to join them in the staff canteen.

"We'll break for 20 minutes, until 16:15," Josh said, "give them time to chew it over."

The staff canteen reminded me of many that I had seen in factories, shops and on building sites around the globe. The paint on the walls was flaked and peeling. The hot drinks machine clanked, whirred and gurgled, overflowing with hot water. It was caked with dark powder, like many I had seen around the world.

Sean summed it up with, "Christ! This is piss awful!"

Josh conversed with the two officers in his native Hebrew and we left the stifling staff canteen. It was a relief. The air conditioning was either broken or switched off and the smell of stale sweat assaulted my nostrils.

Joshua and the female sergeant gained admittance again to interview room two in Tel Aviv Police Headquarters. The prisoner looked smug. Eitan's sister was pale, with dark circles around her eyes.

Josh came on strong. "I am Mossad!" Joshua banged the table. "Do you know what that means?" He stared into the young man's eyes. "It means you are in holy shit!" Josh shouted. "I can make you disappear…you and your sister. You're going to stay here until you tell us everything you know."

Eitan appeared nonchalant and he yawned, cradling his head in his hands. He appeared to have found new strength and courage. It looked as if he believed that he could walk free, that he was winning.

Sean asked the female police officer something, gesturing with his hands until she understood. She left and returned five minutes later with a brown manila folder. Taking the mike connected directly to the interview room, he asked Josh to step out. I knew that whatever training Joshua had encountered with Mossad, he would not win an argument against Sean Casey. But what did Sean have in mind?

Inside Leitz at Strasbourg

Horst Leitz had a lot riding on a bag of leaves.

Some months before, when Hans Kestelmann, a former lab technician at Leitz Pharmaceuticals, had rung, Horst had expected a sob story. The man had used drugs; while within Horst's circle of friends drugs were acceptable, they were not acceptable at work. He chose to be magnanimous and listen, hoping to use the man for some scheme or other.

"You must be kidding!" Horst had gasped. "OK, email me everything and I'll look at it," he said. Look at it he did, and then he looked for a chink in the Morgan armour.

*

When he had introduced Jason Gould to his granddad at their villa in Berne, Horst knew it would be hard work. 'This Jason is a cold fish and a greedy bugger,' he thought. He'd asked Jason to wait in the vestibule while he talked to his grandfather.

Old Karl Leitz, 84 years old, leaned on his cane. Stroking his grey goatee, he said, "What are you thinking? Magic leaves, gardens of Paradise, cures for all. *Sie dumm fuhrt*! You stupid head!"

"Pappa, listen. I didn't believe it either," Horst said, "but I checked it out. I even visited the UK."

"So what are you proposing?" Karl said.

"Let's give this Jason a sweetener," Horst argued. "After all, if we can get our hands on this bag of leaves and our guys test it, analyse it and we find it can be manufactured, well, Pappa, we'll die and go to Heaven!"

Karl nodded. "Do it," he said, "put Gould on the payroll, get him to sign a contract, and ask that ex-employee to come and see us."

*

Hans Kestelmann had been interested when he'd heard from a friend about Eitan's inquiries. A small-time pot dealer, Hans spent most of what he earned on his habit. That was his problem. Approaching his mid-30s, he needed a break in life. The story about the old man's diary interested him, and so he'd contacted Eitan and arranged for the spring on John Morgan at the airport.

When old man Leitz outlined what had to be done, just before Christmas, he'd received a brown envelope stuffed with Euros across the executive table.

"And more will follow if you get the box," Horst Leitz had said. "This is Jason," he showed him a photograph, "who is working with us on this as well. And I want you to take Tim from security with you. Go back to Tel Aviv, snatch the old Jew and make some threats. Don't hurt the old guy, we're not criminals. Keep him safe until you have the bag. Oh, and use the kid, Eitan. Offer him money. We need to keep him quiet."

'Don't hurt him? Hans thought later. 'Sod that. He'll see my face. When I have the bag, the Jew will have an accident and the kid too,' Hans had said to himself as he flew back to Israel from Strasbourg with Tim Mann. Snow was falling outside the airplane window. It was nearly New Year. Together, they plotted how they were going to kidnap Simeon.

The Confession

Five minutes of heated debate resonated around the neon-lit corridor near the cells, and the female officer left the interview room and joined the discussion.

After some further argument, Joshua relented. Sean Casey, formerly a captain with the SAS, and Sergeant Federman, a Special Forces intelligence officer with Mossad, sat down opposite the young thug who had stolen a diary. His sister sat next to him looking increasingly worried.

The youngster's eyes narrowed. Joshua explained again that he would interpret. The teenager's hand trembled. He probably remembered Sean from Heathrow Airport; he certainly remembered being head butted, punched and karate kicked. He whispered to his sister and toyed nervously with a white drinking cup.

Sean placed a brown manila folder on the table. The teenager reached for it.

"Not yet!" Sean said.

There followed a long series of interchanges between Sean and the prisoner. The browbeaten youth looked questioningly at Josh, who nodded in assent. The young woman cried. Sean pressed on with his onslaught. Sentence by sentence he made his points, and Joshua hurried to translate. Eitan paled and grew petrified.

Sean deftly opened the manila folder, taking out a photo.

Sliding it across the table, he asked, "Well?"

He slid another, then another, and finally one more. He arrayed the photos in a line, like a row of playing cards. The young woman vomited loudly and turned her face away. I recognised the crime scene photos from the detectives' area: horrific, gruesome and vicious murders in recent months. The teenager gagged and asked for another drink of water.

"Wait!" Sean said with authority, before the police officer in the room could oblige.

He swung out of his chair and stood behind the scared-witless detainee and his sister. Drawing the writing pad and pen across the table, he placed it squarely in front of the youth, who trembled with Sean's hand on his shoulder. He turned, looking meekly at Sean and then at Josh, both of whom nodded. Then Eitan started to talk and write scribbled notes that filled three pages of A4 lined paper. Josh asked him to sign it. The Mossad officer witnessed the statement and then asked the female sergeant to enter and do the same.

Sean left the room wiping his brow, "I need a drink."

For our benefit, Sean then outlined his methodology. "I painted every picture I could from Madame Tussauds Wax Museum Room of Horror. Using the crime scene photos, I emphasised that the kid would experience it all. I told him that I would make him an offer he couldn't refuse. Either his brains, or information and his signature on the paper."

The female police officer registered shock, but I was not surprised.

Joshua slapped Sean on the back but said, "The confession will not stand up in court. Eitan confessed under duress, but we have vital information. Thank you, Captain."

Josh rang his team at Mossad, ordering them to do a search for a blue van and recently rented properties within ten kilometres of the Maccabiah Stadium going north and east up the coast.

"What Eitan told us is that when the men took Simeon, he wanted no part of it. They blindfolded both Eitan and Simeon and threw them into the back of a blue van. He knew that they had driven past the Maccabiah Stadium because he heard cheering. There was a match on New Year's Day. The kid said they travelled for five to ten minutes, he could hear seagulls, and then they turned right. One man unloaded Simeon and the other returned to Jaffa and dropped the kid at the train station."

The pieces of the jigsaw were coming together for the rescue of Simeon.

*

Darkness was approaching at 7:00 p.m. when we arrived back at the Hilton Hotel on a starlit night. Josh left us to brief his colonel and the team at his base. I rang Joseph to tell him and Esther the news.

I knocked on the door to our room and the chain rattled.

James called out, "Who is it? I only open for Sean." I noticed his eye was absent from the peephole.

"Open up, you plonker," I said. "I need a pee."

Sean and I shared what we knew with James.

I said, "Josh's team is deciphering information and following-up leads. About the blue van, they're trying car dealers and hire companies, stolen vehicles and local businesses. For recently let properties in the designated area, they're making enquiries of the estate agents and letting companies."

At 8:30 p.m., after showering and changing, we descended the stairs to the restaurant. It had been a strange journey since I had first walked down those steps. The box locked in our room upstairs held answers that many sought. I felt strongly that we were drawing closer to the evil people who had tried to steal the healing leaves; drawing nearer to the men who were holding Simeon.

That evening, using Skype, I spoke with Liz. "Liz, I love you now more than ever."

"Aww thanks, hun, I love you too," Liz said and blew a kiss. "You're not worried about this, are you?" she asked.

"Not really," I lied. "But I want us to take a holiday for my 62nd birthday, maybe around the Easter holidays so Becky and Wesley could join us. How about the Royal?"

"That would be lovely, John. You sure you're not worried?" she said.

"Nah, he's not worried. He's got me!" Sean interjected over my shoulder. "And where's Rachel?"

"In Berne still," Becky said. "Where's Josh? In his room?"

"With his colonel," I said, "but he'll be back at midnight."

"Pooh!" Becky said. Then, "OK then, goodnight. Night, John boy." The two females closest to my heart giggled. I chuckled, hoping we were nearing the end of a rollercoaster ride.

I tossed and turned, my sleep disturbed, similar to my first journey to Tel Aviv. On that occasion, I'd been anxious about a meeting with Simeon. Nearly 11 months later, I was worried about his safety. His phone had been discarded. Ruthless men were holding him hostage. St Peter's box, the scrolls and mysterious leaves were deemed to be worth a life.

Being reminded of the scrolls and the interest of so many, including the Mossad Colonel Balak, I made my mind up. James was snoring in his bed. I carefully lifted the box, took out all the documents and maps and placed them in my holdall. Sneaking carefully out in the early morning, I tiptoed to reception.

"Do you have a photocopier?" I asked the night porter, who helpfully pointed to a room adjacent to two telephone kiosks, explaining how to use it with my room card.

I closed the door with a click and lifted the parchments and maps from my holdall. A state-of-the-art Ricoh copier and printer filled one wall. Into a slot I inserted my room card and then placed the sacred parchments one by one on the glass platen, pressing the green button and hoping the photocopying would do no damage to the originals. Fifteen minutes later, I placed the originals and copies in my holdall, and returned to our room.

James was singing in the shower. Our breakfast meeting ten minutes away, I replaced the parchments and maps in the box and packed the copies into my suitcase.

Smartly attired hotel staff, used to our comings and goings, served our party in the restaurant with coffee and took orders for food. Joining us, Josh insisted we try cereal, oatmeal, eggs, hash browns, steak, toast, and pancakes. Arriving just in time, Joseph echoed the Mossad officer's selection. Tucking in to a hearty meal, we caught up with the latest intelligence.

"What was wrong with you last night?" James asked. "It sounded like a jumping frog in the next bed."

"Err...I had things on my mind, and things to do."

"You should count sheep, Boss. It works for me. Me mammy said I could sleep on a clothesline."

"Too much imagination, I suppose. Once a sheep wearing pyjamas or something jumps the fence, I'm wide awake."

"Mine get taken up by flying saucers," James laughed.

"You're two ginger-headed weirdos," Sean said, making sheep noises.

"Anyway, Dad, we're trying Google Earth to locate the van. We could get lucky," James said, "if the camera is pointed in the right direction and the weather is clear. We're limiting the search area to a 50-kilometre-square section grid by grid. Using a complicated programme, one of our online friends, Tealeaf, is limiting the pixels to highlight vehicle-size blue objects."

"Huh? And did you say Tealeaf?" I was gobsmacked that James' chat friends were working around the clock to locate a blue van for us. 'These cyber buffs are not so bad after all,' I thought.

"But I gotta tell you, Dad," he added seriously, "that when I searched Google Earth for Woolacombe, there were kids playing on the sand and holiday-makers splashing in the sea."

"So?" I said. "It's a great beach."

"Yeah, but not in January," he added morosely. "The images we see may be months old."

"OK, thanks, James," I said. "The paper still concerns me though. The *Cheshire Gazette* will shout from the housetops about Wesley's amazing recovery, mentioning a mysterious Middle-Eastern visitor to our home. Delivering a denial may placate the news-hungry wolves, but once the trumpet has sounded our adversaries will be strengthened in their resolve to obtain the box. If the tale spreads, it will jeopardise our search and endanger Simeon's life."

"I may be able to help," Joseph said. "I've been thinking about it. One of my friends from the Manchester synagogue is a substantial shareholder in the *Manchester Evening News*. He's on the board. I believe they own the accumulated *Gazette* brands. Perhaps board pressure will stifle more broadcasts unfavourable to our cause?"

Slapping Joseph on his back, I hugged him, overjoyed at the news.

Encouraged by these developments, we leisurely ploughed into the gastronomic delights. There was little else we could do but eat and wait. Leads, interviews, data, reports, details from snitches and informers, all were appearing fruitless while the sands of time slowly seeped through the hourglass of our Thursday morning.

"The local police are canvassing areas in patrol cars and door-knocking owners of blue vans, as well as checking recent lets. With all searches there are peaks and troughs," Joshua said, "we've made great progress so far. Colonel Balak feels that if we had the CCTV coverage that you have in the UK in your towns, cities and road and rail transport systems, we would have found the criminals by now. Sadly, our people prefer their privacy to safety. I think the colonel is secretly envious of the UK. 'Big Brother' is everywhere in your country!"

"Well, you must use what you have. Let's hope it's enough," I said.

The Farm Hideout

At exactly 2:00 p.m., James arrived at our table in the restaurant amid leaps, spins and punches to the air.

"EUREKA! I think we have it!" he said. Other diners enjoying their lunch looked across at us.

"He's getting married," Sean said. The diners clapped and voiced congratulations.

James hurriedly moved plates, dishes and cups to one side. Coffee spilled onto the impeccable white tablecloth. Joseph dabbed at the dark stain with a napkin. As we gathered around his laptop, James showed his thrilled audience the images that a cyber-friend had sent.

"See this image?" he said excitedly although in a lowered tone. "A bit blurred, I know...but it's a blue van. Google flippin' Earth came through! The farmhouse is in an apple orchard, and get this...the owner is on holiday."

The Mossad agent continued to turn a blind eye and deaf ear to the activities of James' and Aly's cyber friends. He called his colonel and his team, making his way upstairs to his room, two steps at a time, Sean following at his heels. Five minutes later, he and Sean returned, both armed and ready.

Outside the hotel forecourt, Josh extracted from the BMW four lightweight protective vests.

"What? Is it 'buy one get one free' from Tesco?" Sean said, pulling one over his head and fastening it.

"They'll not stop a bullet but they'll lessen the impact," Josh said. "The vests will protect against sharp implements, however." Joseph looked at Joshua and then at his stomach, before Joseph and I struggled into the vests.

Sean said, "Don't worry about John's head, it's as hard as a brick, and his balls are made of iron." Turning to me with a stern countenance, he said, "Stay behind and for God's sake, just remember to duck!"

I smiled, because his reference to my testes was a subtle reminder of the treatment I'd undergone for prostate cancer. I took his hint.

Panoramic views of the swirling blue sea with crashing waves passed us as we hurriedly snaked along the coastal road. As we passed the Maccabiah Stadium on our right, I knew we were not far away. While we travelled, Josh gave clear instructions about the operation.

"Sean and I will enter the building first. John, you and Joseph follow. Booby-traps are possible and intruder alarms, so keep back." Sean checked that I understood and I nodded, moistening my lips.

The BMW turned right through broken gates and we bumped along past apple groves. Slowing the car to a crawl, Josh looked nervous as we parked. The sun was hot on my back when we left the car. The BMW doors closed noiselessly. Following Sean and Josh, my heart beat faster when they pushed open the farm door. Indicating by hand signals that Joseph and I should stay well back, they pushed open the lounge and kitchen doors, pointing their pistols. My body felt detached.

In the corners of rooms were signs of occupancy. The armed duo gingerly ascended a wooden staircase. Sean waved us forwards, his finger on his lips. On tiptoe, we reached the landing and Josh pointed to his left, signalling to Sean to go right. Gently prising open the first bedroom door, Sean tapped his ear and pointed to a room ahead. Josh joined him and they both held outstretched pistols. With a solid kick, the door smashed open.

Josh shouted in Jewish and English, "POLICE! FREEZE OR WE WILL FIRE!"

Through the broken doorframe, I saw Simeon tied to a chair in the corner of the room, naked apart from white cotton underpants. Everything seemed to happen in slow motion. His two kidnappers jumped up. The menacing one lit a Molotov cocktail with a cigarette lighter and threw it at Simeon, smashing it on the floor, and then threw himself through the bedroom window, shattering the wooden slats.

"Josh, window! I'll get the other one!" Sean shouted.

The man at the far door spun, fired, and ran onto the landing. The bullet ricocheted off the wall amidst white cascading plaster clouds and bounced off the floor near to the door where I was standing, breathing hard.

Time froze and eye-stinging fumes filled the room as I watched Sean pursue the kidnapper onto the landing, and then crouch and fire. The kidnapper's skull exploded and he fell to the floor with a dull thud. A coagulated pool of dark blood grew around him. Seeing the congealing sticky mess, I felt sick and turned my face away to dry-retch.

Josh threw himself headfirst through the broken window slats to pursue the escaping man, while Joseph and I raced to dampen Simeon's flames. Choking black flames engulfed us, along with the smell of burning flesh. Joseph beat at the flames with his jacket.

"Simeon...Simeon, it's me," Joseph sobbed. The smoking raging inferno took a few minutes to dampen. Flames extinguished, Joseph wrapped a discarded blanket around him.

Unfortunately, it turned out to be a bad idea. The blanket fibres attached to Simeon's burnt skin, pulling when he moved and causing inflammations to erupt all over Simeon's body. He was shaking violently.

Sean and Joseph assisted Simeon down the stairs as screaming sirens and flashing strobe lights came towards us at breakneck speed. Blue-uniformed paramedics with green crosses on their chest pockets and epaulettes checked Simeon over, placed him on a stretcher, and administered a clear liquid intravenously. Within minutes, the ambulance raced away with Joseph accompanying Simeon.

Outside the farm, Josh and the local police held the other kidnapper: the ex Leitz employee. Pushing him into a police car, Josh called his colonel.

Afterwards, Josh congratulated the rescue team. "Well done!" The local police stretched blue and white SOCO tape around the farm. Forensics staff in white boiler suits and plastic-covered shoes entered the building with carry cases.

Following the ambulance, with Josh at the wheel, we careered at breakneck speed along the country road and as I pulled off the body armour, I called James.

"Well done, son," I said. "Tell Aly and your friends that we've rescued Simeon and arrested a kidnapper."

"WOW! That's ace, Dad." I had mental images of his Twitter feed going viral.

"I just hope the old bugger pulls through," Sean said, expressing my fear.

Skidding the BMW to a halt, Josh dropped Sean and me at the emergency assessment unit entrance and left to meet with his colonel. We raced through the door.

Esther, Simeon's daughter, approached us looking crestfallen, her eyes red and puffy. Joseph placed his arms around her as she informed us, sobbing, that the burns and injuries were horrific.

"The surgical team are doing all they can to soothe his pain while they're removing the blanket fibres as gently as possible." Joseph shook at that last statement and Esther placed an arm around him.

"They've explained to us that with third-degree burns, his skin will become like leather," she said. "Severe burns tighten the skin and the capillaries in deeper tissues leak and cause swelling. Within two days, patients need surgery to remove dead skin and have skin grafts. Dead skin causes a massive toxic load on the body. Bacteria and severe infection will increase. Dad's circulation may collapse. If a patient's age and the percentage of burns to their body add up to more than 100, the chances of survival are slim, virtually nil. My dad is 56 and he has burns to 70% of his body. The score is 126."

Esther looked sad but resigned to her father's fate. Her dad was now in the hands of God.

I felt the bag in my jacket pocket and had an idea.

Intensive Therapy Unit,
Tel Aviv General Hospital

I had spent countless hours in hospital waiting rooms at GOSH when Wesley was sick. In another waiting room, in a different country, I shared my plan with Sean, Joseph and Esther.

"No, John," Esther said. "I can't allow it...it's a nonsensical scheme."

"Esther," Joseph patted her hand. "I trust these people... and time is running out."

She finally surrendered to our appeals, laid aside her training and experience, and reluctantly agreed to our plan. She beckoned us to follow her to the critical care unit where Simeon lay sedated in a private room, hooked up to several drips and monitors. His shallow breathing rattled through his mask. Esther left me in the room, her hands shaking.

I spoke with Simeon, unsure if he could hear me or understand.

"Simeon," I whispered in his ear, "can you hear me? It's John. I'm here with Joseph and Sean."

He opened his eyes and nodded slightly, dazed. The strong smell of cleaning fluid and burnt flesh filled my nostrils. I took a breath, staring at my friend's inflamed skin and blackened body, and gave Sean a nod.

Sean unhooked the intravenous feeds and monitor cables, and the machine started to beep. I turned off the power.

Simeon gasped for air, moaned and struggled when Sean removed the oxygen mask and lifted him up in his arms. I winced at Simeon's grimace.

"Sorry, me bucko, don't fret; it won't be long now," Sean soothed.

In the bathroom, water slapped against the sides of a massive ceramic bath. The steam was damp on my shirt. Esther dipped her elbow in the water and nodded. I pulled the drawstrings of the bag and tipped the entire contents into the bath water: it was not the time to think of saving any.

"OK, let's ease him in." I gently stirred the leaves around with my right hand.

Esther breathed a prayer, "Jehovah Rapha, be our Healer. Be our *Mizpah* today."

Simeon's neck and head were undamaged by the burns. His lobster-like body seemed to relax after a few minutes of soaking. Water spilled over the bath onto the tiles, soaking our feet as he wallowed in the bath water and gradually woke up. Footsteps sounded in the corridor. When Sean gently lifted him out of the water, we gasped. The inflamed and blackened flesh had metamorphosed into that of a new-born baby.

"Quickly, put this on him. Just let it hang," Esther said, passing us a light blue surgical gown from a peg. We surreptitiously walked the drenched and dripping figure along the hospital corridor, frogmarching him towards the exit.

"For God's sake, somebody pull his gown together," Sean whispered. "I can see his wobbly arse." Esther adjusted the gown while we walked, quickening our pace.

Passing a hospital porter adjacent to the main hospital doors, Joseph assuaged his curiosity.

"My brother needs a breath of fresh air." Esther, in her nurse's uniform, nodded with an air of authority.

In the rear of Esther's yellow Nissan, Simeon seemed to grow aware of the car's movement.

"The sedation is wearing off," Esther said, turning the

wheel. When he asked where we were going, Esther replied, "Home, Daddy. We're going home."

At Simeon's house, Sean and I called a cab, leaving Joseph and Esther to explain to the female police officer what had occurred. Apparently, she applauded when told of the capture of the kidnappers but didn't understand why Simeon was wearing a hospital gown. I heard the next morning that Joseph helped to dress him and then he stayed the night.

Both exhausted and elated, we entered the hotel. Our mood changed when Josh met us with a sullen face. He explained that Mossad had tipped him off that the local police were coming to arrest us all on Friday morning. Something to do with jurisdiction.

"What!" I said. "I can't believe my ears!"

Josh shrugged apologetically.

With Josh's room booked for one more night, we assembled and sampled his hospitality bar. James, equally elated at our news but dumbfounded at the impending arrest, called the girls on Skype. They were thrilled at Simeon's miracle.

Overjoyed at the capture of the kidnappers, Liz, Becky and Aly registered shock to hear our other news. Before Sean, James and I retired for the night, I wanted to express a concern.

"I don't know why I was chosen to be given the box." I said. "The healing leaves have certainly proved their power."

"They sure have, Boss. It's a shame we've none left," Sean said.

I think he knew what occupied my thinking. Despite our differences, we did seem able to read each other's minds.

James said, "That's true, Dad. What are you thinking?"

"I think," I said, "we have to face up to the possibility of using the maps and documents one day. We may have to find Eden and its tree. It sounds corny...but I think it's part of my destiny." I felt foolish for saying it.

"It sounds good to me, Boss. If anyone can put a team together with a plan, you can," Sean said, resting his hand on my shoulder. "That's something to think about, huh? But I bet if we get to the garden they won't let me in," Sean added. "Look," he said, showing me the tattoo on his hand. "Mine is the snake, you got angels. Mind you, I'll tell you what's weird, but don't freak out. I went back to that tattoo parlour a few weeks later and it wasn't there, and I asked locals and they looked mystified. They said there never was a tattooist there. Strange huh?"

I felt chills.

The Team is Arrested

Joseph joined us at our breakfast table with a cheery smile, a contrast to how we were feeling.

"Simeon's strength is returning," he said. "Esther says that from being tied to a chair for hours, his muscles were atrophying. But she's amazed at his recovery. He has lived on German baked beans and frankfurters since Jan 1st. My brother is eating ravenously, making up for lost time."

We told him our news and he was incredulous.

"Arrested?" he asked, rubbing his black curly hair ferociously.

We continued to eat our toast, but I felt like the condemned prisoner having his last meal. The sound of boots on a hard surface disturbed our meal. Other hotel guests stared with astonishment when four armed police officers marched across the foyer. I saw Sean's eyes scoping the area and he tapped Josh's hand.

Josh immediately opened his phone, "Yes, Sir. I understand," he said.

A Tel Aviv police sergeant held up arrest warrants while Joshua interpreted.

"We have arrest warrants for you three." They pointed their Uzis at me, Sean and Josh.

Joseph pleaded with hands outstretched, inviting handcuffs. "Please, take me."

"Friggin' heck," Sean said. "Not again," as rough hands

patted him down and searched him. I felt huge relief that Sean's weapons were in a holdall locked in Josh's trunk.

Josh went red with rage when his weapons were confiscated. The police sergeant shrugged. We were frisked, handcuffed and escorted to our rooms. By this time the hotel manager had appeared in a flap with a master key card, repeatedly brushing his hair with his hand.

When the sergeant searched the room and placed the box under his arm, James protested loudly and hopped around, recording the search on the video cam of his phone.

"This is harassment, you pen-pushers! It'll be on YouTube in five minutes!" he bellowed.

I couldn't help but smile, and I believed him. James was not included in the arrest warrant. "It's better that you stay here, James. Keep a link with home," I said.

"Want us to crash their server, Dad?" James' eyes twinkled mischievously. "It'll take a few hours but I think we could try."

Joshua shook his head, making a zipping motion with his finger.

"We'll be cool, son," I said. "But to quote Ian Hislop, 'If this is justice, I'm a banana!'"

"Cool? Who the frigg is that? What have you done with John Morgan?" Sean said. James and I laughed.

Repeating our journey of the previous day, this time we could see nothing through blackened meshed windows and security grilles as we were thrown from side to side in the police van.

"Have you been in one of these before, Sean?" Josh asked. I guessed he was attempting to apologise for the ham-fisted police.

"What, me a trained, experienced and responsible former officer of the UK military?" Sean said. "Yes, to be honest I've been in a black Maria...but it was a case of mistaken identity. They were looking for a drunken para." He winked at me.

A sudden halt announced our arrival, and the rear door swung open and two officers escorted us up the escalator.

They stared straight ahead, prodding us with their sub-machine guns as we made our way to Inspector Maier, Chief of Detectives in Tel Aviv District.

Placing St Peter's ornate box on his desk, the officers left the room but stationed themselves on guard outside. When Inspector Maier rose and came to our side of the desk, I suspected that Josh's ruse had indeed come "to bite us in the arse". He suddenly slapped Josh hard on the cheek and returned to his chair. Josh tensed his muscular frame, biceps twitching under his short-sleeved shirt, his knuckles growing white. But he remained cool. I admired him.

Sean, however, sprang across the desk with the speed of a striking cobra, grabbing Maier by the throat and beginning to throttle him.

"Do that again, you little Dumbo-eared weasel, and I'll break your windpipe."

Josh pulled Sean back and bent close to him, whispering something. I shrugged, wondering at what he'd said.

Sean mouthed, "Balak," to me, and settled back in his chair, twiddling his thumbs and quietly whistling.

Inspector Maier's face glowed beetroot red; he coughed and choked for some minutes, sipping water from a plastic cup. Struggling to remain composed, his lip angrily quivered under his waxed moustache. His sergeant opened the door but was dismissed. Maier was clearly not used to men like Sean.

He picked up the box, turning the lid towards the light. Lifting it, he took out the empty cloth bag and disappointment registered on his face. Fixing stern eyes on Josh, he began a stuttering diatribe in a squeaky, high-pitched voice. Embarrassingly, Josh had to translate at a speedy pace as the tirade tumbled from Maier with staccato energy.

"You have humiliated this police force," he said. "You have lied to me during a police inquiry. You have conspired with foreigners, and one has murdered a German citizen in cold blood. We have a foreign national in custody, arrested by *my* men. He is helping with our inquiries about drugs – phone-tapping, extortion and kidnapping. You have disgraced our nation's intelligence service. Your superiors are on their way here."

Looking at Sean and me, he continued. "You will be immediately taken to your hotel to gather your belongings, after which you will be deported, guarded by my officers until your plane leaves. You will leave the Israeli artefact with me; we do not tolerate those who pillage in our city."

I felt my cheeks growing red, but didn't want to argue or debate the point with him about the veracity of the box. It could be Christian because it belonged to Christ and His apostle. It could be Jewish because it was found in Jaffa and had parchments about Israel's holy places.

It seemed we were in deep shit, as Sean would say. What on earth would Colonel Balak say? Could he help?

*

"Your guests have arrived, Sir," the sergeant said, ducking out of the door as Colonel Balak and a smartly suited man entered the room. We stood up. Sean rubbed his hands together. The colonel eyed the box and then fixed his cold eyes on the inspector.

Sean and I resumed our seats, while Josh stood to attention next to his colonel. Examining the red finger marks on Josh's cheek, the colonel spun around quickly and addressed the inspector in a booming parade-ground voice.

"You have reprimanded one of my men, disarmed him forcibly and arrested him publicly." He spoke in English for our benefit, Josh interpreting for Maier's sake and seemingly taking great pleasure from it.

"Aye, and he slapped him," Sean said.

"You witnessed this?" Balak asked us, a fierce authority in his voice and manner. He was as mad as a hornet. He looked at us with piercing hooded eyes and we nodded. He sprang across the room, reached across the desk and fiercely backhanded the detective's cheeks. Two loud "thwacks" resounded in the air, echoing off the walls. Police in the outer area left their desks and craned to peer into the office.

Before the stunned inspector could respond or call his men, the smartly attired stranger placed a business card on his desk and handed one to me and another to Sean. The embossed card stated, "Israel's Minister of Homeland Security, Secretary to the Knesset, and Adviser to the Prime Minister of Israel."

Sean trumpeted, "Hooray, the cavalry has arrived."

I nudged him to shut up, but smiled. The minister gave a precise summing up in Hebrew, Josh interpreting for us.

"All press releases and media contact must be handled via Mossad or my office," he said. "An Israeli citizen was kidnapped. An attempt was made upon his life. Foreign nationals have committed cyber-crime and phone-tapping. A distinguished lecturer from Cairo University has had items stolen and his personal information has been shared with criminals. A prominent health worker in Tel Aviv has been threatened and required 24-hour protection. Hired killers made an attempt to assassinate a Mossad officer and his visiting friends, one of whom is a decorated officer with the British armed forces and the other a leading businessman and employer."

Sean whispered, "God, he's so dry I bet his ancestors were having a barbecue in Noah's flood." I smirked, listening to Joshua's translation. 'What an incredible memory,' I thought.

"Israel's National Defence Force, working closely with Interpol, put together a specialist team under the mandate of Colonel Balak, led by Sergeant Joshua Federman, who heroically risked his life to rescue an Israeli citizen. Inspector Maier, you are suspended from your position and duties pending inquiries. By publicly arresting and disarming a Mossad sergeant, you have shown disrespect to national intelligence to my office, *and to the Prime Minister himself.* In addition, you have arrested innocent tourists and threatened their deportation with *no* authorisation from IDF."

"Friggin' heck," Sean said. "He's reading the riot act! We might get a medal." The minister scowled at Sean, who made the sign of the cross and then whispered, "He's as cold as ice."

The minister continued. "The Homeland Office of Security will not allow our good relationship with Israel's allies to be jeopardised, nor will it allow the Tel Aviv police to be sued for wrongful arrest. The bumbling of the investigation, compounded by your unwillingness to cooperate, gives me no other choice. You are suspended. Your personal possessions will be sent to you. Now go!"

He opened the door and stepped aside. The police in the detectives' area outside quickly scrambled back to their workstations. Inspector Abraham Maier slouched away, as white as a ghost. His shoulders sagged; his walk was uneven like that of a drunken man. I think his colleagues knew he had made a serious enemy; they avoided him as if he was a leper.

Collecting the box from the inspector's desk, the minister tucked it under his arm. "Is it all here?" he said.

"I believe so, Minister," Colonel Balak replied, turning to Josh. "Is it all here, Sergeant?"

Josh saluted and said, "Yes, Sir. The parchments and maps are all there. The cloth bag is empty, I'm afraid."

"No matter," the minister said. "The antique box is part of our national heritage. The heirloom and its scrolls will be kept and displayed in the national museums of Israel in Tel Aviv and Jerusalem."

Poking his head through the door, the colonel called the police sergeant and commanded him to release the prisoners and return the firearm to the Mossad agent, which he did promptly.

In the squad room, Colonel Balak introduced the minister in his commanding voice and then addressed everyone in the room.

"The kidnapping investigation conducted by Sergeant Federman has been concluded. Thank you for all your hard work. An arrest has been made. Unfortunately, your inspector is relieved of his duties pending a gross misconduct inquiry.

Our guests will be shown every courtesy and any items confiscated will be returned to them." The atmosphere in the room seemed to lift.

The minister invited us all to accompany him and the colonel to the ground floor. On the steps of police headquarters, the minister shook Josh's hand, then ours. He thanked us for our support in the investigation, the subsequent rescue of an Israeli citizen and the return of a precious piece of Israel's history. He asked how Simeon fared. Then he waved to us and entered a chauffeur-driven white Mercedes.

Colonel Balak shook our hands and also thanked us.

Sean said, "And I had heard lightning doesn't strike twice." He roared with laughter and slapped us both on our backs. A friendly gesture, but I stumbled to keep my balance.

"Collect your luggage and my sergeant will take you to the airport," Colonel Balak said. "The bloodhounds within the media are baying. It's to your advantage to leave the frenzy that will surely come. You can keep the photocopies; we are only interested in the original parchments. The minister will revel in the publicity of recovering artefacts and saving an Israeli."

'He knows about the copies,' I thought. But it appeared to me that Balak knew his job and practised ruthless efficiency. I believed he also served the Jewish nation as a loyal servant.

I heard him say to Josh, "Don't trust that snake. The minister will use us to step upwards if he can, but he has no interest in our work. Now, your car is parked just a few metres away. I will see you in the morning. Take the night off, you have deserved it."

Journeying towards the hotel in Josh's BMW 3 Series, I called James, explaining everything to him and asking him to pack and to let the family know the good news. Then I called Joseph with the news; he was ecstatic. I invited him to visit us at our home any time. In a few hours, it would be the Sabbath and I assumed he and Simeon would be going to thank God for Simeon's release.

Journey Home and Thoughts about Eden

When he met me at the door to our hotel room, James was puffing and panting as he lugged the bulging suitcases. He dropped them and gave me a big hug. When we walked down the carpeted stairs carrying our cases and flight bags, I hoped it would be the last visit to Israel for some years.

The manager looked exuberant as he slid a letter across the counter to me. It was from the PM, thanking us but also mentioning that a German pharmaceutical company had made a donation of 7.5 million Euros to a new burns unit at Tel Aviv Hospital, to be named the Leitz Burns Unit. I felt sick.

I shook hands with staff and expressed my appreciation. The manager was brimming with pride when informed by Josh that the personal adviser to the PM had praised the hotel. Homeland Security would encourage foreign dignitaries to Tel Aviv to stay at the hotel. The manager pressed some vouchers into my hand. I gave him Ahmed's card, hoping his taxi business would grow.

Outside the hotel, I breathed a sigh of relief as the porters placed our luggage into the BMW and Sean dropped a black holdall into Josh's trunk, winking at him as it closed.

At Ben Gurion Airport, James, Sean and I shook hands with Josh.

Sean joked, "I'll see you soon, Sergeant Joshua Federman, and I'm sure there's a black-haired beauty in the UK who fancies the socks off ya."

I added, "Josh, you're always welcome to come and stay at Kirmingsham Hall anytime." I hugged him.

*

The ticket gave our ETA at Ringway Airport as 6:15 p.m.

"Our two Jewish friends will now be in their synagogue," I said.

"You know, Dad," James said, "Simeon's healing is like Naaman in the Bible. He had leprosy but the prophet Elisha immersed him in a river, and his flesh became like a child's. Awesome, huh?"

I nodded, wondering where this was going.

"By the way," James said as he tapped on his laptop, "I think Aly and I want Simeon and Joseph to come to our wedding and say a Jewish prayer. And Josh said he'd like to come, but I'm not sure about this colonel…he sounds like a nasty piece of work."

"Colonel Balak?" Sean perked up from his semi-dozing. "Nah, he's a pussy. You should invite him. But don't turn the other cheek!"

James scratched his head.

"I didn't know you read the Bible, James," I said.

"You're kidding, right?" James looked across at me. "Aly and I are really into that stuff. Not the same as her adoptive parents, the Wickhams, who are like, 'do this, do that'…I'm talking about the cool stuff."

"Like what? Sean and I want to hear it."

"Not me," Sean replied with a grin. "I'm not a Cat-a-holic, I love dogs!"

James and I convulsed with laughter. Other passengers stirred.

"Well," James said, moving forwards on his seat. "Take Noah's Ark. What are the chances of finding enough wood to build a craft that would house all the animals in that area and withstand a flood? Did you know that all ancient civilisations have a story passed down about a flood?"

"I'd heard that," I said, "so what are you saying?"

His fingers flew across his keyboard and images appeared one after the other.

"See that?" James said. "Spaceships. The arks were shuttles: big and strong enough to save many species during a great flood event. It happened all over the earth, with dozens of ships, not just in the Middle East. And what about the Tower of Babel?" he asked, showing us more images. "Who would build a tower like that, and what for?" James said.

"An early rollercoaster," Sean said with a glint in his eye.

Reaching to tap Sean on his head, James said, "It's a comms tower, you nutter. Don't you get the clues about Babel's 'many languages'? Did you never watch *Close Encounters of the Third Kind*? But we're not gonna play the tune next time. We're talking binary, programming and code." James looked expectant.

"Did you say 'we'?" I asked.

"Yeah, me, Aly, our online buds…we figure that every now and then these 'beings' or 'gods' visit earth to give the human race a technological kick up the behind," James said. "Copernicus, Galileo, Leonardo Di Vinci, probably many more: superior intelligence that has advanced our planet. Think about it, guys. Who built the sphinx in Egypt and the pyramids of the Incas?"

James showed us images of the Great Sphinx of Giza and large stone heads discovered around the world.

"OK, mastermind, what's your theory about Eden…the box and leaves? What's your theory about that?" I asked.

"Jesus Christ is one of us *and* one of them," James said. "Don't you see, Dad? He wanted us to know about the life they have, that's why he came, and why he left the box: peace, health and everything humans need to survive."

"Live long and prosper, huh?" Sean made the Vulcan sign with his fingers. "I'd better stop using his name then, in case he hears me, right?"

"Exactly, Einstein," James responded. "Watch this space!

Lots of stuff in science fiction is becoming reality. We reckon Jesus left you the clues and the leaves, Dad. The other guys are so excited to be part of this. Our online buds are buzzing with it. It's a shame we can't Tweet it. We'd have millions of followers!"

"WOW," I said. "That IS epic."

James punched my arm.

"Why me, huh?" I asked.

James' ideas intrigued me, but I favoured the traditional beliefs. After all, I had prayed at a clock tower, and two miracles had happened. Many would mock the story of the antique box, maps and leaves that Jesus Christ of Nazareth had entrusted to St Peter. We knew its reality. Two lives had been raised from deathbeds; those were facts, not myths.

In Jaffa, we had made friends and enemies. Those enemies were either dead or incarcerated awaiting trial. Our friends in Israel had forged lasting bonds of affection in our hearts and minds. Certainly one member of my family evidenced a growing affection for a Mossad sergeant.

Sean ferried us home and my daydreaming continued. My heart overflowed with relief that alongside my wife and daughter, my grandchild Wesley John waited excitedly for us at home. Regular tests at Great Ormond Street Hospital had confirmed what we already knew as a family: the disease had been defeated.

James' intended, Alyana, had been instrumental, via her internet friends, in tracking down the kidnappers. I felt proud that my son had found his soulmate.

I had once again witnessed Sean's awesome efficiency to be lethal when the situation demanded it. His Irish wit had kept us sane, and sometimes driven us insane. But we would accept Sean with his strengths and weaknesses. I planned something special for his birthday on April 2nd.

Becky, my elegant and fun-loving daughter, had come through a very dark patch in her life. With new energy, she was now grabbing life's opportunities. Morgan Fashion would fulfil at least part of her life. Would there be a match made in heaven with Josh Federman, the Mossad sergeant? I thought she could do a lot worse.

Walking through the door of Kirmingsham Hall, I saw Liz, the dream of my life, pottering around the kitchen, keeping busy.

She leapt into my arms. "You're home! I am so glad. I thought I heard the car."

"Mmm, me too," I said, as we embraced. "I love you now more than ever. And we will take that holiday!"

The cord that bound us lodged in the centre of our hearts, pulling us ever closer. I felt profound relief to be in her arms again.

Royal Hospital at Gwent

With the Kindle Liz had given me for my 62nd birthday, I sat up in bed reading *The Life of Pi* by Yann Martel. Several nights into the book, not understanding the plot, I had read the words: "Oncoming death is terrible enough, but worse still is oncoming death with time to spare, time in which all the happiness that was yours and all the happiness that might have been yours becomes clear to you, you see with utter lucidity all that you are losing…"

The next day the family had the sad news that Liz's father had experienced a mild stroke, and I read the passage again. I suddenly knew what Yann Martel meant. Those words encapsulated exactly how Bill must have felt.

Liz and I travelled down the M5 and M4 to the Royal Gwent Hospital in Newport, Gwent, on the last Sunday of February, passing farms, fields and light industry.

Liz said, "I thought he would live forever, it's hard to think of him as old."

In his hospital ward, we were pleased to find Bill in remarkably good spirits, his mobility and speech unaffected, although he appeared confused.

Later, the issue of what arrangements to make for Bill became a prickly subject. Whilst her dad could manage on his own, we had to grasp the nettle of the future.

"All families around the world have to face this, Liz," I

said. "I know he values his independence but this Bron Afon Community Housing seems pretty good from what I've read."

"Well, being a strong Labour supporter all his life, he'll admire the fact that the people own it."

Visiting the housing association, Liz and I were very pleased with the staff, the open-style management and the facilities. All this persuaded us to apply for a supported bungalow for Bill.

"Dad," Liz said, appealing to him in a gentle voice. "The major advantage is that everything in the two-bedroom bungalow is on the ground floor. You'll have a support intercom lifeline installed with a pendant alarm if needed."

"And my pigeons?" Bill asked, concerned.

"A Bron Afon tenant with an allotment has agreed to house them there," Liz diplomatically answered, and you can see them anytime."

Liz's dad moved into his tenancy four weeks after his stroke.

Wedding Preparations

Liz and I took a holiday at Devon, staying at The Royal Hotel in Woolacombe as we often did. We loved the food, views, entertainment and nearness to the beach. By the time we returned, James' and Aly's wedding preparations were well underway.

They were planning a disco and after the wedding ceremony, all the guests would don fancy dress for the reception. But they weren't giving away what the fancy dress theme was to be.

As the wedding day approached, I tried to find out more about the disco and the fancy dress theme. One day in the office, my PA let slip that she thought the wizard and warrior costumes in Morgan Fashion's upstairs studio were marvellous. I knew from then what James and Aly were planning for their epic disco.

"I must share this with Sean," I hummed merrily.

Together, Sean and I planned a covert mission. At Morgan Fashion, when everyone was distracted, we sneaked upstairs and walked silently past the office area to behold racks of costumes: orcs, goblins, warriors, hunters, thieves, and wizards in various sizes, fabrics and colours, waiting for guests to try them on.

"I am definitely going as Gandalf," I said confidently to Sean.

"And I am going to be Robin Hood or a thief," Sean stated with pride.

One evening after dinner, I could hold back no longer and spilled the beans that I knew what they were planning.

James quite smugly said, "Then you don't mind if my best man is a mage called Petros who is coming from Greece?"

"I'll come as a cat burglar," Sean said.

"That's not a…oh forget it," James said.

*

Kirmingsham Hall faced a challenge with a celebration the size of a wedding.

At the rehearsal, Liz said, "It'll be like squeezing size ten feet into size seven shoes."

In the UK, villages make up a unique part of society, some dating back to the Magna Carta. Pressures of employment, increased mobility, lack of affordable housing, and the creation of out-of-town superstores has altered village life but some, like Kirmingsham, have resisted some aspects of change and maintained their uniqueness.

Kirmingsham boasted a population of 168, which was about to be nearly doubled with the 150 invited guests coming to James' and Aly's wedding. Villagers, school friends who weren't invited to the reception, well-wishers, and probably others would squeeze into St Luke's Church in Goostry village on Saturday May 11th.

"Can we fit them all in?" Liz asked. Not wanting to interfere, she had encouraged James and Aly from a distance.

"Well, I hear at least 200 people are coming and the church is designed for 120 pew seats. Extra chairs can be placed around one side and at the back by the font," I said. "They'll see most of the wedding."

We ignored fire regulations, sure that the old stone building would never burn. It had stood since the 13th century. I didn't think our small bash would harm it and we were, after all, paying for the vicar, the choir, the organist, the bell-ringers, and the caretaker. Despite that army of paid-for personnel, we'd been told that confetti was banned in the church grounds. I hoped the wind didn't blow on the day. Becky, Liz, Rachel, and Wesley had two boxes each.

"What time are the Wickhams arriving today?" I asked James and Aly, referring to Aly's adopted family.

"They're flying direct from Austin to Manchester, arriving at 7:00 a.m."

Later that day, James and Aly returned home looking pale and exhausted.

"My life!" James said. "They had a trolley piled high with luggage!"

"I'd told them that the Nissan wasn't a big gas-guzzler, ya'll," Aly said. "In the end Mom Wickham sat in the front passenger seat with a flight bag under her legs, Pop Wickham squeezed into the back seats with his flight bag under his feet, and I sat on a case on the other back seat with my head pressed against the car roof. The other three cases fitted in the trunk."

Liz and I laughed and offered the young couple our support. "How did you get on at the Mucky Duck?"

"What?" James asked.

"That's what your granddad called the Old Black Swan," I said.

The village of Kirmingsham, originally a small farming community, had grown with the development of the railway between Manchester and Crewe, and over the past four decades, by the advent of the M6 motorway. Two pubs, two churches, a primary school, a post office on the main road, and several shops were at the centre of the village life. The duck pond in the centre of the green was hugely popular, with villagers and friends relaxing with a pint in the summer.

"That's the best of it, Dad," James said. "The Wickhams were very unhappy that they were staying at...get this...a distillery."

Liz giggled. "What did you do?"

Aly replied, "He told them that the pub did not 'distil', and anyway James pointed out that the hotels further away were charging £60 or £70 per person for B & B. They surrendered their opposition and went to lie down due to 'jetlag'."

Liz and I hugged them both. "Well done you two, you've passed with flying colours!"

We didn't hear a peep from the Wickhams until the wedding ceremony. It appeared that they did not allow their religion to interfere with their lives.

*

While the Wickhams may not have promoted the harmony of togetherness, many other family and friends made the effort to cross the globe and join the celebration.

The two brothers from Tel Aviv and Sergeant Joshua Federman flew into the UK in the afternoon. My heart warmed when my eyes landed on the trio making their way through arrivals, lugging their cases. Standing behind the security tape across the airport corridor, I waved frantically and then greeted them in the Middle Eastern tradition by hugging them and kissing them on their cheeks.

I dropped Simeon and Joseph at the train station in Holmes Chapel. They were going to stay with friends in Manchester.

Driving Josh to Kirmingsham Hall, I inquired about his colonel and other colleagues. "How is Colonel Balak?" I asked.

"The colonel is well, thank you, John," Josh replied. "He sends his best wishes."

"What have you been up to since we met?" I asked. "If you can tell me, of course." I turned in the driver's seat and winked at him.

"I've actually been in the US for a NATO conference and recently in the embassy in Jerusalem. How are your family, John?"

"Everyone is well, thanks, and looking forward to seeing you. Especially Becky."

His face brightened.

At our home, introducing the Mossad sergeant to my family went easily. Wesley's reaction was the most heart-warming. After 20 minutes, he had shown him his bedroom, demonstrated all his toys and games and suggested they take Bourne and Aunty for a walk. At that point, Becky suggested she could go with them.

Josh replied, "Yes please, that would be good."

Beholding the muscular dark-haired soldier alongside my raven-haired lithesome daughter, I caught my wife's eye. Liz gave a knowing nod. She looked euphoric. Wesley grabbed Joshua's right hand and led him across the lawn, the dogs racing ahead and Becky close by.

As we stood at the door, a blue minibus arrived with luggage strapped precariously to the roof and black smoke belching from the exhaust. Waving hands appeared behind windows when the vehicle jolted to a stop. The door creaked open and the driver strode towards us, hand extended.

"Hi, I'm Martin," he announced in a Merseyside accent. On his grey hoody, a white label announced "Thudd". I shook his hand while others disembarked.

All were greeted with hugs or backslaps from James and Aly. Martin, from Liverpool he told me, had met the passengers at the train station, some arriving via Eurostar, others from Stoke-on-Trent, Nottingham and County Durham. They were a handful of James' and Aly's online friends and fellow players of the game WOW.

They unpacked drinks from their rucksacks, slurping as they spoke, and the conversation buzzed. I noticed that on their jackets, hoodies, anoraks, coats and fleeces, all wore white printed nametags, courtesy of Aly's initiative. "Because we've never met in real life before," she explained. I walked amongst them eavesdropping, hearing varied accents, and checking out their nametags. Thudd, Wickedgypsy, Brunson, Tealeaf.

Their friends were shown around Kirmingsham Hall, much to the initial consternation of Liz. She observed the motley crew carefully as they entered every room amidst exclamations of "cool", "awesome", and "epic".

James rounded up their gaggle of guests and marched them off towards the lawns and lakes. They resembled a party of schoolchildren on an adventure ramble. The sun's rays reflected off the waters as geese flapped and honked and ducks waddled away from the noisy group.

Sean and Rachel pulled into the driveway. "Who the frigg are they, Boss?" he asked, scratching his crewcut. "Aliens and super beings, I guess." Rachel punched his arm.

A dirty white Ford Transit clunked up the drive churning up pebbles and shale. Faces peeked through dirty windows. Suitcases, rucksacks and cardboard boxes nearly tumbled out when the sliding door banged open. James and Aly hurried to meet it.

"Hi, James," the driver said. "And you must be James' dad. Sorry we look a bit ragged, we've driven from Greece. This is my girlfriend and a friend from Sweden."

Incredulous to hear that they had driven from Greece, travelling through Spain to Santander, and arriving at Portsmouth the previous night, I shook the driver's hand. His name was Petros, who was the best man, and his girlfriend was Orcslayer. With them was a slightly overweight passenger called Dorke. He looked like a boy but James assured me that he could be in his 20s or even 30s.

"No one knows, Dad, how old Dorke is," James said, "and we don't know his real name."

"...but he's a loyal friend," Aly butted in, "and one of the best IT guys on the planet. He helped us with our 'problems', John. Remember?"

"Yeah, I think," I said, "anyway, if he's a friend of yours, he's welcome."

The overweight passenger looked right and left, drinking from a coke can.

"Did I fall asleep and wake up in *Star Wars* or *Lord of the Rings*?" I asked Sean.

Slapping me on my shoulder, Sean said, "They sure are a queer bunch." He quickly leashed the barking dogs, who had returned from the jaunt with Wesley, Josh and Becky, as Bourne was jumping excitedly around the guests and Aunty was sniffing new "meat".

*

World of Warcraft® had come to Cheshire, to my house.

Spread across our lounge on two couches, two recliners, cross-legged on the carpet, seated at the breakfast bar in the kitchen, and on chairs from the dining room, wedding guests were relaxing, making conversation and having fun. Wesley was grinning from ear to ear.

I passed amongst them and gleaned the residences, occupations if any, major skills, and interests of the 20-odd online friends. Liz warmed to them and she and the girls made some easy-to-serve dishes, thrilled at the polite thank-yous and the offers to do the dishes.

In Liz's Nissan, James took the friends who had no transportation to their accommodation at the YMCA hostel in Stockport. With the hostel being in the process of refurbishment, the manager had been happy to accept the exclusive rental of rooms, dining room and gym for five days and nights.

I was impressed with the way that James and Aly had managed the logistics of getting folk from all over Europe, coordinating their arrivals, and sorting out accommodation practically with military precision, and asked Sean for his comments.

"Military my arse," Sean said. "In the Falklands it took them seven weeks to send us night vision goggles. Jesus, we were 12 miles from Port Stanley by the time they arrived."

On the Friday night before the wedding, Liz announced that she and the girls were going for a spa and pampering session at a local hotel. For his bachelor party, James was meeting at the YMCA with his buddies, where Sean, Josh and I joined them. Sleeping bags, suitcases, rucksacks, empty pizza boxes, discarded coke and Budweiser bottles, clothes and footwear, were scattered around the periphery of the hall. The smell of sweat and muskiness hovered.

In the centre of the room, tables were arranged in a rectangle. Laptops were placed on the tables, facing inwards, power cables and extension leads trailed to sockets around the hall. A Wi-Fi routing device flashed in the middle of a table. James' computer friends were sitting at their workstations waiting for him. Sean, Josh and I, the uninitiated, were about to be introduced to the World of Warcraft®, WOW to the initiates.

"WOW is not for me," Dorke said, "though 12 million don't agree." He laughed at his own joke. "I don't play, but it's cool. These guys are playing on the European realm. On every continent there are WOW players, with realms in different languages. Millions of players worldwide."

The players, with headphones and microphones, communicated with the other team members. I overheard comments which were clarified by Dorke.

"They are in an old-style raid in Karazhan, gradually killing bosses until the final. At the moment they are killing Little Red Riding Hood."

Josh clapped and made enthusiastic comments while he peered over various players' heads to witness the scenes unfurling. Sean was not quite as enthusiastic.

"It's not a proper stag do unless it's a booze-up," he said. I was relieved that Sean's Achilles heel would not require me to carry him home. However, even Sean enjoyed himself eating pizza and answering questions about his experiences.

"Only thing is..." he said, "...when I kill 'em, they stay dead."

The players were in awe.

I asked Martin, alias Thudd, "What do you do, Thudd...err Martin? In real life, I mean."

"You may not believe it, Mr Morgan," he said, "but I am a 30-year-old married man from Liverpool with two children.

I'm a civil servant with the Department of Work and Pensions, managing a job centre. The minibus is an employment scheme bus."

"And I believe that you helped us with the local newspaper?"

"I know nothing." He winked.

The only member of the YMCA group who had no employment, and apparently had no intention of seeking any, was Dorke from Sweden. Amazingly fluent in French and English, at times he seemed in his own world yet at others, he became animated and verbal, beating down the opinions of others. Despite his appearance – plump, greasy-haired, slovenly dressed – he was reputedly, we were assured, one of the finest computer brains in Sweden and the best hacker on the planet.

After several hours, Petros insisted it was time for everyone to leave. Most of the friends objected, but Petros said, "Come on, guys, there's a wedding in the morning!" Everyone started singing, "I'm getting married in the morning!"

James and Aly had drawn together an interesting and diverse group. The Morgan circle was growing.

The Wedding

"For God's sake, take the dogs to the lake," Becky said to James and me. You're giving us all the jitters," Becky said.

She and Rachel, a blonde and a brunette, looked radiant in their peach-coloured bridesmaids' dresses.

James was pacing the floor nervously, the prototypical bridegroom. Aly was to be collected by Rev Wickham from her digs in Stockport.

"That's a good idea," Sean said, in reply to Becky. "Josh and I will come with you, John, and on the way back we can see how Becky's bell works." He was referring to Becky's studies in psychology and what she'd told us about Pavlov's dogs being conditioned to come for food at the sound of a bell.

He looked at her and she nodded, and then he wheeled Wesley's bike into the kitchen by the door. Sean had expressed his doubts about Pavlov's theory, and he and Becky had made a wager that if by the time of the wedding the dogs did not respond to the bell, she would have to dive into the boating lake and swim in the buff. I sensed that Sean planned to win the bet against Becky.

We strode to the middle of the lawns with Bourne and Aunty, and then the sound of a bicycle bell rang out from the house. Bourne went bounding, tail wagging, into the house. Sean spoke discreetly to Aunty and she sat on her haunches unflinchingly, as immoveable as a rock.

We arrived in the kitchen to a barking Bourne jumping up and down, his backside moving from side to side.

"Sorry, Freud," Sean said. "You've failed. Bourne is not salivating – in my opinion – and Aunty is nowhere to be seen."

Becky admitted defeat and announced that she would jump into the lake in the buff during the disco. Josh smiled when we told him about the bet.

When Becky explained to Wesley, he stated with a gasp, "Nude, Mummy? With nothing on?" It pacified him when the challenge was explained. "Oh I see," said Wesley. "It's a dare."

*

Wesley, attired in waistcoat, perfectly creased grey trousers and black, newly polished shoes, was escorted to the front of the church doors where he waited for the bridal party. His first occasion as a pageboy, he seemed a bit nervous about his responsibility. Repeatedly annoyed by the white buttonhole poking his cheek, he finally pushed the flower heads to point downwards. He tugged at the maroon dickie bow. "Nan, can you carry my basket?" he asked Liz, who acquiesced and picked up a wicker basket with red petals inside.

James, Petros and I, uncomfortable in morning dress, sat on the hard church pews for 20 minutes before the bells started to peal. James wiped the sweat off his hands onto his handkerchief.

"You OK?" I whispered.

The sun gleamed through the stained-glass windows. I sensed the generations that had attended here, and wondered who had been the first: probably the earl after the Norman Conquest.

"Yeah, I guess," James whispered back.

In top hat, necktie and tails, we were making an effort to keep calm. Sean, Josh and Thudd were escorting people to their seats and placing the service sheets in their hands.

"It's cool, James," Petros said in his Greek accent. "It'll be awesome."

A voice proclaimed from the back of the church, "She's here!"

Turning to look around, I was awestruck that the church had filled with people while we had sat transfixed with our eyes on the cross and communion table. Several high-heeled clicks sounded on the stone nave. My eyes searched the room for familiar faces. Liz took her seat a row behind us on James' side of the church. She looked amazing in a peach two-piece suit with a frilled blouse. On her head, she wore a band with feathers.

At precisely 2:00 p.m., the vicar, in his white cassock and dog collar, took his place at the front of the church and when the organist struck up Wagner's *Here Comes the Bride*, he invited James and Petros to stand, and then the whole congregation.

A dazzling white apparition came walking slowly down the aisle. Aly, escorted by Rev Wickham, was wearing a tiara and her long dark hair was styled into a bun. Her gorgeously sequined and billowing silk dress with traces of silver thread and angels floated down the aisle. From the crown of her head and gently falling across her face, a thin lace veil with a butterfly pattern partially concealed her face.

James and Petros took a sneak backwards glance and James loosened his bow tie.

Wesley had preceded the bride, sprinkling red roses from the wicker basket, blushing as people spoke with him and dodging their pats on the head. Following the bride were Rachel and Becky, holding the bridal train. The girls could have graced any catwalk.

Passing the bunch of posies to Becky and lifting her veil, Aly looked towards James. The couple trembled slightly when the vicar asked us all to stand and sing *The Lord's My Shepherd* to the Crimond tune.

At every wedding I had ever attended, I had never experienced an interruption, but on that occasion, the large oak door of St Luke's church in Goostry creaked open on its iron hinges and slammed against the stone walls.

I craned my neck to see two figures standing in the vestibule. One of them was a giant of a man who had to duck and
turn sideways to enter the nave area.

*

A hushed silence permeated the church after the big oak door
slammed, followed by an uncertain but expectant pause.

Two hundred heads turned to gaze at the two male strangers. James and Aly looked nervously around to observe the
reason for the disturbance. The vicar, unperturbed, called
some order back into the ceremony and proceeded with his
charges to the couple.

"Do you, James…"

Sean, in the pew behind me, whispered, "Two foreigners
in suits, and one appears to be packing." He choked a laugh.
"Mind you, he doesn't need a weapon. Looks like he could rip
the door off its hinges and eat it."

I gave him the nod to go and make inquiries tactfully.
Everyone looked askance at Sean tiptoeing up the aisle, smiling and nodding left and right, using his customary thumbs
up gesture. The vicar continued with the ceremony.

"Will you…"

I looked behind me to see Liz staring daggers at me and
mouthing "hush". I shrugged. When Sean returned five minutes later, he sat down with a smirk.

"You're not gonna believe this, Boss," he whispered. "I'll
tell you later." He chuckled and slapped his thigh. "You're
really not gonna believe this!" His body shook with suppressed
laughter.

The vicar finally declared James and Aly "man and wife"
and I breathed a sigh of relief.

The chords of Mendelssohn's *Wedding March* were thumped
out on the organ as we formed a procession from the vestry.
Following the newly married couple, the bridesmaids and
pageboy, I walked next to Mrs and Rev Wickham, with Liz

behind us. The bridal train dragged along the stone aisle, Rachel trying to keep up. Wesley tugged his red bow tie off and passed it to his mum.

Outside St Luke's church, as the cameras snapped, I caught Sean's arm and steered him towards the two men in black suits. The Mossad sergeant joined us. I think he sensed that there could be trouble.

The five of us made our way to the graveyard, forming a circle next to a crumbling gravestone covered in green moss.

I said, "OK, tell me, Sean. What's going on?"

The ex-SAS captain, moving his two hands like a conjurer towards the two men, announced, "Voila! Meet the in-laws." He was grinning broadly.

"What?" I asked loudly.

The smaller of the two men raised his voice, due to the loud pealing of the church bells, and said, "Please allow me to introduce myself."

His appearance and accent were markedly eastern European. His black suit and shoes were immaculate. The younger man had to be over seven feet tall, but he was equally smartly dressed.

Sean moved towards the two men. "Before you say anything, ask your friend to leave his piece somewhere."

"*Unë kuptoj*," the man said, then added, "I understand."

The smaller man gave his companion an order, indicating a car with his eyes. The man-mountain walked down the church path, crunching on the gravel. He took long strides towards a sleek black Mercedes Saloon with darkened windows.

Josh whispered in my ear, "Albanian."

Sean struggled a few steps behind the giant-like creature who pulled open the limousine door, took a pistol from the pocket of his huge jacket, and threw it inside. Turning to Sean, he nodded and the two of them returned to us.

"Have you seen that guy's neck?" Sean whispered to me. "It's like a tree trunk. Mind you, size isn't everything. Our martial arts trainer was the skinniest bloke on the planet, but he could break your neck with one finger."

Holding my finger to my lips, I said, "Sshh."

"My name is Sallos, or Saul," the smaller man began, "my friend is Goliath. It may surprise you to know this, but I am Alyana's uncle."

I gasped. "What?"

He carried on undeterred. "I hoped to get here in time to establish a relationship with my niece, but we have been delayed."

Sean folded his arms and smirked with a 'told ya' expression.

The man extracted a brown envelope from his inner pocket and opened it. He passed to me a stiff paper document with the official Albanian seal. It was a birth certificate. A woman named Dorina Lushi, it stated, gave birth to a baby girl, born in Durres in Albania. On the certificate, the father of the baby had scrawled his name: Alexander Pernasksa. Sallos showed me his passport. The name meant nothing to me.

"I am Sallos Pernasksa," he said, pointing to the photo in his passport, "the father's brother and therefore Alyana's uncle."

Josh gasped, "Pernasksa," and appeared to regret it. "*Mund ta përsërisësh, të lutem*?" he said to the smaller man, then said, "Please say that again."

The man repeated himself, his face pained. The man-mountain, appearing to sense the anguish of his comrade, crossed the graveyard to stand next to him. He blocked out the sun as he stared with cold but watchful eyes.

The smaller Albanian frowned and looked sterner.

"I see, Mr Morgan, that your friend has heard my family name. Be assured that I'm not like my brother. I regret to say that Alexander was a wicked man; wicked all his life. On his deathbed, he recanted his crimes. Many of his trespasses were known to me, but not all. I was unaware that 22 years ago he made a hotel worker pregnant."

He inhaled, scanned our faces and continued.

"The girl ran away to a centre for expectant mothers in

Durres. She gave birth to Alyana. When Alexander found out, he demanded to be on the birth certificate. I think reluctantly, Dorina agreed. When Alyana reached a month old, unknown to her mother, Alex took her to an orphanage in Tirana. She remained there for six months until he sold her to an American family for $3,000."

The details were starting to make sense to me.

"I am not my brother. You may know that the meaning of "mafia" is "a safe place, a refuge". But my brother did not give a refuge. His life was given over to violence and vendettas. The last conflict with a family in Naples became bloodthirsty and ultimately ended his life. I didn't know about Alyana until my brother told me just a few days ago on his deathbed. We got here as soon as we could, once we heard the news. We came straight after his funeral."

Having by now regained my composure, I said, "Thank you for explaining everything so clearly, Mr Pernasksa. We appreciate how difficult this must be for you. Now, how about we rejoin the wedding party and we'll just play it by ear." I saw Saul talking with Goliath. Probably explaining 'play it by ear'. From a distance, we saw the photographer taking family shots. I suspected that the next photos would be earth-shattering.

*

Saul was shadowed by his gigantic friend, nudging the three of us out of the way to stand beside him. He moved with agility but reminded me of a grizzly bear.

Saul raised a hand. "Please excuse Goliath," he said. "He doesn't speak much English and he is zealously protective. He has been with me since I found him begging on the streets when he was six or seven."

Sean responded, "Aye, I bet his mammy couldn't feed him."

When this comment was translated to the gargantuan bulk, he chuckled and his huge 56-inch chest quaked. He looked at Sean and nodded. Relieved that the tension had dissipated, I proposed that we should join the photographic session and tell Alyana the news later at the reception.

I took hold of James' elbow and drew him to one side. "You've two more guests, for the top table. Get them in on the family photo and I'll explain later."

James replied, "Whatever."

The photographer looked through his lens and asked us to take several steps further back, in order to fit in the giant.

James shrugged as his friends inquired about "the big guy".

Wesley threw confetti on the couple and Aly turned to cast her bouquet over her shoulder. Becky and Rachel both jumped to catch it like rugby players in a lineout, but the flowers landed in the hands of one of the villagers. Her partner looked in despair when she waved it under his nose.

On the short journey to Kirmingsham Hall, I told Aly's story to Liz and Becky, who both gasped. Sean, travelling behind us, would be doing the same with Rachel. The innocent voice of my grandson expressed his awe from the back seat next to his mum. "Wow! So one is Aly's uncle and the giant is, like...her cousin."

Only a child could sum up a problem, which appeared so complicated to grown-ups, so simply.

Our two dogs joined the wedding reception. Bourne bounded around like a prisoner set free after a long incarceration. Aunty walked confidently into the space occupying the edges. She made her way towards Goliath, growling and sniffing.

Sean called, "LEAVE!" and she came to his chair and sat on her haunches looking back at the huge man.

After the toasts, speeches and introductions, the inevitable could not be delayed any longer when Aly approached Saul and asked him for his name.

Gathering Saul, Goliath, James, Aly, and Sean into the disco marquee for privacy, I asked Saul to recount his story. The perplexed couple stood near the flap as Saul spoke. James grew pale and Aly's lips quivered while she examined the birth certificate and Saul's passport.

Overcome with emotion, she picked up the white hem of her bridal dress and ran from the disco marquee sobbing. James pursued her towards the lake. Her Uncle Saul's countenance was etched in pain.

Entering the tent and taking me by the arm, Liz said, "John, some of the guests are getting restless. People want to know what's happening."

"OK. Can you go and talk with Aly? Try to calm her down? We'll go back in now."

Mingling amongst the guests and slapping a few backs, I assured everyone that the speeches would resume shortly. Sean noticed Dorke patting Aunty.

"Don't do that, son. She'll have your hand off." When instead Aunty licked Dorke's hand, Sean was surprised. "It must be because he speaks the same language."

*

Aly had calmed down and returned to the reception. Petros tapped his fork against a glass and called, "Quiet please!"

Aly Morgan took the microphone and announced, "I would like ya'll to meet my Uncle Saul and my cousin Goliath." Several people gasped, others tittered.

The announcement sent a ripple of astonishment through the guests. Aly and James left their seats. James shook Saul's hand and reached for Goliath's. Aly grabbed her Uncle Saul and kissed him on both cheeks. Goliath lifted Aly bodily to kiss her cheek. Her feet dangled two feet in the air and one of her wedding shoes fell off.

James and Aly and took their seats again. With curled lips, her adoptive parents showed every sign of disapproval.

Any apprehensions faded as we drank more wine. Rachel and I kept our eye on Sean, who was drinking orange juice. Saul and Goliath made friends as more guests made their way to the celebratory table to shake their hands. Apart from the Wickhams, everyone seemed delighted at the news.

Then, a piercing scream echoed across the lawns. We rushed out onto the grass to witness a distraught Becky pointing to a man running towards the boating lake carrying a little boy under his arm.

Sean commanded, "ATTACK!" to Aunty, signalling to the fleeing figure.

"You too, Bourne!" I shouted, and both dogs gave chase. Fearing that the boy was Wesley, I ran as fast as I could. Sean and Josh overtook me after a few yards. A huge bulk bounded past us all with huge strides. The ground trembled with every step as Goliath charged like a raging bull.

We arrived to witness Aunty with her paws on top of the man, her panting breath and fangs in his face while he struggled on the ground. Bourne yapped and nipped at his ankles and pulled at his trousers. The boy was not Wesley but Alan, our gardener's son. We had all been afraid that we faced the possibility of losing our grandson a second time.

The Albanian giant give the man a gentle thump on the top of his head, and the little boy squirmed away. I felt afraid to behold Goliath's anvil-size fists over the man's face. He lifted the man by his shirt collar and trouser belt, and started walking him towards the lake, the man's legs thrashing.

"No!" I shouted to Goliath. Josh cupped his hands to his mouth, shouting a few words in Albanian. The 360-pound giant dropped the whimpering man onto the ground like a floundering fish.

While we interrogated the man and waited for the police, Liz assured our guests that things were well. The disco would begin in three hours, giving all guests time to change into fancy dress. The group staying at the YMCA boarded the minibus and the transit van and sped off to Stockport, black smoke trailing behind them.

The child abductor was the boyfriend of Maria, Tony's wife. The couple's marriage problems had erupted volcanically, causing malice and envy towards Tony as well as us. Hatching a desperate plot, she had decided to take her child, run away and make money demands upon Tony.

Frightened by the near abduction of a child who could have been our grandson, Liz and Becky secured a promise from me to improve our security. Security gates, CCTV linked to our study, infrared lights in the trees and bushes, PIR sensory lights to light up the house and grounds at any movement after dark, and a pendant for Wesley to keep on a chain around his neck which, if pressed, would send an alarm signal to a receiver from a distance of two miles away.

*

With the emotional turmoil over, Sean suggested with a wink that it was an opportune time for Becky to fulfil her part of the bet.

"Let's get it over before it gets too dark," Sean stated innocently. Rev and Mrs Wickham had sneaked away from the rest of the nuptials.

Liz and I made our way arm in arm to the large lake. Becky slowly stripped, her cheeks glowing red despite the cold. Finally, reluctantly but bravely, she jumped with a splash into the cold, dark, rippling waters. "GOD!" she exclaimed when she surfaced, her teeth chattering.

Ducking her head under the lake water, she swam a few strokes and then made her way back to the jetty. Dripping wet and shivering, she pulled herself out of the water. Josh held out a white beach towel for her.

While she pulled on her jeans, Josh whispered something to Becky and she said, "NEVER!" Then she called in a loud voice, "COME 'ERE CASEY!"

Sean, I think sensing defeat, humbly made his way to the jetty. In a loud voice, Becky proclaimed to her audience that Sean had commanded Aunty to "stay" so that Becky would lose their bet over Pavlov. Sean shrugged his shoulders, cupping his palms in prayer towards us.

Seeing the funny side, Becky said, "OK, Casey, get your kit off and get into that water."

Saul and Goliath were mystified by it all but roared with laughter when they learned the truth and that Sean was about to pay his debt.

Defeated, Sean stripped off and, with no more embarrassment than a man alone in a shower, dived into the water. He made no sound cutting through the water with a strong front-crawl stroke. Suddenly a loud splash resounded and a blonde head bobbed alongside Sean.

"Gosh that's c-c-c-cold!" the blonde woman screamed, and immediately turned for the jetty. Sean swam towards her and standing waist-high in the lake, he settled between her knees while she sat on the woodwork drying her blond hair with a towel and shivering. Rachel had stripped to her underwear and jumped in. She could have made a centre-fold pinup.

"Now everyone has seen your knickers, I suppose I'll have to marry you," Sean said.

"Is that a proposal, Captain Casey?" Rachel mocked.

We all shouted in unison: "YES!" Liz clapped her hands and she and Becky linked arms and danced like Morris dancers.

Rachel then said, "If so, the answer is YES – with one condition."

She whispered to Sean and he hollered, "Bugger!"

Walking back to the house, he told me that Rachel had insisted that she would only marry him if he promised to stand at the Queen's anthem and sing *God Save the Queen* at Christmas.

We had another wedding to plan, but first we needed to don our World of Warcraft® and *Lord of the Rings* outfits for the disco at 9:00 p.m.

*

With the costumes designed or hired by Morgan Fashion, my lack of familiarity with the World of Warcraft® characters was not a disadvantage for the fancy dress disco.

My grey garb, long white beard and pointed hat were incontestably those of Gandalf the Grey. Aly donned the garb of Arwen Evenstar to partner James' Aragorn, son of Arathorn, and my wife Liz transformed into Galadriel, a very wise and alluring grandmother. However, she refused to wear pointy ears and protested, "No way I'm looking like Spock!"

Rachel became Eowyn, an elfin hunter with bow and arrow. Sean, refusing to wear green tights as Robin Hood, had morphed into a World of Warcraft® rogue, donning grey Lee jeans, a red shirt, brown leather jacket, and a red bandana on his head. Rachel strapped her arrow quiver to her side and carried a bow in her right hand. Sean buckled his belt and inserted his combat knife. The dogs accompanied Rachel the huntress as her World of Warcraft® pets.

Upon leaving the house for the party, I had tried out my gnarled wooden staff, uttering, "KAZAM!"

Liz pointed her wand at me. "Be Brad Pitt!" and giggled, "Oh! That didn't work!"

Josh was dressed like Robin Hood, although in green combat trousers rather than tights, and Becky was a very radiant Maid Marian.

Wesley came as himself with his friend Alan, conscious that they could only stay an hour due to it being past their bedtime. Both boys had a play-fight with plastic swords during the evening.

Photographers and reporters from the *Cheshire Gazette*, forgiven by the family for the publication that had nearly cost the lives of our Jewish friends, interviewed many of the guests. Uncle Saul and Goliath stayed out of the way of the media.

Once the press had gone, the huge man demonstrated his prowess and terpsichorean skills on the dance floor. He lacked grace but not agility and enthusiasm.

It was to be a day and a night of unexpected guests.

*

"And just what do ya think you're doin', Sean Patrick Casey? You're makin' an eejit of yourself prancing about!" A young woman had arrived who nobody recognised. She was not attired in fancy dress but in a Laura Ashley white, red and green floral-print dress, and a white cardigan. On her head, she wore a grey waterproof waxen hat with a felt band and bow. In her right hand, she carried a brown leather suitcase that looked the worse for wear.

Liz shot her eyes across to me, mouthing, "Who? Patrick?"

I shrugged.

Sean had been dancing with his fiancée Rachel, attempting the refineries of disco dancing. Embarrassed by the arrival of the young woman, a flushed Sean took her through the open flaps of the marquee. Rachel looked at Liz and me with a querying look. We had no answers nor any idea who she was.

After a few minutes, I poked my head through the tent flaps. Observing the two absconders in an affectionate embrace, I drew my head back quickly.

Approaching Liz I whispered, "I hope she's not his wife."

Sean seldom mentioned his background apart from referring to his "mammy" in jest. I knew he came from Cork but had no knowledge beyond that, except for snippets he had shared in Afghanistan. He kept his past locked in a private vault labelled "Do not disturb".

Sean and the young woman re-entered the tent holding hands, to the obvious consternation of Rachel. Drawing near to us, Sean invited us to join him in the refreshment tent. Liz, Becky, Josh, Rachel, James, Aly, and I assembled in a semi-circle around the two of them. Until now, I had barely seen Robin Hood and Maid Marion during the reception. They had taken several walks along the lakeside in the moonlight.

Sean swallowed and proclaimed, "Friends, say hello to my Aunty Colleen."

To the dumbfounded shock of his tiny congregation, Sean

elucidated. "My grandfather was a randy bugger. He got a local girl pregnant, and she had a baby girl in 1984 when I was 22 in the parachute regiment. Colleen," he indicated towards her, "lived with her mum but then she ran away from home because of her mum's new boyfriend. She lived with my mother Kathleen, who was fully aware of Granddad's indiscretions." Sean sat, seemingly emotionally exhausted, on an empty metal beer barrel.

Colleen continued the story. "Sean's mother passed away a few weeks ago. The solicitor, wanting to settle the estate, contacted the parachute regiment, and the SAS at Hereford gave me his forwarding address at Kirmingsham Hall."

With revived energy, Sean stood and said, "She has journeyed by coach from Cork to Dublin, ferry from Dublin to Holyhead, and coach to Manchester. From there, she caught a train to Goostry and walked from the station. She has travelled across Eire, traversed the Irish Sea, journeyed across England, and undertaken a 20-minute walk at 10:00 p.m. with hardly any streetlights on the country roads. She has Casey blood in her!"

I admired her immediately.

All the girls hugged Colleen, and Rachel especially made her welcome. Re-entering the disco marquee, James asked the DJ to halt the music. Taking the microphone in his hand, he introduced Colleen. The girls then insisted that Colleen, who looked pale and tired, freshen up in the house.

"You must stay here in our guest room, Colleen," Liz pressed her. "It's too late to get a hotel room, besides you're like family and you're very welcome."

The guests clapped when Colleen rejoined the party.

Goliath was slapping Sean on the back, saying one of his few intelligible English words, "Aunty!" and quaking with laughter.

When the celebrations were coming to an end, Sean approached the DJ and handed him a CD. "We have a special request," the DJ announced, and Sean took Colleen by the hand and led her to the middle of the dance area. She looked out of breath and tired, which I assumed to be from the journey.

The speakers in the two tents blasted out an Irish jig, to which Sean and Colleen demonstrated dancing equal to Riverdance without the clogs. Partway through, Colleen sat down, exhausted, but all the guests, apart from Saul and Dorke, joined in, Goliath's feet pounding the ground.

Dorke amazed me by shaking my hand and kissing Liz, announcing: "Best gig I've ever been to, man."

Journeys

The next morning after breakfast, we said farewell to James' and Aly's friends. Martin from Liverpool shook hands and everyone on the Department of Work and Pensions minibus waved. The springs creaked and the windows misted over as it drove away.

Saul pressed an embossed business card into Sean's hand. "Get in touch in a few weeks. I want you to recruit and supervise security in our hotels on the Black Sea. Fly to Albania as soon as you can."

Turning to Liz and me he said, "I'm sorry for the shock and disruption to the wedding. In the meantime, I would like Goliath to stay and get to know his half-sister and learn more English. Is it too big a favour to ask that he stay with you until I can rent a house nearby?"

"Err, well…"

Liz took over and said, "Yes, of course he can stay. He can sleep on the floor in the guest room until we find a larger bed."

Saul conveyed the news to Goliath, who took Liz's hand in his dinner-plate hands and kissed it.

"We're off then folks," James said through the window of Liz's white Nissan. "The Mumbles at Swansea for a few days. We should get there by lunchtime." Liz and I waved. They intended taking a longer honeymoon in Ireland later in the year.

Joshua Federman was the last to leave. Becky drove him to Manchester airport to catch a noon flight to Amsterdam to connect with his flight to Tel Aviv. I felt sure that we would see him again.

That evening, Liz and I relaxed in our lounge and chatted with Sean, Rachel and Colleen. Sean announced, "Rachel, Colleen and I are off to Cork tomorrow. Rachel still has a few days before she needs to travel to the Philippines." This was to be her last assignment with UNICEF, before she joined the Morgan Foundation fulltime as CEO.

"Colleen has never flown before," Sean said, touching her shoulder as she bit her lip.

My friend then told us more than I had ever known him to. He said that his father, a corporal in the parachute regiment, had been killed in 1967 when Sean was five years old. His mother, Kathleen, died after a long battle with liver cancer, and Colleen had lived with her since she was 14 and cared for her when she became ill. "We are the only beneficiaries of her will," he explained.

*

After his journey to Ireland Sean and I were travelling to Cebu City in the Philippines on Morgan Business. Afterwards, he was going to catch up with Rachel, but she didn't yet know why.

On the plane, Sean's knuckles were white with tension and his cold grey eyes were focused. I smiled. He looked as though he was on a mission.

Cebu City, the oldest in the Philippines, was the main centre of commerce, trade, education, and industry in the Visayas. A travel magazine in 2007 had voted Cebu the 7th most popular tourist destination.

"A great place for a honeymoon," Sean said.

"A honeymoon first and a wedding afterwards, only you could think of that," I replied.

When we disembarked, a blast of heat hit us as if we were stepping into an oven.

Sean and I were meeting government ministers, negotiating with governments to alleviate their bulging prison populations by using our floating prisons, which were converted former passenger liners.

Our talks were positive. I recalled one of my dad's sayings, "Find a problem and solve it at a profit."

We took a stifling cab to our accommodation, which we had sourced quickly on the internet before leaving the UK, and the online descriptions were not perfectly accurate. The receptionist, Manuel, gave us a room key and pointed to the stairs, indicating the lift was broken. We were offered no help with our luggage.

The next morning, we prepared to leave the hotel.

"OK, can we go, Rambo?" I asked Sean.

"Aye, let's rock n' roll," Sean said, grinning.

Sean and James had schemed most of the night on Skype over Sean's great mission.

The taxi ferried us to the two-storey UNICEF building. The driver promised to wait while Sean and I entered the drab concrete building. We were greeted by a couple of women with "UNICEF" emblazoned on their tee-shirts. On the ground floor were a dozen girls, one as young as 11, unpacking boxes of bottled water. Blankets, tents, food bags, first aid kits, and equipment for making wells was spread across the floor.

Sean whispered to one of the girls, "Rachel. Is she here?"

"Sí," she pointed to a flight of wooden stairs. The girls stopped working and started to chatter. They excitedly showed us Rachel's camp bed in a corner. Her laptop was open on her bedside table. The girls clapped their hands, understanding our mission when Sean explained. We gathered Rachel's belongings and laptop and tiptoed upstairs.

"Who? What?" Rachel said. Immediately a small mahogany-coloured boy sprang at us, glaring and barring our way.

"Amigos, Ignacio," Rachel said to him, "amigos," she

repeated. The boy, dressed in a UNICEF tee-shirt and red shorts, sported a blood-stained bandage on his head, was bare-foot, and looked like a street urchin.

"Been in the wars, have we?" Sean said. Rachel flew across the room and hugged him. "Who is the Artful Dodger?"

"That's Ignacio," Rachel stroked Sean's back. "But we call him Iggy. I found him in the city a few weeks ago when two men tried to mug me. Iggy jumped at them from an alley-way, swinging a dustbin lid. I think that's his home, he's very territorial."

"Good God," I eyed up the small, bedraggled child. His fists clenched. I think he knew Rachel was recounting his tale.

"The men attacked Iggy," Rachel said. "But he fought back with the dustbin lid, smashing them, kicking them and jump-ing at them with his little fists flailing."

"Dos grandes hombres," Iggy piped up, proudly pulling out his tee-shirt with his thumbs.

"He says two big men," Rachel laughed.

"OK, we get the gist," Sean said. Then he looked into Rachel's eyes and said firmly, "Now the reason we're here..." he paused as if expecting a drum roll, "...is to take you on our honeymoon and then get married." Sean breathed out.

"Err...isn't that the wrong way round?" Rachel asked, rais-ing her eyebrows.

"Told ya," I said.

Sean and James' plan would come together over the next few hours. A honeymoon followed by a wedding.

"Only Sean and James could think of that," I spoke to the air.

*

James had negotiated the journey with the helicopter pilot for $5,000 on American Express. I waved the Amex card under his nose to assure him he would be paid.

At the private airfield adjacent to Ninoy Aquino International,

Sean squared his shoulders and smiled as Rachel, Iggy and I boarded, and then he negotiated with the pilot to sell him the use of his emergency life raft and helicopter survival kit. From this transaction, the pilot made a further thousand. The average wage in the Philippines was 150 pesos or two US dollars per day. Even taking into consideration his fuel costs, the pilot would still have earned seven years' wages in one night.

"What about the other thing?" Sean asked. "Another thousand?" The pilot looked left and right, and then passed a brown paper parcel across the seat to Sean.

I saw Sean open it and pull out a handgun with two 15-round magazines. He stuffed the gun into his waistband and the clips in his shirt pocket. The hot weather survival kit from the helicopter would be a huge bonus, especially the canned water, food packets, shovel, sunblock, frying pan, and above all, the water desalinator. We all knew clean drinking water was essential for survival, honeymoon or not.

Rachel dragged Iggy to the helicopter. "Es OK, mi amigo," she placated him, tousling his hair.

"Friggin' gooseberry! Some honeymoon this will be." Sean smiled and Rachel overheard his mocking comment and pursed her lips.

Taking his place in the rear next to Rachel, Iggy noticed Sean's weapon. He mimed a shooting gesture and blew on his fingers.

The helicopter flew low over the foliage. Its whirring blades disturbed fruit bats in eucalyptus trees, and the helicopter lurched as we made a quick turn.

"Madre de Dios," Iggy called out, crossing himself three times.

As the pilot hovered ten feet above the beach on the island we were soon to land on, the wind generated by the rotating blades blew up sand and water. Like so many of the Visayas islands, there were rocky promontories north and south. In the centre of the island, dense forest proliferated.

Sean threw out the emergency life raft and the survival kit, jumped out of the helicopter and forward rolled in the sand.

The helicopter landed with a bump. Rachel took Iggy's hand and they disembarked, keeping their heads low.

I threw Sean a satellite phone and shouted above the noise, "Call me if you need to, otherwise I'll see you on Sunday." The helicopter ascended, blades spinning, and I waved to the trio on the beach.

Darkness came quickly as I journeyed back to the private field near the airport. I caught a flight to the capital and thought of something I had read in *The Life of Pi*: "Survival starts with me. It is a mistake to hope too much and do too little."

I knew that Sean would relish the survival experience on the island. But would Paradise Island be an island paradise for Rachel and Iggy?

*

Sean sat Rachel and Ignacio down under the shade of some acacia trees and gave them basic instructions for their next few days. The orange life raft became their sleeping quarters, on a grassy area covered in cogon grass that Sean and Ignacio flattened under other acacia trees for shade.

"Staying for periods in the shade after noon is important," Sean lectured, "the sun will be scorching hot. The temperature soars to 32 degrees Celsius or 90 degrees Fahrenheit. The effectiveness of sunblock is limited, so use wet mud if you feel your skin is burning. Dehydration is our real danger and will be until the water desalinator is set up. I'll demonstrate that afterwards. Seawater or urine must not be drunk, however desperate we may be."

"Yes, Sir," Rachel mocked a salute. "Did you book this honeymoon all by yourself?"

"Pissing or shitting is not allowed near the camp," Sean said, eyeballing Ignacio while Rachel translated.

"No sheet...no pees," Iggy said.

"I'll take Ignacio and we'll build latrines. Urine scent

attracts rats, which attract snakes. Faeces brings flies which carry diseases."

Rachel appeared worried at the thought of snakes. Sean stressed that many snakes were harmless but that there could be poisonous snakes on the island. The party had no anti-venom, so avoiding danger was critical.

"But we have the bat phone, right, Sweetie?" Rachel pointed to the dingy. "We can always phone home like ET."

"Phone home, ET phone home," Iggy mimicked. He knew some English.

Sean ignored them and said, "Nobody must enter the forest area or sea alone, or walk barefoot. Animals will not attack unless a person makes a threat. Insects and snakes could be more likely to bite a naked foot. Corals, spiky fish, jellyfish, rocks, all can injure, so nothing must be eaten unless I approve. There are poisonous plants, fungi and bacteria."

"This honeymoon gets worse and worse," Rachel said, rubbing her eyes and feigning tears. "Can we go back?"

Again, he ignored her. "I'll light a fire, showing everyone how to use matches, kindling and twigs.

"The fire must be kept alive at all times. If the fire goes out and all our matches are used up, we'll use a magnifying glass or flint to relight the fire."

"You light my fire," Rachel said teasingly and blew Sean a kiss.

"Our main priority is drinking water," Sean said. "We have a few water cans with the emergency survival kit, and some water purifying tablets if needed. Rain can be collected and drained into the spare water bag, but if we have too much rain we could be in the shit."

Rachel tutted, "Language, Mr Casey", she said, and wagged her finger. Ignacio laughed at Sean's mock bow.

The start of the monsoon season could bring massive challenges.

Sean took the solar-powered water desalinator and showed it to his yawning audience. Then he took a pocket guide out of his pocket and passed it to Rachel. "The SAS survival guide can show you what to eat, what snakes are dangerous and how to find water. There's water in fruit and vegetables. Most healthy adults need between one and a half to three litres a day. You can judge whether you're drinking enough by the colour of your urine. If it's a pale straw colour, then your fluid intake is probably fine. If your urine is dark yellow, you probably need to drink more."

When Rachel translated, Ignacio said aloud, "No sheet, no pees." Once Sean had shown Rachel and Iggy how to operate the desalinator, Rachel took the bucket to the water's edge and filled it.

"It's like playing with buckets and spades at Western on Sea with my mum and dad," Rachel said, joy written all over her face.

"Well, I know you're Bristol born and savvy, but from what I remember there are no wild animals at Western on Sea. There is a proliferation of wild animals here and some can be very dangerous," Sean said.

"You're a real party poop sometimes, Mr Casey, but don't worry, I have Iggy to protect me." When she translated, Ignacio beat his chest. She laughed and then Sean laughed.

*

Iggy lay down on the beach, using his tee-shirt as a pillow.

"Tell him he'll be eaten alive by sand-flies," Sean said.

"Moscas de la arena," Rachel called.

Iggy got up and sat with Rachel and Sean, their backs against the inflated survival raft, its bright orange tubes and canopy contrasting with the green foliage behind it. Iggy walked to the sea, his bare feet slapping on the wet sand. Bending down he drew seawater to refill the desalination contraption. Sean was growing to like him.

"Mi casa es tu casa," Sean called to him, smiling.

In the evening, squashed together in the life-raft tent, the three of them bedded down for the night. "No nookie tonight then," Rachel giggled.

The chatter of the monkeys the next morning woke them up, the animals swinging in the tree branches and jabbering. Ignacio imitated them and then spotted a lizard a few yards from the camp. He chased after it with a large stick.

"Leave that, it'll do us no harm," Sean said, "come on, let's lay some traps."

He laid a few snares in the forest areas where there were small tracks. On the way back, he spotted a large durian fruit, weighing about ten pounds. The skin had long sharp spines so Sean inserted his combat knife blade, separating the fruit into two halves. He peeled the fruit and removed the spikes while Ignacio, the eager apprentice, watched with fascination, his eyes on the knife.

At the camp, the pair made coconut shell containers for preserving any meat they happened to snare, adding sea salt from the cone of the desalinator. While Rachel prepared salad for the evening meal, they resumed fishing. As the sun was sinking, Ignacio tugged at Sean's arm and pointed at a fin near their fishing pool.

"Tiburón, Meester Sean. Beeg Jaws!"

The pair raised their lines and watched the fin. Incredibly, the fin lay submerged a few feet from the water's edge and then instead of a shark, a turtle's head and scaly neck broke the surface with a spurt. It pulled itself slowly up the beach, leaving a shallow trench behind it.

Sean discouraged Ignacio from chasing the turtle. Carrying him kicking and struggling back to the camp, Sean asked Rachel to translate his gibbering.

"He wants to ride it, like in the Swiss Family Robinson," Rachel translated.

Iggy nodded, "Sí," and mimed riding.

"Jesus. Does he get all his words and ideas from the TV and cinema?" Sean asked.

"He was abandoned as a toddler at an orphanage," Rachel

said, "he spent some time in foster homes but kept running away. From what I can make out, he's about 11 and he's lived on the streets since he was eight years old. Maybe he sneaks into cinemas. It's all he has."

"God in heaven," Sean uttered. "OK, tell him he can ride it if we can catch it. These things are fast," he added with a wink.

Following the turtle's trail along the beach, the three of them arrived at the place where the turtle was busy excavating the beach with her flippers. Sand was flying upwards in spurts and a small hill emerged.

"It's a medium-sized sea turtle which could be good in soup for days." Sean wiped his hands on his pants. Rachel's face showed horror at the thought. Slowly they crept towards the turtle, keeping some feet away.

"Aww, it's going to lay eggs," Rachel said, her eyes moist. "I read that females nest a few weeks after mating, usually during the warmest months of the year. Most females return to the same nesting beach each year." The turtle heaved sand with her huge flippers, creating mounds.

"Aye, and from what I remember she deposits 50 to 200 ping-pong-shaped eggs into the cavity. The eggs are soft-shelled and are papery or leathery in texture. What it means is that we'll have scrambled eggs for dinner. We won't take them all. We'll leave most to hatch. Tell young Mowgli here what we're gonna do. He can have his ride when she's done."

Rachel explained what Sean had said, and Iggy pointed to his chest, "Mowgli."

Around the campfire that night, Sean told stories of Robinson Crusoe and Robin Hood. Rachel talked of King Arthur and his knights. Ignacio had no stories to tell but his face lit up when Sean talked about Robin Hood and his Merry Men.

"What day is it, my fair knight?" Rachel asked. "And I wonder what Little John is doing?"

"It's Thursday June 14th," Sean said. "Good night, and good night John boy wherever you are."

Ramada Inn, Manilla, and Leitz, Strasbourg

The rainy season – the monsoon – was coming.

In my bedroom in the Ramada Inn in Manilla, I thought of Sean. He was a natural, a trained and experienced survivor in all terrains and regions, but I wondered how the rainy season would affect his "operation".

From the mini-encyclopaedia acquired at the hotel shop, I looked up "monsoon" and read a few paragraphs. After that, I slept fitfully.

*

A storm was also brewing in the boardroom of Leitz Pharmaceuticals. Sitting around the executive polished mahogany table were Horst Leitz, Jason Gould and a third man.

Standing by the ornate fireplace, Karl Leitz leaned on his cane. "Well, what do we know?"

The man opened his briefcase with two clicks, placed a blue folder on the table and opened it. Karl Leitz sat down. The table seated 20 comfortably, but the man sat a few feet away from the plush velvet-covered wing chair of the chairman of the board and CEO.

Horst and Jason sat opposite the third man, their backs to windows that extended from the floor to the ceiling. On the fireplace shelf, a clock ticked. Above it on the wall were framed certificates from various business organisations.

"Well?" the old man asked.

"OK first, Tim Mann was buried today," the man began, taking a sheet from his pile, "I visited his family and gave them your cheque."

"Good. At least someone is doing something right," Karl snarled with a scowl.

"They did go over the top, Poppa," Horst said. "They were too enthusiastic."

"He had some fire in his belly, for sure," the chairman chuckled. His face changed as he realised he had used the word "fire", thinking of Simeon and his injuries. He muttered under his breath, "He was a Jew, for God's sake. OK, and what about the punk?"

"The damage is done there," the man with the papers said, taking a second sheet. "We think he told the police about the van. But how they traced it to the farmhouse we don't know."

The old man stood up and leaning on the table with his left hand, he swung his cane and hit the table. "Don't tell me what you *don't know*. I want to know what you *do know*." He struck the table again, causing the glasses to topple and spilling water.

"The kid is not the problem now, Pappa," Horst intervened. "He told them what he knows and that's the end of it."

"So finally we get to the problem," the Leitz CEO said. "What about this Hans person. This drug-dealing son-of-a-bitch."

The man with the papers took a third sheet, stapled to a fourth, and sighed, "Hans Kestelmann could be a problem. Up to now he has kept his lips sealed, but if he faces trial he may blab. We don't have the law of silence here like some of our Colombian friends, and I think he will talk."

"I assume bribes have failed?" Karl asked. The other three men nodded. "OK, can we get to him while he awaits trial? How safe is the remand centre?"

"If he was in jail we could certainly get to him," Horst said, "but remand is not easy."

Jason coughed. "Can I speak?"

The old man groaned.

"I've made some friends in an extreme right-wing group," Jason said. "For a price they would get to him."

"Shaven-headed tattooed thugs in bovver boots?" The old man banged his cane on the floor enthusiastically. "Let me hear it."

Jason said, "These people are nasty thugs, I know, but one of their leaders is on remand, awaiting trial for armed robbery. For a price, he will get to our friend, making it look like a suicide or an accident."

"Do it! For God's sake, do it!" the old man yelled. "We don't want our stakeholders getting nervous."

"Stakeholders? Like shareholders?" Jason asked, immediately regretting his ignorance.

"Stakeholders, you cretin!" Karl snarled. "Our retailers like Walmart and your Boots. Government officials in South America where we're clearing acres of trees to grow bushes that give us laxatives, and regulatory bodies that can close us down. If Leitz is shown in the media cavorting with murderers, we could be in deep shit. Our stakeholders would run a mile." Turning to the man with the papers he asked, "Did you do what I asked?"

"Of course," the man replied. "A cheque for 7.5 million Euros was donated to a new burns unit at Tel Aviv Hospital."

"And it's to be named after us," Horst smirked, "can you believe it?"

For the first time, the old man smiled. The smile became a chuckle and then a belly laugh. He pointed his cane at Jason. "Now find those leaves!"

Hunter Gatherers, and
the Honeymoon Ends

On the Friday morning, Sean introduced Ignacio to "fishing how my daddy used to do it".

Pushing Ignacio behind a rock, Sean threw a stun grenade into the water near the coral. A torrent of seawater exploded around them, along with cascading pieces of rock and seaweed. Fish were cast into the air ten feet, some landing on the sandy beach, others splashing back into the sea. Sean and his small helper gathered the stunned fish from the surface of the water and those on the beach that remained intact. Their bucket full to the brim, they looked up when they saw Rachel running down the beach towards them to investigate the noise.

Ignacio jumped up and down, shouting, "KABOOM!"

"When I was three years old," Sean explained to Rachel, "my da', on leave from the parachute regiment, took me to a lake and demonstrated 'fishing the way ya da does it', by throwing a dynamite stick into the water."

Rachel laughed, her hands holding her sides. "But is that legal?" she asked.

"Err...I think the Filipino government banned the use of cyanide and dynamite by fishermen because dynamite damages the coral and seriously reduces fish stocks. But water, food, shelter, and wellbeing are more important to us than legislation," he replied meekly, although with a hint of mischief.

Leaving the bucket of flopping and splashing fish with

Rachel, Sean went to help Iggy who was struggling up the beach with a five-foot-long black marlin that had been stranded on the beach in the explosion. It was still alive and was dangerously turning its lithesome silky body to bite young Ignacio as he pulled it by its tail towards the camp. Sean dispatched it quickly by driving his combat blade through its head.

Sean explained as best he could to his young comrade that the island region was a dangerous place. The sea harboured stinging jellyfish and sharp coral. In addition, there were venomous sea snakes.

That night Rachel learned how to gut fish, no longer squeamish. "You know how to give a girl a good time," she said, holding her nose.

After an afternoon nap in the afternoon, Sean and Rachel went for a romantic stroll. Coming across a turtle's nest, Sean asked Rachel if she had thought about having children.

"Well I don't want 200 like that turtle," she joked.

Sean took her in his arms, kissing her tenderly on the lips, whispering, "Practice makes perfect." She slapped him playfully on the arm, running away and giggling. Sean chased and caught her. Breathless and hot, they arrived at the campfire at evening mealtime. Ignacio seemed quiet; it was the first time there had been any tension in the camp. He walked away morosely in the failing light, kicking at the sand furiously.

Rachel announced, "I'll go look for him."

Ten minutes later, Sean was worrying.

Suddenly a voice yelled, "Meester Sean! Meester Sean!"

The young Filipino was sprinting towards the camp followed closely by Rachel. Both were running as if their lives depended on it, churning up the sand in their wake. Taking in the situation, Sean retrieved his pistol from the campsite and ran hurriedly towards them.

A wild boar, fiercer and more bloodthirsty than a Rottweiler, was pursuing them, its muscular haunches working ferociously as it skidded left and right.

223

Bravely, Ignacio jumped up and down, waved his arms and continued to shout and throw rocks at the panting monster.

Sean shouted, "Rachel, lie down now!"

He crouched and took aim. "CRACK!" The first round sailed over Rachel's prostrate form grazing the pig's back and leaving a red streak. It squealed in pain but did not slow down. The large hairless mammal, its sharp teeth protruding from a slobbering jaw, was now just 15 feet from Rachel.

"STAY DOWN!" Sean shouted. "CRACK!" The second round flew through the air and hit the beast in the forehead. A small hole oozed blood, the exit wound as big as a man's hand. The animal skidded to a halt, rolling over, splattering blood, bone and gristle all over Rachel. A dark pool appeared in the sand and an awful mixture of smells followed: cordite, blood, faeces, and animal stink.

Ignacio was still jumping up and down shouting at the pig. He mimed shooting a pistol and shouted "BLAM! BLAM!" Helping a shaky Rachel to her feet, he walked her back to Sean.

Ignacio's excited chatter ceased after a few minutes and he again became sullen and morose, standing with his arms crossed. Sean shrugged at Rachel, who took Iggy to one side. Finally, Iggy wandered off down the beach, his shoulders slumped.

"What was that all about?" Sean asked Rachel as she sat on his lap and they cuddled.

"He feels when we leave he has no one. For the first time in his little life, he has a family, and he'll lose it in a few days. I have an idea, Sean, but I don't know how you'll feel about it." She whispered something in Sean's ear.

"Mmm, OK, I can't stand women crying," Sean said, going to get the satellite phone.

"John? Yes, it's me, who do ya think it is, Einstein?" Sean spoke into the black handset, a cord stretching to a yellow box. "No, sorry, it's not an emergency. No, we're not having a row. Listen, John, you're the planner, the calm forward thinker. Listen to Rachel's plan and see what you can do."

Sean passed the handset to Rachel, who outlined her plan.

Before it became too dark, Sean invited Iggy to help cut up the wild boar. Carrying the heavy carcass to the snare area, he showed him how to skin and cut up a large animal, tying cross pieces of acacia to suspend the beast.

That night, the trio had starters of fish and a main meal of fried pork and vegetables. Pudding was bananas. Around the campfire, they had a singalong, Sean and Rachel singing The Righteous Brothers' *Unchained Melody* and Ignacio singing in Spanish Gloria Estefan's *Rhythm is Gonna Get You*, his hips moving in time to the music.

Later, Iggy asked Rachel to translate his story. There followed a harrowing tale of eight brothers and sisters, an alcoholic and violent father, a mother washing wealthy families' clothes for a few dollars, and the breakdown of the family unit when Iggy was taken to an orphanage as a toddler. Any foster parents only wanted Iggy to work for nothing, so he ran away five times and at the age of eight, he was thrust onto the streets where he survived by his wits for four years.

Sean said, with Rachel translating, "My father was killed when I was five. I was a rebel until eventually I joined the paras. They became my family."

Ignacio rose from sitting cross-legged in the sand and hugged him, although neither of them was used to shows of emotion.

On Saturday morning, after coconut and bananas for breakfast, Sean decided to check the snares. The island was becoming familiar territory to Sean and they had just one more day to explore.

Rachel turned to Sean. "By the way, how did you find this place...no, don't tell me, you bring all your girlfriends here."

"James used Google Earth," Sean said, "and you're the first, and the last."

Approaching the snares, Sean could tell that animals and reptiles had been through the cogon grass. He drew near to the area bloodied by the pig's entrails and noticed a fresh but faint trail in the grass.

"Stay here in the sand, Ignacio," Sean indicated with his eyes, "it may be a harmless snake like a green tree snake, a rat snake or a bull snake." He breathed a sigh of relief when he saw the olive brown body with lateral stripes of a harmless garter snake. "OK, come on, Mowgli," Sean called.

Ignacio joined Sean and excitedly pointed to the snake. The amphibian had stretched its mouth around the rat caught in Sean's snare, partially swallowing it, but the wire noose held the rat aloft. Rats had been introduced to the islands, like many animals, by sailing ships from Europe. Sean clubbed the snake with regret, knowing that it would not release its hold and that it would die anyway trying to swallow the snare wire.

The hunters then ate, slept, fished, and explored for the rest of the day. They loudly munched on sugar apples with ravenous appetites and ate fish with pechay cabbage. That night they all finished the remainder of the turtle eggs. The desalinator had provided fresh drinking water for the island group for the days they had been there. They were starting to lose track of time and checked their watches for the time and date.

"Last night on Paradise," Sean said, easing into his sleeping bag.

"Aww, I'm gonna miss our little island," Rachel spoke in the darkness.

The following day was Sunday, the day they were going home. Informed of the day, Ignacio went onto the beach, knelt and prayed. Considering the hardships he had known it amazed Sean and Rachel that he maintained his religious beliefs.

Rachel translated the boy's rowdy petitions. He was praying for their safe and speedy return home, for a baby for Sean and Rachel and that he would find his mother and father. Maybe, they thought, the answer to Ignacio's prayers was closer than he realised.

*

"It's our taxi," Sean said. "Good job it's the navy; I've no more traveller's cheques."

The sun had been hidden by clouds during the morning, presaging a storm just a few hours away. Rachel heard what she thought was thunder but Sean pointed to the skies as a chopper approached with a "WHOOP! WHOOP!" of its blades. The trio hugged one another and watched as a blue Filipino navy rescue helicopter descended towards them.

The grass near the beach was flattened by the draft from the blades and a sandstorm whipped up and stung their eyes as they waved to the pilot. Diesel fumes filled the air. Rotors slowing, the pilot called from the cockpit and made hand signals.

Sean left the emergency kit on the beach. "You never know who may need it." Ducking their heads and shielding their eyes, they clambered aboard and headed for civilisation and a wedding.

The navy helicopter landed with a judder and bounced on an "H" circle at a navy base on the outskirts of Cebu. Sean asked the pilot to deliver the borrowed equipment to the commercial airport, and then shook the navy captain's hand. He carefully placed the handgun on the passenger seat, pointing to it with a nod and a thumbs up.

A battered yellow and white Audi taxi took them to the UNICEF building for Rachel to say her goodbyes. Sean asked the taxi to wait. Young Ignacio swung open the rear door and bounded away, his legs pumping incredibly fast. Sean and Rachel called him back but he paid no attention to them, turning left on a street corner and vanishing. A black and white police car idled outside as they entered the building.

"It's the police, Sean," Rachel pointed to the patrol car. "All his life he's learned to avoid them."

After Rachel said her farewells, they returned to the taxi, which took them to their B & B accommodation, passing markets, mobile food vehicles and hordes of wandering people. Sean told the taxi driver to wait again and climbed the stone steps to the B & B. The owner appeared at the top, grappling with a young Filipino at the front door. The owner was losing, nursing his shins from repeated kicks from the urchin.

"Leave him alone," Sean commanded with a smirk, "he's a friend."

Ignacio ran to Sean and Rachel, hugging them both. He stared daggers at the owner of the guesthouse and gave him a rude sign. The manager retrieved Sean's luggage from the cellar and struggled with it to the taxi. When they pulled away, Sean laughed as the man on the stone steps rubbed his leg.

Rachel showed Ignacio the blue and white airline tickets. Ignacio looked nervous, never having been beyond Cebu City's streets, apart from their stay on the island.

In the airport lounge, they ate flame-grilled burger and French fries. The flight number was announced and the three of them walked down the departure corridor. On the plane, Iggy stared out from his window seat, clearly nervous. The helicopter had been a thrill, but then he could see all around him: the plane was different.

As the powerful engines roared and the plane sped down the runway, Iggy gasped, "Mama mia!" going pale when the plane banked.

A Wedding and a Funeral

I met Sean, Rachel and the small Filipino boy at the arrivals area at Ninoy Aquino International.

With their cases on a trolley, the wheels clattering on the cobbled road, I steered them towards a taxi rank. A short drive of 20 minutes in the navy-blue Volvo 744 and we were established at the Ramada Inn in Manilla. It was a whitewashed modern hotel with palm trees on the paved area outside.

"I've spent the last few days visiting various offices and making calls," I said to Sean and Rachel in the lounge while Iggy played a video game. "The orphanage sent the paperwork and the adoption service gave me the forms, which you both need to sign."

They signed and I witnessed. Persuading Iggy to have his photo taken in a booth, we all rushed to the UK Embassy. Passport papers were authorised for Ignacio and a passport issued.

He was in a whirlwind, not fully understanding at first but now he repeated, "Mi familia...my mama and papa?" his face brighter than the sun.

Monday June 18th at 9:35 a.m., Sean, Rachel, Ignacio, and I boarded a United Airlines flight to Las Vegas, a 20-hour flight with a brief stopover at Vancouver. Ignacio Gonzalez, leaving his homeland for the first time in his life, would within weeks be the son of Mr Casey and the soon-to-be Mrs Casey.

I notice that Iggy wasn't eating any of the in-flight meals and asked Rachel to ask him why.

"Aww, he thought he had to pay! Está pagado (it's paid for)," she explained.

Looking incredulous, Iggy remembered the phrase they'd used on the island and asked, "Free food?"

"Aye, son, it's all free, like on the island," Sean said, looking emotional.

"Free food! Free food!" Iggy called out, and we all laughed as the lad scooped as much as he could into his mouth and then into his pockets.

*

Sean and Rachel's wedding ceremony at a chapel on the main boulevard was simple. A kilted Scots piper played *Amazing Grace* as the bride entered at 4:30, beautiful in her white gown. A small Filipino boy held her wedding train aloft, licking his lips nervously, having never officially attended a wedding.

In a marvellous Southern drawl, the black-shirted reverend with his starched and well-worn dog collar pronounced Sean and Rachel husband and wife.

Ignacio whooped and whistled, managing a backward somersault before he crashed into the floral display. We paid for the damage along with the service, as Sean tucked the marriage licence into his hired suit pocket.

I texted Liz with the news, knowing that in the UK it was after midnight but also knowing she was waiting for the news.

For the honeymoon meal, the four of us wined and dined at All the Restaurants of the World, opting for Japanese teppanyaki. Wide-eyed, Ignacio watched as the chef placed steak, tomatoes, onions, and sliced potato onto the hot plate, and then theatrically tossed the salt and pepper shakers high into the air and caught them again.

Iggy accidentally placed one of the condiment shakers on

the hot plate, where it burned, melted and emitted a noxious cloud before becoming a discoloured lump.

"Sorree Meester Sean." He bowed his head. He also assumed the clear liquid in the glasses was water and downed a glass of saki before we could stop him, soon experiencing drunkenness for the first time.

As Sean carried him to bed, he said, "And I thought I was supposed to carry my wife over the threshold!" Rachel laughed and mock punched him.

The next morning after steak and eggs for breakfast, we caught a cab to Las Vegas McCarran International Airport and caught our Virgin Airways direct flight to Manchester, arriving at 8:00 a.m. after a nine-hour flight.

I collected our luggage, wheeling it through the concourse and thinking about all that had happened in just a few days. Rachel, smiling radiantly, had learnt survival skills on a tropical island during her pre-marriage honeymoon. She would soon become an adoptive parent.

I knew that Ignacio would be both a challenge and source of joy to the Morgan family. Wesley, my grandson, would have a new friend. I was a little apprehensive about what he would learn from the Filipino.

My friend Sean, I could tell, was relieved to be heading home. Though wild at times he had demonstrated his single-minded ability to use all his knowledge and experience to get a job done. It was a characteristic that benefited all in the Morgan circle of family and friends.

Not long after we returned home, Bill, Liz's dad, died. The family comforted Liz as best we could. I helped to make the funeral arrangements. Grieving is a journey that must be travelled, and family and friends can relieve some of the anguish.

As we waited for the cars to take us to the church for the funeral ceremony, we reflected that Bron Afon Community Housing had looked after Bill well in the months he had lived there. Family memorabilia occupied the bungalow: vases, knick-knacks, mirrors, photos, and clocks adorned sideboards and dressers. His cap rested on a peg, his walking stick leaned against the wall in the hallway. On the mantelpiece, a signed picture of Nye Bevan reminded us of Bill's social commitment and happy memories came flooding back to Liz, despite the sorrow.

"He was a good man, John," Liz cried, her head nestled on my chest.

"He still is," I said, "probably looking down at us now."

"Cars are here," James called, as several black cars pulled up outside Bill's housing association red brick bungalow. We silently climbed in. The cortege left Bill's bungalow, travelling along the main roads, arriving at Bill's home town of Ebbw Vale. Silent mourners lined the streets outside their terraced houses and bowed their heads as the gleaming funeral hearse slowed down. White roses landed on the top of the coffin-bearing vehicle as we drove slowly along.

Looking at the sympathetic well-wishers, Liz shed a few tears as I held her hand and patted her shoulder. Becky and James were sitting in the rear of our funeral limousine. Wesley, we felt, was too young to attend but would come to the wake later.

Josh, Aly, Sean, Rachel, and Ignacio followed us in a second funeral car. We resembled a mafia procession with Goliath driving a third car, the black Mercedes Saloon behind us, and Mike the solicitor as his passenger. Leaving Ebbw Vale, our cars and a long line of other mourners' cars hugged the inside lane of the Swansea dual carriageway, moving slowly. Turning through the crematorium gates 20 minutes later, we arrived and the undertakers carefully placed the coffin on a silver trolley and opened the limousine doors for us.

Walking arm in arm, Liz and I approached the open wooden doors. *Men of Harlech* was playing over the speakers. As we walked slowly behind the coffin, the sounds of the melancholic voices of the Tredegar Male Voice Choir were like electric waves. Members of the congregation were wiping their eyes and blowing their noses.

"Jesus said, 'I am the Resurrection and The Life'," I heard, but my mind was floating elsewhere. With the acquisition of the healing leaves, we faced moral dilemmas.

We were certain that healing my grandson and sparing his life had been the right thing to do. We were equally convinced that delivering Simeon from sure death was a good thing. The Morgan household and extended family had held fascinating discussions about the issues of life and death. If we'd had more healing leaves, for instance, would we be a judge presiding over who lived or died?

After the vicar had recited the final words of "Dust to dust", Liz went forwards and threw a rose on Bill's coffin, kissing her fingertips towards the mahogany coffin, and sobbing, "Bye, Daddy."

Becky and Rachel sobbed behind me.

Leaving the crematorium for the wake, I sighed and said under my breath, "Glad that bit's over."

Keep the Red Flag Flying was playing over the sound system as we departed the church.

Liz smiled and waved to the heavens. "Good on ya, Dad."

The wake held at the West Monmouthshire Golf Club near to Ebbw Vale accommodated 60 people officially, but there were about 90. Locals popped in and out, sharing stories about Bill. In huddles around the room, people balanced paper plates containing a variety of buffet food and held glass pint mugs. Goliath bumped his head several times on the golf club's chandeliers, the locals staring wide-eyed as he strode to the buffet.

"Sit there, my giant friend," Sean suggested, "I'll get Iggy to fetch your food. You might break something."

Ignacio grinned from ear to ear as he became the giant's runner, repeatedly bringing more plates of chicken legs, pork pies, potato salad, beetroot, pickled onions, and other delicacies.

"Free food," he grinned towards Sean and Rachel, who laughed. I laughed too, watching Iggy deposit some chicken legs in his trouser pockets.

Watching Goliath and Ignacio play fighting over grapes, Sean reminded us that in the Bible, a little boy had killed Goliath.

Goliath said, "If it's God's will, God's will be done."

Sean and I were amused that both Goliath and Ignacio Gonzalez were religious.

Goliath, with his frame and his strength, reminded me of a silverback gorilla while Ignacio looked like the younger, smaller pretender.

Family Fun in Cheshire

At Kirmingsham Hall, with Sean's and Becky's permission, Iggy taught his new friend Wesley the wonders of catching fish from the lake. I insisted that they free most of the fish they caught to resume their life in Cheshire waters. Iggy also taught Wesley how to swim: our grandson had never learned due to his hospitalisation. Liz, Becky and I stood watching on the lakeside near to emergency floats, but found them unnecessary.

The little Filipino legally became the adoptive son of Sean and Rachel Casey. His new parents explained his name could be changed by deed poll if he so wished. "Of course, Rachel and Mr Sean, I want to be Casey!" the lad said, jumping up and down. Thus, another Casey joined our circle.

One evening just as Liz, James, Aly, and I were tucking into lasagne, Saul paid us a surprise visit.

"I have bought the house Goliath is renting," he announced, "and I wish to gift it to James and Aly as a late wedding present." To James' and Aly's astonishment, he passed the documents and a key to James. "Goliath and I need to return to Albania to sort out some business matters."

I wondered exactly what those "business matters" were, at the same time unsettled that the brother of a mafia don had bought my son and daughter-in-law a house. I wondered whether Saul's investment might come back to haunt us. James and Aly had been living in Sean's former apartments above the garages while Rachel and Sean were living in the bedsit next to his workshop, with Iggy sleeping in the main house.

As Goliath packed that evening, James, Aly, Liz, and I inspected the four-bedroom detached house that Saul had bought, while Saul stood by a radiator. "Epic," said James, "thanks, Uncle Saul." James shook his hand and Aly kissed him on both cheeks. "When you return to the UK you can move back in if you like," James said to Goliath, who had finished packing. The happy, jubilant man-mountain lifted James and Aly, one in each arm, and twirled them around. Their arms encircled his 26" neck as they bounced on his 56" chest.

"I think that's a yes," Sean said, transfixed by the biceps as huge as a basketball. "That means I can have my attic back and Iggy can move into the workshop."

"Sean's tree house!" Iggy said, as he and Wesley ran into the garage block.

Typically, James and Aly's main concern was the broadband connection, which I immediately organised back at our house over coffee.

Before Iggy started school, Sean and Rachel took him aside in our lounge, with Liz and me as moral support. "We're organising a place for you at the local high school and a home tutor in English for you. There's six weeks before school term begins."

The young Filipino resisted. "I need nothing. Sleep, eat, it's enough, no?"

"No it isn't enough, Iggy," Sean said, and Rachel translated. "Like you, I used to live by my wits from the age of five, skirting trouble with the Garda by the skin of my teeth. I spent nights, sometimes weeks away from home, eking out a living where I could. I can teach you some things the school can't, but they can teach you things that I can't. You need both."

"OK, Mr and Mrs Sean. I weel go to school."

Sean said, "God help them."

Attending school proved fraught for Iggy. Mockery he would not accept. There were regular fights in the playground. Coping with the high school curricula, when he had never attended a learning establishment, was massive for the young boy. There were tempers, tears, absences from class, and frequent meetings with teachers.

Sean refused to place his son in a "special needs" learning environment. He and Rachel worked tirelessly with their boy to bring his education to a decent standard. Gradually he settled in and began to learn, and he became popular, remaining fiercely competitive in sports.

I was told that apart from Ignacio "snoring like a hippo" in the workshop bedsit, Sean and Rachel were well settled in Sean's tree house.

Colleen Comes to Stay

Colleen had remained in Baltimore, living in the house bequeathed to her and Sean in Sean's mother Kathleen's will. Unbeknown to Colleen, she had inherited another legacy: a deadly one.

As a 14-year-old, she had fled in the middle of the night to Sean's mother's to escape from her mother's live-in boyfriend. He had been abusing her for months and had brutally raped her on the night she fled.

The emotional and mental torment lingered beyond the scars on her body. Becoming weak a few days after her visit to the UK, she had struggled on until finally, her physician in Baltimore did some tests and discovered that she had HIV, the legacy of her mother's boyfriend. She was in danger of developing AIDS. The local hospital could not offer treatment so she was referred to a specialist unit attached to Victoria University Hospital in Cork.

Sean arrived back in the UK, having spent several days with Saul reviewing the security of his hotels in Albania. Rachel met him at the airport looking worried. She had received a call from a doctor at the hospital in Cork.

It was clear that Aunty Colleen needed their help. Sean's conversation with the specialist was brief. Client privilege prevented the doctor from disclosing the details of Colleen's illness and although both Sean and Rachel tried speaking with

Colleen, she was not forthcoming and urged him not to travel to Ireland. The specialist had assumed they knew something and had mentioned AIDS.

"Sean," I said, "Liz and I both agree that you and Rachel must go. We'll look after Iggy. Don't worry about a thing."

The Caseys made plans to travel to Ireland and I dropped them at Manchester airport. Iggy insisted on coming in my car. The boy would miss half a day at school, but he was stubborn and tough once he had made up his mind and he would not be persuaded to miss the journey.

*

From Cork Airport past Farmer's Cross, Sean and Rachel drove in their hire car the 20 minutes on the dual carriageway and then to the hospital just off the city link road. Sean strode confidently to a pleasant receptionist and inquired about Colleen Casey. She gave him the ward number with a sympathetic look.

Colleen was sitting in an easy chair in the ward, wearing a light-blue woollen dressing gown that contrasted with her pale skin. Seeing them, she laid aside a *Hello* magazine and rose unsteadily to greet them.

With moist eyes she said, "Ya needn't have come."

Sean struggled to hold his emotions in check. Colleen had lost several pounds since the party at Kirmingsham Hall. Other patients, some with drips and machinery attached, looked over at them. Disinfectant, floor polish and some putrid unidentified smells assaulted their nostrils.

"Let's talk," Sean said, and beckoned Colleen to show the way. Rachel took her arm as she slowly walked along a corridor, her slippers slapping on the hard floor. In a small waiting room off the ward with the walls papered in a diagonal shaped pattern, a senior nurse brought tea on a tray. The three sat at a round table and supped the tepid brew.

With dry lips and in a weak voice, Colleen told them her

story. Sean's emotions went from shock to deep sorrow and then to fury, as she poured out her heart to her nephew. Her mother's boyfriend had died years before, but the virus lived on. Rachel had seen her fair share of catastrophic epidemics like HIV and AIDS in her work with Save the Children in Uganda, Nigeria and Kenya.

"OK, I've heard enough." Sean took Colleen by the hand. "You're coming with us to the UK where we can look after you."

Reluctantly she capitulated, got dressed behind a screen, and discharged herself from the hospital.

It was not the first time that Sean had taken a patient out of a hospital to save a life.

The trio spent the night at Colleen's house in Baltimore, allowing her to pack and gather some personal items as well as rest for a while.

That evening, Sean and Rachel went for a walk around the fishing port. "This is where I grew up," Sean said, pointing out some of the local attractions in the moonlight. Moored boats rose and fell with the tide and red and white buoys bobbed up and down.

"Not sure you ever grew up!" Rachel said. "And what's that smell?" She leaned over the harbour wall surveying the nets glistening from the day's activity. The smells of freshly caught fish and crab drifted in the mild breeze. Seagulls cawed and fought over fish carcasses on the cobbled jetty, which was overlooked by a ruined castle. They bought fish and chips in greaseproof paper and sat on the jetty eating.

"My God, this is the life!" Sean proclaimed, his concerns temporarily laid aside. Sean had the ability to compartmentalise his life: a segment for fun, a segment for action, a segment for worry. Worry would return in the morning.

*

The next morning I met their early flight to Manchester from Cork at 8:30.

While we would all accept, love and care for Colleen, we knew she needed a miracle, a healing miracle.

Maps, Charts, Drawings, and Notes

Over the following weeks, Colleen took her prescription medication and was visited regularly by our GP but she grew weaker. Her rasping cough resounded at the top of the stairs. Her fragility and weight loss worried us all. The Morgan household shared Sean's concern for his aunty. A family meeting was called, our practice whenever issues that affected us all needed to be discussed. I also welcomed Josh into our gathering, as he was practically part of the family now. His Israeli background and knowledge would be hugely useful. Goliath had taken Wesley and Ignacio fishing with the dogs.

"I've got to go and look at least," Sean pleaded. He was putting forward a strong argument to travel to Israel to obtain leaves from the Eden Tree. "John, Liz, you know what the leaves can do. This is Colleen's last chance."

"And of course I'll come," I said, "you may need me."

Sean looked relieved.

"We'll need the photocopied maps, drawings and notes from my safe." I ran upstairs and brought all the documents into the lounge, spreading them out on the carpet.

Sean and Rachel sat cross-legged on the floor; James and Aly were half sitting, half lying. Liz and I picked up papers individually and read them from our recliners. Becky and Josh relaxed on a couch. As we finished reading, we passed the papers around. Each person studied the sheets with interest and with gasps of fascination. It was the first time that Rachel, Josh and Aly had seen them.

These were the copies I had surreptitiously made at the Hilton in Tel Aviv when I had realised that Colonel Balak, Josh's superior in Mossad, would demand St Peter's box and its contents. Caleb, Simeon and Joseph's uncle, had left us a wealth of his research on his laptop, which James had copied by mirroring his hard drive. With copies of the original manuscripts and Caleb's detailed research papers, there were dozens of items to examine. I made notes on an A4 pad.

"I don't think we can doubt the power of the leaves," I said. "Wesley and Simeon would both be dead without them. If they were not given to the disciples by Jesus, then where did they come from? We've got to decide if the Garden of Eden existed at all. There are various views on this. The undeniable fact is that the mysterious leaves have wrought these two miracles of healing."

"Jesus was an alien, a superior life-form," James said, confidently putting forward the same arguments he had done on our return flight from Israel. Aly was nodding. "The parchments are maps and details of where he landed and where he left a sort of encampment with a tree from his planet," he said. We all gathered around his and Aly's laptops as they showed us the photos Sean and I already had seen: images of pyramids, large stone figures, various maps.

"OK," I said, "if we accept your view we still need to ascertain where the garden is."

Josh cleared his throat. "I believe that many of the stories in the Pentateuch, the first five books of the Bible, are partly historical and partly religious. Debate has raged for centuries about the Cradle of Humanity and the Genesis account of early man. The location of the Garden of Eden is as elusive as that of Atlantis the sunken island." He cleared his throat. "I'm returning to Jerusalem. I'd like to come with you. You may need official backing for this quest, which I can provide." Becky stroked his hand.

"There ya go," James said, "Atlantis is another site. It may still be under the sea."

"Like in the film *The Abyss*," Aly added.

James sat up, "Exactly...nice one... alien city miles down, with a superior species. There could be gardens under the sea."

"Yes, James," I emphasised, "but the garden we're looking for isn't," thinking that we were going off at a tangent.

Becky said, "I'm travelling with Josh so count me in! I'm going to meet his parents. Mum's OK with minding Wesley." She looked across at Liz, who nodded and smiled. Clearly, mother and daughter had discussed this already.

"Now regarding the leaves – for which I'm very grateful, as you know – I accept some of the religious arguments and am open-minded about their origin and a Tree of Life," I said.

Liz stood up, her hair falling over her shoulder. "I agree there is much we do not know, but we do know the healing virtue of the leaves. And why would anyone bury a box in Joppa in the very house where Jesus' disciples met? The original parchments and scrolls were very old. I think the whole story could be true and if so, it's possible the maps will lead you to the Tree."

A debate followed, as painful as it was to Sean under the circumstances, concerning whether we had the right to determine whose life we would prolong or whether someone lived or died. Rachel pointed out that people made those very decisions every day in medicine. She added that some countries lacked certain advancements in medicine and that because of it, children died needlessly of illnesses that immunisation, mosquito nets or condoms could prevent. There was a parallel here that we could draw with the healing leaves.

At lunchtime, we adjourned to the dining room. Rachel took a tray up to Colleen's room. When she returned we knew a decision had to be made.

I took comfort in the knowledge that Jesus Christ had entrusted the leaves, through His followers, to me, and so the decision became not whether the leaves should be used but when we would go to Israel. We also still had no answer to the centuries-old riddle: the location of the Garden of Eden.

X Marks the Spot

The "Israeli task force" of Sean, Josh, Becky, and me, along with Liz, James and Aly, spent Sunday afternoon and evening studying in detail the maps and copied documents along with the extensive research downloaded from Caleb's computer.

One document referred to a work and a map dated 1695 from the British Library. The work, *Paradise or the Garden of Eden with the Countries Circumjacent Inhabited by the Patriarchs,* was by Joseph Moxton. At first glance, it seemed to be a straightforward map of the Middle East but closer inspection revealed an illustration of Adam and Eve in the top right-hand corner.

Sean read from some notes that Caleb had made: "More recent discoveries in 1994 in Turkey were believed to be at the heart of the Paradise of Genesis. Tending his flock, a Kurdish shepherd found a large oblong stone. Dusting off the sand, he was amazed to find text and pictures of people. The man looked around the area and found 45 stones. The site at Gobekli, named the Turkish Stonehenge, was of paramount importance to archaeologists around the world. Carbon dating showed the stones to be at least 12,000 years old, meaning the site was constructed in 10,000 BC. As a comparison, Stonehenge was built around 3,000 BC and the Pyramids of Giza in 2,500 BC." (Curry, Andrew, 2008.)

I said, "Gobekli Temple was certainly an important discovery but does it help our quest?"

"Maybe you have to search for some pillars in the sand, Dad," James said.

"Look here folks," Becky said, "Caleb has written some notes in italics. 'Genesis 2:10-14, And a river went out of Eden to water the garden; and from thence it was parted, and became four heads. The name of the first is Pison: that is, it which compasseth the whole land of Havilah (Arabia), where there is gold; and the gold of that land is good; there is bdellium and the onyx stone. And the name of the second river is Gihon; the same is it that compasseth the whole land of Ethiopia (Africa). And the name of the third river is Hiddekel: that is, it that goeth towards the east of Assyria (north of Babylonia). And the fourth river is Euphrates.'"

"I know those passages," said Josh, "they're part of Jewish history."

Following the biblical references to the four rivers, Caleb had added detailed maps of the earth's plates and land mass changes since biblical times. He had added a comment in the margin, "It's a fact that many precious stones and gold have been found in India and Australia, former fragments of the land known as Havilah or Arabia."

There followed a long debate regarding the four rivers. James and Aly were convinced that the ancient rivers, the Euphrates and Tigris being the two remaining, had originally flowed into the Persian Gulf. They were equally convinced that Kuwait was built near to a space ship and that the US military knew about it but had kept the details secret.

Becky believed the centre of the rivers, in Turkey, to have been at the base of Ancient Armenia. She read Caleb's notes about a fertile plain near a village called Harput, in Eastern Anatolia, which had been destroyed by an earthquake. She was sure we should search there.

Josh, with his Jewish background, gave by far the most persuasive argument. Quoting Caleb's notes and biblical references in Ezekiel, he believed Eden to be in Lebanon, south of Jerusalem. "In Ezekiel 28:12-19, the prophet sets down God's word against the king of Tyre," Josh said. The king was the 'seal of perfection, adorned with precious stones from the day of his creation, and placed by God in the Garden of Eden on the holy mountain as a guardian cherub. But the king sinned through wickedness and violence, and so he was driven out of the garden and thrown to the earth, where now he is consumed by God's fire. All the nations who knew you are appalled at you; you have come to a horrible end and will be no more.' The trees of the garden are mentioned in Ezekiel 31, and scattered passages from Ezekiel, Zechariah and the Psalms refer to trees and water in relation to the temple without explicitly mentioning Eden."

Josh continued, "All four of the rivers in Genesis had one thing in common. They were all connected to the Great Rift system. And that is the key to the mystery! Two rivers presently originate out of Turkey to the north and two other rivers flowed south of Israel. The latter are now underground or else they have dried up. The geographical centre of these four points of flow is neither Turkey nor Kuwait; the centre is somewhere near present-day Israel and Jordan. The Bible says that the river flowed out of Eden, but nowhere does the Bible give a geographical size for what constituted the area of Eden. Therefore, the actual source of the waters could have been south of Lebanon. More specifically, those waters could have originated near Jerusalem in present-day Israel."

The four rivers, Josh explained, would have sprung forth from the ground in Messiah's reign, flowing through the City of God, the New Jerusalem. Josh reminded us that according to the last book of the Bible, the Book of Revelation, the river that flowed through New Jerusalem had a tree in its centre and it was a commonly held belief of the Israeli people that its leaves would bring healing to the world.

Following our discussions, we decided to fly to Jerusalem and start our search south of the city. It would also allow Becky to meet Josh's family. Josh arranged a week's leave from his work in the Israeli Embassy in London. Mossad had a special relationship with Jewish embassies around the globe.

Colonel Balak in Tel Aviv was interested to hear that his sergeant was travelling to Tel Aviv with his friends. He immediately deduced the purpose by commenting to Josh on the phone, "Ah. You intend to find Eden and acquire more leaves."

It was pointless to deny it.

Jerusalem

Monday September 16th

Early Monday morning, Sean's brown Range Rover churned up the gravel on our driveway. He and Josh came into the kitchen carrying boxes with NATO labels.

"OK, from the NAAFI at Hereford, we've beef and carrots, tuna and potatoes and sweet biscuits. The Halal chicken tajine is nicked. I've added energy bars, fruit jelly, chocolate bar, chewing gum, caramels, sweets, Puritabs, heating kits, packs of paper towels, and four first aid kits from supplies."

Liz was driving us to the airport. Loading four rucksacks into the trunk of my BMW, we waved goodbye to the rest of the family. It seemed that a large part of our lives had been spent travelling from the UK to Israel. This time, we were going there to follow maps to a lost garden.

We arrived in Tel Aviv at 3:10 a.m.

At Ben Gurion International Airport, we climbed into a hired Land Rover Discovery and drove to the Hilton. Pulling into the car park Sean looked at me knowingly, his eyes saying, 'here we are again, another stay at the Hilton'.

"Why, hello again, Mr Morgan," the deputy manager greeted me, passing across two room cards, "here again?" I recalled his flattened hair, tiny moustache and the smell of garlic on his breath.

Josh had insisted he share a room with Sean and me for propriety. In the early hours UK time, I called Liz from our room and left a message on her mobile.

"Hang on before you two fall asleep." I held up the vehicle rental agreement and commented, "Guys, we're not covered for parking in East Jerusalem or the West Bank."

"Because of the tensions, I'm afraid, John," Josh said, "and of course we're famous for being terrible drivers. More Israelis die every year on the road than have died in all the wars combined."

"That's OK, I'll use my horn," Sean said, pulling the duvet over his head.

On Tuesday morning after a fitful nap, we entered the familiar restaurant, ate a tasty breakfast and went over our plan once again. Both Palestinians and Jews were suspicious of strangers, so it was decided that Sean and Josh would don the garb of Bedouin guides and Becky and I would kit ourselves out like typical tourists.

Boarding the Discovery, I noticed a car in the car park with the Leitz Pharmaceutical insignia. 'What are they doing here?' I wondered. Had they followed us here? Were they still intent on acquiring knowledge of the Eden Tree? I pointed to the Leitz car and Joshua noted the registration.

We drove the 26 miles to the Holy City, passing cars adorned with blue and white striped bumper stickers as reflective warnings. In the passenger seat next to Josh, I observed the traffic and remembered what he had said about Israelis being terrible drivers. They were certainly impatient and aggressive.

Josh wound down the window and shouted, "*Ben-zona!* You son of a bitch!" His horn blasts joined other angry horn blasts. "Sorry, Becky," he said, looking at her in his rear mirror.

As we climbed up into the Jerusalem hills in the last third of the trip, the temperature began to drop and it seemed like winter. We were entering a different world.

"Is it just me or is it getting colder?" Becky asked, zipping up her jacket.

"WOW, it's amazing!" I said, transfixed by the beauty and aesthetics of the city.

Josh manoeuvred the vehicle through streets and interpreted signs which stated that "By a law dating from the time of the British mandate (1919-1948) all buildings must be faced with Jerusalem stone."

The modern part of the city, bright and bustling with crowds of ordinary looking people along with Orthodox Jews in black coats and hats, beards and braids, felt safe despite the tensions hovering beneath the surface.

Josh's parents lived in a wealthy suburb where the houses were large and beautiful. His parents' house had a decidedly European feel about it, with its spacious living room and atrium, picture windows looking onto a lush yard and a flourishing grapefruit tree growing just outside the kitchen window.

Josh kissed his mother on both cheeks and said, "Hi Momma. This is Rebecca – she likes to be called Becky. And this is John, Becky's father, and this is Sean."

Josh took Sean upstairs, saying, "Toilet."

Mrs Federman's face showed concern when they returned: both he and Sean had pistols tucked in their waistbands. I suspected that she knew her son's job was dangerous.

Mrs Federman served us a lunch of homemade meat pie along with sparkling water to drink. For pudding, we had fruit strudel.

The typical Jewish mother, Mrs Federman fussed around her son like a mother hen, to his obvious embarrassment and our muted chuckles as he translated. His hair was too short... he had lost weight...why hadn't he called before...when could she expect grandchildren?

At the last question, she looked towards Becky who smiled politely.

At the end of the meal, she kissed us all on both cheeks and gave us her blessing. She hugged Becky the longest and whispered loudly, "He's a good boy."

We set off south for the Israeli-occupied West Bank. Outside the city, Sean and Josh changed into their tribal outfits of blue and white stripes and dark brown ponchos.

Would we find the Eden Tree here?

Pillars in the Sand

I held Caleb's and St Peter's maps in my hand. On the former, a red-inked circle indicated an area just east of Hebron. Caleb's notes, made after his meeting with his nephews, indicated an uncharted area. A collection of sand dunes skirted the road.

"Let's go off the road here." We bumped across the wilderness to explore. The area was truly 'off road', making me glad we had a vehicle that could handle the terrain. Clouds of sand blew up as we drove. The air conditioning blew strongly on our faces. On the skyline, palms stood tall.

"A wadi," Josh said, "let's head for it, but be careful what you say. We'll see if we can stay here the night."

Sean pulled hard on the steering wheel and the Land Rover jumped, skidded and blasted sand as it lurched forward. Goats bleated as we approached the oasis. Some of the goat herders, clothed as I imagined people would have been in biblical times, stood up as we approached. We parked the Discovery and walked through the sand, which was like walking through treacle. Under the shade of the palm trees, the goat herders shared their food and water with us, smiling and chatting with Josh in Yiddish. He told us they had agreed to let us spend the night at the oasis.

I shivered and drew nearer to the campfire as I read aloud from a pamphlet in the moonlight. "Hebron, a city south of Jerusalem, was where Abraham buried his wife Sarah, also where David was originally crowned king, and where he reigned for his first seven and a half years." Hebron, I explained, was spelt 'chevron' in Hebrew and one of its meanings was to join or unite.

The goat herders led their flocks to a small pasture area and lay down to sleep.

"I need a wee," Becky said. We cautioned her to be careful and to take our torch.

Becky trudged through the sand, pointing her torch beam on the ground. Over her head, bright stars twinkled in the moonlit sky. She passed some small rocks and walked a few steps, searching for a discrete place to pee. Under a rock overhang, she took another step and stubbed her foot on a rock. Tumbling head over heels, she fell several feet but managed to hold on to her torch. Rolling down a high sand bank, she landed in a trench. Annoyed at her predicament, she dropped her pants and urinated. Then she stood up on her painful ankle and thought she saw a reflected surface in the moonlight. "What on earth?" she said.

She limped through the heavy sand, her torch beam illuminating shapes ahead. Slowly taking a few laboured paces, to her dismay she saw that the shapes had vanished. "A mirage," she said, "it must be." Then in the moonlight, she saw reflections again. She wielded the torch beam in her right hand, feeling her way ahead with her left. There, she discovered two very thin pillars joined by an archway.

"It's not marble, or metal, or stone, or wood. It feels solid yet pliable too. It's cold and yet it feels almost liquid smooth. What on earth is it?" she asked herself.

Then she saw the writing and drawing under the arch and knew she had found the gateway to Eden.

We were getting very anxious by the time we saw Becky's torchlight beam coming over a dune 30 minutes later. She was so excited by the discovery that the words tumbled out and she barely noticed Josh tenderly examining her ankle, until he strapped it up and she winced.

"Two pillars?" I asked for clarity, when she came to the part about the archway.

Becky smiled and nodded.

We were perplexed how no one else had so far discovered the pillars and determined to explore the area the next day at sun-up.

*

The next morning at dawn, we were woken by the sound of men's voices and the jingling of bells. The nomadic goat herders were awake and watering their flocks, and would soon be on their way. Eager to return their hospitality, we shared our food with them. Josh explained what each army ration package contained and they ate with gusto.

Lifting our rucksacks onto our shoulders, we followed Becky into the desert, spreading out but keeping within sight of one another to look for the rock overhang. I noticed some nesting birds hovering and then saw them drop out of sight.

"Let's try over here," I called out, estimating where the birds had landed. We fought against the sand as if it was swamp mire and were relieved when we found the overhang. Becky came panting and hobbling behind us.

"This is it," she said, and looked for the place where she had stumbled. Sean forward rolled down the sand dune and stopped at the trench. We were just beginning to feel discouraged and were about to look for another trench when Sean shouted, "Here!" and pointed to the pillars and the archway jutting out of the sand.

Quickly digging around the two obelisks, we found they were taller than a man, similar to the ones at Gobekli. There was a drawing on each stone and writing across the archway. Josh interpreted the words. "The joined hands." The shapes and material were like nothing I had ever seen. We walked around the stones, through the arch and under it, examining the area from every angle. The stones were as thin as a wafer, so it was no surprise they had remained undiscovered if they had only ever been seen from the front. The writings and drawings were identical to those on the other side. I dusted off the drawings and noticed under each drawing a shelf-like indentation.

Unsure whether this was something important, we sat under the shade of the stones and tried to fathom the mystery. Then Becky, who was examining the drawings again, remarked that they looked like a serpent and a devil on the left stone and a golden angel with leaves on the right stone.

"Don't you see, Dad," Becky said with a confident smile, "it's your and Sean's tattoos!"

Sean and I took a careful look and saw that she was correct. We were in the right place! The drawings matched our tattoos. But where was the garden?

"Try placing your hand on the shelf," Josh suggested, "the arch mentions hands". Sean inserted his left hand into one stone and I inserted my right hand into the other. Nothing happened.

"Try holding your other hands," Becky prompted, "the arch says 'Joined hand of God'. Hebron means joined, doesn't it?"

"This doesn't mean we're swapping spit in the shower," Sean said.

We joined hands, feeling foolish until we noticed something happening like miniature lightning. Under the archway between the pillars, a swirling blue haze appeared like a whirlpool. The opaque mist cleared, leaving a circular image of a beautiful garden that was as tall as a man.

"Wow!" I said. "James, eat your heart out!"

Sean, whistling the *Indiana Jones* theme tune, placed his hand through the portal. He pushed up to his elbow, and then further, winking at us as he walked through the picture. Each of us followed in turn. Once through, we looked backwards and could see the two pillars and the archway but without the picture. Were we trapped? We felt it was not a trap but a doorway.

The Garden of Eden! We floated more than trod on the

softest and greenest grass I had ever seen. It was like walking on silk. The rolling lush grassland hill led up to an oasis. The clear blue sky above had a rainbow, yet no clouds. We were mystified how this beautiful location could be hidden in the dunes. We walked along a pathway made of what looked like marble, but it was not marble. It felt like being in a science fiction plot.

Sean said, "Sorry folks, I know this is serious 'n all but I can't resist this," and he started singing, "We're off to the see the wizard…"

We were not on a yellow brick road, although I suspected a supernatural encounter awaited us.

The Tree of Life

When I'd first heard the story from a flower seller at a market about St Peter's last will and testament, a hidden box, magic leaves, and maps to the Garden of Eden, it had sounded incredulous. But here we were, walking on ground that had not seen a human footprint for thousands of years.

We heard no calls of animals or birds, just the gentle sound of rippling water. Several sparkling oases appeared. A few hundred yards ahead, nearer to a large garden, a crystal-clear river flowed through the grassland. It poured into pools and wadi waters. Prolific foliage and fauna grew on its banks.

Sean stood in stunned silence. "You see that water? It's flowing, but coming from nowhere. It's like a clear liquid with rainbow colours reflected in the water. I've never seen anything like it in my life!"

"The River of Life," Joshua said. "It's mentioned in Ezekiel and the Christian book of Revelation. I never dreamed it could be true, but here it is!"

We floated further and I felt overwhelmed by peace. Euphoria burst forth like bubbles from my innermost being. I couldn't stop smiling.

"Anyone feel different?" I asked. "I feel the same as I did as a child on Christmas morning. It's like having a child's innocence and trust."

"I feel light as a feather, wheeeee!" Becky said, and started to twirl and dance like a ballerina. "I feel the same as I felt when I first held Wesley." Her face had a healthy glow.

Sean knelt in the lush grass and wept, his shoulders shaking. I had never seen him cry; not even during Wesley's illness.

"I feel like I am being washed all over," he sobbed, "waves of warmth. And I feel a heavy load has fallen off my shoulders." He stood up moments later, and taking Becky's hand, he began to dance around with her, leaping and spinning like a child.

"Like a blind man who can now see," Josh said, "experiencing the world for the first time –excited, thrilled and confident in a good world: a world where people care for others."

"I must video some of this," Becky said, holding up her phone camera.

"I have some great photos of the SAS captain dancing," Joshua laughed. "And John, you look slimmer!" Turning to Becky he said, "Come on, I have an idea."

He took her by the hand and they ran ahead to an area surrounded by plants, flowers, shrubs, fauna of every size and colour. The whole area was resplendent in reds, yellows, oranges, whites, an abundance of colours and shapes. Small stalks, huge stalks, tiny leaves, massive leaves, the garden like every garden in the world gathered in one place, displayed in wonderful abundance.

On the soft green velvet garden, under the shade of a resplendent tree, Josh knelt down on one knee. "Rebecca Morgan, will you marry me?"

"Of course I will," she said, joining him on her knees as they kissed passionately. But it didn't seem out of place.

"Dad," Becky said, "can you use my phone and take Josh proposing again?"

"That will be one f...f...great snap," Sean said. "You know I can't even swear here!" He laughed and laughed, and we all joined in.

Photo session over, we drew near in hushed reverence to two trees where Becky and Josh had knelt. One strong and healthy tree with medium-sized flat green leaves. The other tree withered, blackened and gnarled. Underneath the dead tree, a plaque of tree bark was etched with ominous lettering.

Josh translated, "'Beware the children of Eve and the Nephilim'. I think the first part refers to a race of Amazonian type women."

"Amazonian women, huh? And what are Nephilim?" I asked.

"They were," Josh said, "according to Genesis six verse four, offspring of 'the sons of God' and 'the daughters of men', gigantic men apparently who inhabited Canaan. David fought one called Goliath, and he had several brothers."

"Well if they're anything like our Goliath back home, they would be awesome," Becky said.

"Aye, that would be a fight and a half," Sean said, taking a leaf from the healthy tree and examining it shiny and moist in his hand.

Within seconds, it disintegrated and vanished, and as each of the others reached to take a leaf, exactly the same thing happened. However, it did not happen to the ones I took.

"Ah, see John, you *are* the Chosen One." Sean bowed his head in mock surrender.

Becky stroked my shoulder. "He's right, Dad. Think about how you met Joseph and Simeon. Think about the words in the parchment." My neck hairs tingled.

Reaching for more leaves, I then found the same thing happened as Sean had experienced. I could only take a few leaves.

Josh said, "It's like the manna in the Old Testament. A family could only collect what they needed. Anything more was forbidden."

I placed what I had taken in the cloth bag.

We behaved like children, laughing and snapping more photos in the pleasantly warm sunshine.

"Me now, Boss, and then you," Sean said.

The phone clicked as I snapped one of him standing under the gnarled tree, pointing towards the sign and flexing his biceps. Sean took a photo of me under the Eden Tree, looking up at the leaves and pointing.

In that place, an indescribable peace, a tranquillity I had never known, permeated everything. I think we all felt it, as we sat silently under the shade of its branches.

The Bible says, "Be still, and know that I am God." And we were still. And we did know.

Homecoming

"It's so good here," Becky said. "I think it's always like this. Sun and blue sky, never night. I feel protected and so rested."

"I think we all do, Becky." I looked at the other faces around me and knew that we would all be changed from that moment.

"But it's time to go home," I said. "We came here for Colleen." We returned to the two pillars and archway, where Sean and I repeated our previous actions. The shelves were mirror versions of the entrance. We inserted and linked our free hands, and a mist appeared. Staggered, I realised the image appearing in the swirling whirlpool was not Eden's Garden but Kirmingsham Hall.

"We're going home!" I proclaimed.

We each looked back and then entered the swirling gateway. We were deposited on familiar lawns, to the shock and consternation of Bourne who ran yelping into the house, his tail between his legs.

Alerted no doubt by the barking, the rest of my family came running out of the house and stood amazed on the steps as we approached them. James jocularly asked where we had left our time machine.

It took hours to explain all the events of our journey, a jaw-dropping tale. Wesley and Iggy were woken up by the noise and joined our celebration.

Remembering the reason for our escapade, Sean asked for

my rucksack. Taking one of the leaves, which he placed in a tissue, he made a pot of tea with it and took the pot with a mug and a jug of milk upstairs.

After ten minutes, he returned from Colleen's room. "She says it's sweeter than honey, smells like pine, and is stronger than Typhoo."

By early evening, Colleen appeared and announced she had a ravenous appetite.

"I'm starving," she said, chewing on a slice of pizza.

In our family lounge, everyone gathered to share in our bewildering events. We looked at the photos on Becky's and Josh's camera and roared at the sight of Sean dancing with Becky like a madman. Rachel hugged him.

When we showed the video of Josh on one knee proposing to Becky under a magnificent tree, Liz said, "WOW!", and we all hugged the happy couple.

Wesley exclaimed, "I knew it!"

I looked at Wesley and thought of the tree mural. Was it possible that he had been watched over by the mysterious tree even when he was in the womb? The healing leaves had saved his life.

I realised for the first time in my life that I couldn't plan everything; I was not really in control. Some aspects of my life were planned by another, by a higher being.

Mark Twain had said, "The two most important days in your life are the day you are born, and the day you find out why."

I had found out why I was born. My destiny was linked to a box and a tree: the Eden Tree.

One day maybe we would return to Eden, but that would be another story.

Epilogue

Liverpool FC had a new home match steward: a seven-foot-eight-inch giant who weighed 26 stone. It solved the problem of broken and damaged seats. We sat at The Kop end, singing, *You'll Never Walk Alone*, and shouting at the referee. At the Black Swan, we often saw and chatted to our soccer stars.

I heard from Josh that the Leitz family was still running Leitz Pharmaceutical. I wondered if they were still chasing a bag of miracle leaves, and if Jason Gould was there too. He never called or visited his son. We heard a rumour that he was in a relationship with a German girl.

Wesley was learning new skills from his Filipino friend, notably catching, gutting and cooking fresh fish over an open fire by the lake.

James and Aly were kept busy with IT consultancy work, often using the skills of others to test systems. They were also trying for a baby; their potential babysitter was a seven-foot-eight-inch giant with a specially made bed. Aly, I knew with distaste, never heard from her adoptive family, the Wickhams. I knew she did however hear often from her uncle Saul.

Colonel Balak, through Josh, told us that former Inspector Abraham Maier spent his time gardening. When asked about his demise, he would snarl indiscernible words about a box. Reports suggested Tel Aviv police crime prevention and crime solving was 20 percent higher than usual.

Simeon and Esther had located the hire car, following my email about the location. They did not stop to explore the area and told everyone they were in Jerusalem to meet friends. People commented that since his kidnap, Simeon looked ten years younger. Colonel Balak was informed of their trip but decided not to follow them.

I was saddened that Hans Kestelmann was found hung in his remand cell. The trial on charges of drug dealing, kidnapping and murder did not go ahead.

Joshua flew to the UK whenever he could, his assignment in London finished after six months. He and Becky chatted almost daily on Skype. No date for their wedding was yet set. Becky's fashion shop was full most days, and there was always a crowd in the Art Cafe listening to young musicians. Her psychology studies continued.

Sean and Rachel lived in Sean's tree house with a noisy Filipino underneath in the workshop. They were also trying for a baby. Iggy was doing well at secondary school. His favourite subjects were Spanish (at which he excelled), domestic science, geography and sports. He loved every sport, viewing each game as a personal challenge, sometimes too personal when he was tackled. Sean and Rachel coped well with his frequent spats. Colleen Casey had bought a terraced house in Goostry, a few minutes away.

Liz and I walked the dogs daily, holding hands like young lovers. Bourne was still playful, bounding here and there, while Aunty followed. I had soon seen that Floating Prisons was not financially viable, so I had outsourced Kenya to Securitas and was looking to sell. Morgan Steel and the Morgan Foundation occupied me daily.

I often perused the maps and notes about Eden and wondered if one day I would return to the Tree. Meantime a cloth bag with brown powder was secure in my safe.

The Sequel: Return to Eden

The honeymoon couple were taken in the middle of the night. Their screams and shouts were muffled by strong hands, as they were bundled into a transit van.

The honeymoon was over.

The bridegroom, thrown side to side in the darkness, reached for his bride with his foot. With blindfolded eyes, hands bound, he wriggled across the hard metallic surface until he found her. Reassured that she was still breathing, he nestled his body close to her, feeling her warmth, the scent of fresh soap still clinging to her skin.

With no mobile phone, he wondered how his family or friends could trace him. 'It was a stupid idea to come here,' he thought, blaming himself. His bride stirred and moaned. 'Had they hurt her?' he wondered. 'Who were they, and why had they abducted them? It must be money.' Moving his hips on the floor, he could not feel his wallet in the back pocket of his jeans. His wallet was missing. 'Of course,' he said in his mind, 'they took it. They took everything.' He remembered the brutal search: money, watch, ring, phone, all taken. His tied wrists clenched. 'But', he thought, 'they didn't check my sock. Big mistake.'

The new bride moved her legs and tried to speak through the cloth, muffled words that sounded like, "You OK?" Typical of her, he thought, to be denying her bruises and to be more concerned for him. The stench of metal and diesel burned his nostrils.

"Uh huh, I'm perfect," he said, reaching her again with his foot. The van turned a sharp corner, rolling them closer, pressed against the cold metal side. The van was starting to climb. Several sharper turns hurled them around more. 'The driver must be belting along,' the bridegroom thought, 'what's his hurry? Are we being followed from the guest house?'

Through the cloth, he could tell it was still pitch black outside. They climbed higher, and then the road noise changed. Tyres churned up gravel. There was the sound of metal clanking. 'A gate is being opened', the honeymooner thought.

Through the van's windows misty lights appeared: the beam of a torch. Metal hinges creaked as the doors opened. The woman was lifted out first, followed by the man, both struggling to walk blindfolded, slipping and falling as they ascended stone steps.

They were forcefully pushed into a building where some lights filtered through the cloth around their eyes, and then the blindfolds were roughly removed. The couple were pushed onto a cold hard floor. It was a kitchen. Another door opened to their left. The couple gasped as they looked up to see the largest man they had ever seen, towering above them.

References

Blizzard Software and World of Warcraft®: http://www. blizzard.com.

Bron Afon Community Housing: https://www.bronafon.org.uk/

CfAN: http://www.cfan.org.uk.

Chambers of Commerce: http://www.britishchambers.org.uk/

Curry, Andrew (November 2008). "Gobekli Tepe: The World's First Temple?" Smithsonian.com. Retrieved August 2, 2013.

Debenhams: http://www.debenhams.com/

Encyclopaedia Britannica: http://www.britannica.com/.

Google Earth: http://www.googleearth.com

Great Ormond Street Hospital: http://www.gosh.nhs.uk/.

Harnden, Toby (23 March 2010). "Gen Stanley McChrystal pays tribute to courage of British special forces". The Daily Telegraph (London). Retrieved 25 March 2010.

Hilton Hotels: http://www.hilton.com

Kenyan Prison Service: http://softkenya.com/law/
kenya-prisons-service/

Life of Pi by: Yann Martel

Liverpool Football Club: http://www.Liverpoolfc.com.

Morrisons: http://www.morrisons.co.uk

MOSSAD: http://www.globalsecurity.org/intell/world/israel/
mossad.htm.

Private Eye: http://www.private-eye.co.uk

Royal Hotel: http://www.royalhotelwoolacombe.co.uk/

SAS Survival Guide (Collins Gem) Paperback – 1 Mar 1999
by John 'Lofty' Wiseman (Author).

SKYPE. http://www.skype.com

Tel Aviv Police: http://www.police.gov.il/eng_contacts.aspx

The NIV Holy Bible, New International Version®, NIV®
Copyright ©1973, 1978, 1984, 2011 by Biblica, Inc.® Used by
permission. All rights reserved worldwide.

The Porsche Experience. https://www.porschedriving.com/
experiences/driving-experiences.

Sacred Geographie or Scriptural Mapps, (London, translated by Moxon, 1691) (one of a series of six biblical maps
published in Dutch by Nicolaes Visscher in 1671 were
published in this atlas).

UNICEF: http://www.unicef.org.uk/.

Lightning Source UK Ltd.
Milton Keynes UK
UKHW010614060519
342177UK00002B/981/P